Foolishly YOURS

RACHEL LEWIS

Editing: Sadie (Dot The i Edit)

Cover Illustrations: Isabelle Diaz (@procastle_studios)

Cover Text and Layout: Amber D'Ambrosio (@whatambersreading_)

ALSO BY
Rachel Lewis

The Bardot Siblings Series

Yours, Unexpectedly (Book 1)

Merrily Yours (Book 1.5)

Entirely Yours (Book 2)

AUTHOR'S NOTE

To my amazing readers,

This was the book of my heart, and I'm so thrilled it is finally in your hands! Ben and Cole captivated me as soon as I wrote their interaction in Merrily Yours. I have been itching to begin their story ever since. You are going to enjoy your trip back to Sassafras, I guarantee it!

First things first, though. I like to list out content warnings and spicy chapters so every reader has a choice in what they consume! I will say, if you skip any of the spicy bits there is a chance you might miss important information. Always do what's best for you!

Content Warnings:
 –Divorced/Low Contact Parent Relationship
 –Homophobia (from a parent)
 –Ignorance/Prejudice from Friend Prior to Autism Diagnosis (off page, past)
 –On Page Sexual Content/Light Consensual Kink
 –Swearing

Dicktionary:
 –Chapter 8
 –Chapter 9
 –Chapter 14
 –Chapter 18

–Chapter 19
–Chapter 26
–Chapter 31
–Chapter 35
–Chapter 36

xo, Rachel

PLAYLIST
Available on Spotify

This playlist is meant to be enjoyed as you read, but it also has great vibes in general! There's one song for each chapter and I hope it gives you an immersive reading experience. Happy listening!

1. Manchild—Sabrina Carpenter
2. 10 Things I Hate About You—Leah Kate
3. feel anything—vaultboy
4. Panic—NOTD, Corbyn Besson
5. Greek Tragedy—The Wombats
6. Lean On—Major Lazer, DJ Snake MØ
7. Want You In My Room—Carly Rae Jepsen
8. bad idea right?—Olivia Rodrigo
9. we're not gonna be friends—pj frantz
10. love me from a distance—Emily Vaughn, Joseph Tilley, we're ok!
11. Sweet Talk—Saint Motel
12. why u gotta be like that—vaultboy, Nightly
13. Silk Chiffon—MUNA, Phoebe Bridgers
14. Dirty Little Secret—The All-American Rejects
15. So Bad—Ethan Dufault
16. Falling Apart—ARMNHMR, RUNN
17. keep the memories—ehren
18. Casual—Chappell Roan
19. Strawberry Blonde—chloe moriondo
20. downbad (2am)—pj frantz

I, BENOIT, TAKE THEE, COLETTE

Cole

GOOGLE SEARCH

🔍 What are the rules of beer pong? 🎤

12 Years Ago

Benoit Bardot is the bane of my existence and most certainly *not* the object of my desire. In fact, he has incessantly perturbed me ever since I first met him in middle school. He was gangly then, the same height as I was, all limbs and floppy hair.

Though I will deny this until the day I die, when I first saw him, I actually thought he was attractive… cute, even. It was summer and his skin was sun-kissed, his hair a little bit lighter than I would learn it gets in the winter. He had a mouthful of braces, each rubber band a different color—I didn't even know they let you do that. I was in the middle of a traumatic period in my life.

Now I know better.

My dad lugged me out to Sassafras right when I was on the cusp of puberty, and ever since, Benoit Bardot has been a thorn in my side.

He was used to being the best… but so was I.

Our motivations were probably even predictably similar. He needed to work for attention to distinguish himself from his close-knit family that all had talent or beauty—or talent *and* beauty—oozing out of every pore.

I also sought attention. But where Benoit actually received it from those closest to him, I did not. My parents were going through the most cliché of divorces, fighting all the time, exhausted whenever I required any bit of them. In my formative years, I quickly learned not to be another issue for dearest Mother and Father.

We have so much going on right now, Colette. As if I was something my mother could categorize and file away for dealing with later.

Some kids rebel when their parents divorce. I excelled.

My parents weren't going to praise me? Fine. My teachers and coaches sure would. And all of that was working well for me.

Until Benoit motherfucking Bardot strutted in with his stupid multicolor braces.

He made me fight tooth and nail for the title of valedictorian. I worked my ass off for it, agonizing over every damn percentage point on every damn assignment. In the end, I got exactly what I'd been working toward for four years. I *was* valedictorian and I had to sit on the stage next to Benoit, our class salutatorian, and his stupidly smug face.

As if everything was going exactly to plan for him.

It was incredibly irritating.

That's what I'm thinking about while I stare absentmindedly at the grass bending to the will of the wind in the front yard of my best friend Maya's house. Maya is my antithesis, which is precisely why I like her so much.

Where I do my best to never get in trouble, Maya is constantly in trouble. Her parents are out of town this weekend, so obviously she is hosting a summer kickoff bash or some other completely juvenile name. I can hear her voice in my head saying, "We *are* juveniles, Cole!"

But it was loud in there, and I haven't felt like a juvenile since I was… well, I can't remember a time when I did, honestly. And as one of the youngest in our grade, I always felt like I had something to prove.

My parents divorce didn't help, either. The therapist I was required to see post-divorce told me I had been forced to "grow up too fast." I didn't feel much different, though…

I huff out a breath because, damn, I'm moodier than usual tonight. I take a look at the drink in my hand. Some sort of trashcan punch. I've never had a sip of alcohol before tonight, always too scared of the repercussions of underage drinking. My worst nightmare was getting kicked off of one of the many teams I was on.

We've graduated now though, and this punch is strong…

Suddenly, a shadow casts over me briefly before someone is sitting down beside me on the top step of Maya's porch.

"Fancy seeing you here, Red."

Great.

Benoit is a frequent flier at these parties. He's been to many of them, had many a drink, but he never got kicked off of anything. That feels unfair. I've been *so* good. For what? It all feels pointless now.

"Benjamin."

"That's not my name, Colette."

I feign surprise. "What?! It's not? My entire life has been a lie."

"You haven't known me your entire life," he counters.

That's how it is between us. A volley, back and forth and back and forth. Until someone comes out on top. Usually him—it drives me crazy.

I scowl and he catches it. "C'mon, Red. Loosen up, you're at a party for fuck's sake. Come let me beat you in beer pong."

Taking a long draw of my drink, I watch him over the rim of my cup. He's certainly not that lanky pre-teen anymore. He and his twin, Julien, have significantly bulked up in the last year. They're identical except for Jules' long hair and cropped beard. Ben tends to keep his hair shorter, but still just as floppy as it was when we first met, and face clean shaven. It does wonders for his jawline, which pulls my eyes in like a magnet.

I hate that he's so pretty.

"Where's your flavor of the month?" I ask, refusing to acknowledge his command to *loosen up*. I know he said it just to rile me.

"Ah, we broke up." He clutches his chest but doesn't seem at all upset by the news.

My eyes roll on their own volition. I don't think Ben has ever dated someone for longer than a month.

"What was wrong with her this time?" It's always something. Even if he's never told me directly, this is a small town and gossip travels fast.

"She wasn't my type."

I actually scoff at that. I can feel his eyes roam my face when I do, and a revelation breaks through my alcohol-addled brain—he's teasing me.

"Oh okay, Zoey Carter wasn't your type. The modelesque head cheerleader doesn't do it for you. Mhmm." I nod. "Makes sense."

He smirks at me. "Jealousy looks good on you, Red."

"Jealous?" I reply, indignantly. "Jealous! Please. Come on, if she's not your type, who the hell is?"

The smirk slowly melts off his face. He morphs from the happy-go-lucky party guy to another of his personas I'm very familiar with—the problem solver. The competitor.

I feel much more evenly matched with this version of him.

His eyes sweep from the ponytail on top of my head, all the

way down to my lips. Brows furrowing, he seems to have a million scenarios running through his head. And I can't figure out what any of them could possibly be.

"Do you think you'll ever get married?" he asks, surprising me with the deep timbre of his voice after so many moments of silence.

That is not even close to what I thought would come out of his mouth. Gaping at him, I question, "Married?"

"Yeah. You know like 'I, Benoit, take thee, Colette,' white dress, flowers, et cetera, et cetera."

An honest-to-God record scratch happens in my brain. The fuck did he just say?

"I-I—" I'm floundering. Because this man—Boy? Man-boy. Boy-man—I hate just recited vows using *my* name. Whatever scenarios I was preparing for, this one was definitely not in the galaxy of possibilities. "Who is Benoit?" I finally reply.

Ben quickly dips right back into his easy-going side, booping me on the nose. "Funny, Red." He runs a hand through his hair, and I watch as it flops haphazardly back against his forehead. "Zoey started talking about wanting to get married and it freaked me out."

She *what?*

"We're eighteen. What on earth did you do to make her think about marriage?"

He looks me right in the eye, deadass serious. "I've been told I have a magical d—"

"Don't finish that sentence!" My hand pops up to cover his mouth, and he *bites* it. Bites! It! Yanking my hand away, I tuck it safely underneath my thigh because obviously it cannot be trusted after two sips of alcohol.

The motherfucker tips his head back and laughs. "Sorry, I forget you have delicate sensibilities. I can't possibly use the word"—he mouths *dick*—"in front of you." He contemplates for a moment. "You've never had a boyfriend."

Not a question, a statement.

"Who says I'm into boys?" I counter, receiving a quirked brow in return.

"You into girls, Red?"

I shrug, because I still haven't quite figured that out yet. Looking away, I admit, "Maybe. Maybe both. Maybe no one." The truth is, I've never felt like I've known someone well enough to feel a deep attraction to them. To want to date them. No one I've gotten to know well enough, except—

"I can work with that."

"Work with what, Benjamin?" My exasperated sigh floats between us.

He eyes me again. I look his way, trying to figure out what is going on in that brain of his. As hard as I try, he remains a mystery to me.

"Can I tell you a secret?" he asks instead of answering my question. I open my mouth to answer, but he just plows on. "I think I do want to get married… just not to Zoey."

I peer into the empty solo cup in his hand. "How many of those have you had?"

He pushes his hair back again, stupid bicep bulging. "I'm being serious, Colette."

"So am I!"

He turns to me fully. "We should make a pact."

"A… pact…" I'm really not following now.

"A marriage pact. If we aren't married by the time we are—"

I'm gobsmacked. "Benoit Bardot! You have lost your mind. I am *not* marrying you!"

"Well not right now, obviously, Red." He looks at me as if *I'm* the crazy one. "Do you want that, though? Want a partner?"

"I… I'm not sure."

"Let's give it until we are thirty," he suggests. "That way, you have time to decide if you want a partner. I have time to find someone. Worst case, we get married for the tax benefit—"

"There's not always a benefit," I interrupt.

"—and best case, we have someone we don't hate to fuck around with."

"Who says I don't hate you?" I snap, genuinely curious.

He smirks. "The way you look at me says you don't hate me, Red."

I shake my head in disbelief, noting how Ben's eyes watch the swing of my ponytail. "You have actually lost your mind," I repeat.

Unfortunately, instead of deterring him, this statement causes Ben to get a twinkle in his eye. "What if we bet on it? I win beer pong, we make our pact. I lose, you can walk away from here and never think about me again."

An actual growl leaves me. He knows I can't turn down a competition. "Fine," I grit out. "But I will win, Benjamin. And I'm so looking forward to never thinking about you again. It will be so peaceful. So quiet…"

"So boring," he finishes, breath coasting across my face. I've somehow leaned entirely too close to him over the course of my little rant. He licks his lips and the smell of peppermint assaults my senses. If I leaned just a tiny bit closer…

"Cole! Come back insi—oh!"

I jump back about six feet, but Ben, to my chagrin, stays exactly where he was.

"So sorry to interrupt," Maya says, a coy smile playing on her lips. "I noticed you slipped out, and I was coming to force you back into the fun."

Ben stands, still staring at me but regarding Maya. "We were actually just about to come inside and play beer pong."

My eyes dart back and forth between Ben and Maya, both of whom have their eyebrows quirked at me. I clumsily stand, a little drunker than I initially thought. A strong arm comes around, gripping me by the opposite elbow. Belatedly, I register that it's Ben helping me up so I quickly yank away, falling right into Maya this time.

"Woah, Cole. Maybe beer pong isn't the best idea!" Maya giggles.

"Of course it is," comes my feeble reply as I use Maya to steady myself. "Benjamin here needs a reminder that I always win. And then I never have to think about him again."

"Ooookay," Maya drawls out, giving me a *we'll talk about this later* look.

I turn and poke my finger at Ben. "Are you ready for me to kick your ass?"

The asshole winks and says, "You can do whatever you want to my ass, Red."

Thirty minutes later, I've lost miserably at beer pong.

For the next twelve years, Benoit Bardot does not let me forget about him, but he never once mentions our pact.

Chapter One

GET FUCKED, BARDOT
Cole

GOOGLE SEARCH

🔍 Tips to relieve sexual frustration.   🎤

December, 12 years later

How much *Dateline* is too much *Dateline*? I feel like I should worry about the amount of murder I'm ingesting, but it's just so damn addicting.

Want me to watch a scary movie? Absolutely not.

Give me a *Dateline* episode about a man who murdered his wife, and I'm all ears.

My love for true crime is actually part of the reason I decided to go ahead and get my masters in psychology. It was a surprise to everyone when I announced I was leaving my prestigious engineering job to pursue this degree.

But to me, people are puzzles to be solved much like an engineering problem.

In one, I might be trying to figure out how to support infrastructure that was never meant to hold the number of people using it, and in the other I'm evaluating someone's need for validation in an increasingly invalidating world.

A puzzle to be solved… some might say people are more volatile, but isn't that what keeps things exciting?

My entire life I spent insane amounts of time trying to figure out why people make the decisions they do. I couldn't understand why my parents got divorced. It was always hard for me to make friends because the trivial problems of girlhood didn't ever resonate. And I certainly never understood why…

Never mind.

I've been back in Sassafras now for six months, and I forgot how fucking cold it gets here in the winter. Part of me misses the moderate California climate that kept me company for over a decade. I had only just gotten used to not having seasons when I got the acceptance letter to Hawthorne's psychology program.

So, here I am. Needing to purchase a new winter coat because the one that's been shoved in the back of my closet since I left Massachusetts no longer fits. It's my only option though, so I simply opt not to fasten it around the tits that only appeared after undergrad. I most likely have post-grad stress-eating to thank for that.

Once my episode of *Dateline* is over, I look in the mirror, admiring how good my aforementioned tits look in this sweater. I'm going on a date this morning. The first one I've been on in… years.

Brody is in my program at Hawthorne. He's the only other student that didn't immediately jump into their masters degree after undergrad, so he's a bit closer to my age, though I'm not sure exactly how close.

I was definitely surprised when he asked me out for coffee. I'm still not great at reading signals when it comes to my personal relationships. Looking at a psychological problem from an outside perspective—I'm great at that. Not so much when it comes to what's right in front of me. Something I've worked on with my own therapist since getting my autism diagnosis in college.

Honestly, it was a relief when I first found out. Finally, a word for all of the things that didn't quite make sense in my brain. Well, they made sense to me, but they didn't make sense to everyone else. Now I have tools to help when I need it, and I love the strengths that come with being autistic. I've gained a confidence I didn't have when I was in high school, even with all of the accomplishments and accolades that were under my belt. My exploration of myself and the world around me looked a bit like a checklist, but it worked for me. I actually *like* who I am today. Mostly.

Looking myself over once more in the mirror, I grab my bag from the hook and give my dog, Ernest, a few scratches under his chin.

"Be a good boy, okay? Maybe I'll bring someone home for you to meet later…" I pump my eyebrows at Ernest, who licks my nose in response. It's been years since I've been on a date and also quite a while since I've had sex.

Sexual intimacy is not typically something I feel a need for—something else I learned about myself in college, but recently there's been a bit of an itch that needs to be scratched, and the vibrator isn't really cutting it.

Brody is handsome… not my usual type, if I even have one, but he's age appropriate and, you know, *here*. And though I don't typically crave physical intimacy with a new partner, I have had the help of… *viewing materials* to learn some things about what I like, and currently Brody is the best candidate for exploring that. With the holidays coming up, I know I'll need something to take the edge off—being low-contact with my parents makes this time of year especially lonely.

Several minutes later, I've parked and am walking into The Coffee Shop—a truly uninspired name for a literal coffee shop—to meet my date. Spotting Brody through the window, he looks objectively attractive. Blond hair slicked back, a bit of scruff, bright blue eyes.

He looks a bit like a Ken doll.

When I walk in, I see that he's already gotten a coffee for himself. "Hi!" I greet, setting my bag down in the chair across from him. "I'm going to grab a drink. Need anything else?"

"Hey, Cole!" He stands, giving me an awkward side hug. "Good to see you. Sorry for not getting you something. I wasn't sure what your order was."

I wave him off. "No worries. I'll be right back."

At the counter, I order what I know will be a subpar double espresso from the college student currently working. I watch as she fiddles with the espresso machine and wonder if it's her first day on the job. I'm so focused on how much she's fucking up my drink, it takes me by complete surprise when someone walks out of the broom closet and straight into me.

I catch a glimpse of Ethel, the longtime owner of The Coffee Shop, as I attempt to stop my inevitable fall. It briefly crosses my mind that I need to find out her exercise routine because she doesn't look even slightly off balance from our run-in, whereas I am bracing for my ass to hit the ground.

Suddenly, strong arms steady my off-kilter body while one single word is uttered into my ear. "Colette."

My head whips around a little too quickly because my long ponytail smacks me right in the eye. I can't even register the pain because dammit, why the fuck is he here? I take half a second to steady my breathing. "Benoit. I didn't realize you were home."

He's not supposed to be here. He's supposed to be in Boston, far enough away that I don't have to worry about running into him in town.

"It's Christmas," he deadpans.

Oh. Right. That.

"You don't always come home for holidays." As soon as it's out of my mouth, I want to grab the words out of thin air and shove them right back in. Maybe he didn't notice.

I could never be that lucky, though. He smirks, eyes running up and down the length of my body. "Keeping tabs on me, sweets?"

Sweets?! "Don't call me that," I hiss.

In response, he crowds my space even more than he already had. "Hmm, what should I call you instead?" he whispers, sending goosebumps out in waves from where his breath hits my neck, forcing a gasp from my lips. An indignant gasp, I tell myself.

"Cole?" Brody's voice says my name all wrong. Ben and I turn our heads toward the sound but don't move away from each other. I feel Ben's thumb smooth across the skin at my wrist, where he's still holding me steady, and that's all it takes.

Hastily, I move away from him, but Ben stays still, taking Brody in. Scrutinizing him. Brody's eyes move back and forth between the two of us uncomfortably. Clearing my throat, I pull Ben's attention back to me. "I'm on a date."

His eyes don't move away from my lips. "Of course you are. You're almost thirty, aren't you?"

Almost thirty... I scowl. So he does remember. The idiotic, godforsaken pact that he's never once brought up since we made it nearly twelve years ago. How convenient that he decides to bring it up now! While I'm on a date!

Glaring, I turn away from him without another word, guiding Brody back to our table. For the next forty-five minutes, I sip my mediocre espresso and listen to mediocre stories about Brody's adventures in day trading. The entire time I can feel Ben's eyes on me like a brand. It heats me from the outside in, my face probably turning bright red alongside my rising anger. This was supposed to be a *good* date. Brody was supposed to fill a void. And Benoit is ruining that by simply existing in the same room.

I grit my teeth, desperately trying to focus on Brody when I hear Ben call, "Remember our deal!"

Now that catches my attention. I turn my head so quickly, I

might get whiplash. Ben notices and looks smug as hell as he saunters toward my table. "I wasn't talking about you, sweets, but I'm glad to see I'm top of mind."

He can tell that calling me "sweets" rankles me, and the fleeting thought passes that I would prefer him to call me Red like he used to. Before I can gather myself, Brody asks, "Uh, can we help you with something?"

Ben doesn't deign to look at him. "I don't know… Colette, can he help us with something?"

"That's not really what I…" Brody starts, but Ben and I are both ignoring him now.

"What is wrong with you?" I hiss, fiddling with the rim of my mug.

His hand comes down to cover mine, tan and veiny. Fuck, I bet nurses love him. "I'm just sick of watching you practically fall asleep over here. You need to be stimulated, Cole." He leans in closer, whispering conspiratorially, "He's not very stimulating, is he?"

Vaguely I hear Brody mutter, "What the fuck? I can hear you."

"And how would you know what I need?" I snap. "You might have known me in high school, but you don't know me anymore, Benoit."

"Oh but I do. And you hate that, don't you?"

Yes. No. Yes!

"I hate *you*," I seethe.

"Woah, maybe I should…" Brody stands, his chair scraping loudly across the floor, pulling me out of whatever haze I've been in.

Fuck.

Turning back to Brody, I desperately try to get him to sit back down. "No! Brody, don't leave. Benoit is the one who is going to leave." I give Ben my most pointed look.

Instead of listening to me, the fucker pulls up a chair, turning it around so he can prop his elbows on the back. "Nah, I think I'll stay," he says, dropping his chin into one hand.

"Yeah, I'm out of here," Brody says. He gives me a look of pity that leaves me feeling mortified. I have to go back to classes with him like none of this ever happened!

Ben keeps staring at me, throwing a "Bye, Ken!" over his shoulder. I hate that Ben also noticed Brody's doll-like looks.

"Wait, Brody!" I stand but immediately realize it's too late, the door already swinging shut behind him. Instead, I turn toward Benoit—the true object of my wrath. "Get fucked, Bardot."

"I'm trying, Red," he replies without missing a beat.

I scoff, trying to hide what that statement ignites in me. "As if. I would never touch you with a ten-foot pole."

He looks down pointedly, and that's when I realize my finger is pushing angrily into his shoulder. I pull it back to a knowing smirk from Ben. "You're an asshole."

"And you're too good for that dickhead."

"Complimenting me now, Benoit? You've lost your touch."

Ben stands, what used to be a lanky body has now turned into lean lines and muscles towering over me. Slowly, he reaches past my shoulder and grasps a strand of my hair between his fingers. The room stills as he wraps it once around his finger and tugs. Whatever he sees in my eyes makes his pupils blow wide.

"Hmm…" he muses, giving one more pull, angling my head up toward his. "I don't think I have."

A mix of anger and disappointment wash over me when he lets go. He gets all the way to the door before turning around. "Seven months and two days, Colette."

Mother. Fucker.

Chapter Two
I QUIT MY JOB
Ben

GOOGLE SEARCH

🔍 Colette Russell   🎤

It might make me the world's biggest asshole to put in my two weeks notice at Scott and Williams Financial Group on Christmas Eve, but that's exactly what I'm doing.

It has absolutely nothing to do with my run-in with Colette Russell and everything to do with the fact that Ethel, longtime owner of The Coffee Shop, won't sell it to me unless I plan on moving back to Sassafras. After one look at my twin brother, Jules, the decision was made.

He's been fucking miserable in his teaching job, and after constantly taking care of everyone around him, it's my turn to do something for him. I have more money than I know what to do with after renting a run-down apartment in Boston for the last several years while I worked my way up the career ladder of the financial group.

I did really well for myself... Like, *really* well. I've barely spent any money these last eight years so it's all just been sitting in investments, making me *more* money.

I'm successful, I'm good looking, and I'm so goddamn bored. No one challenged me in Boston. No one has really challenged me since high school.

Hitting send on this resignation email sends a zing up my spine. I think I'm… excited? And it feels good.

"Why are you smiling?" Gabe, the oldest and most definitely not the wisest of the Bardot siblings, is splayed out on our family couch, head dangling off the side, throwing a baseball up in the air before catching it in his other hand.

"I quit my job."

The baseball completely misses Gabe's open hand and smacks him square in the forehead. "Fuck. Ow! Wait—shit that hurt—you did what?!"

"I quit my job," I repeat. "Do you need an ice pack?" His forehead is reddening quickly, probably killing the few brain cells he has left.

He sits up, rubbing at the mark but completely focused on me. "No, I don't need an ice pack. What I do need is for you to tell me what you're talking about. You can't just quit your job!"

"I just did."

"To do what?" he asks indignantly. Gabe and I have—well, I guess *had*—similar jobs in finance, but he works for a much smaller firm in Sassafras. His job is something he's actually happy with, whereas I've felt the crushing weight of Corporate America slowly sucking my soul out for the better part of the last decade.

He's also here. With our family. And I'm very much alone in Boston.

"To move back. Be closer to the family."

"I mean for work, asshole. What are you going to do for work?"

No one in the family really knows just how much money I've made and saved over the years. I technically don't have to work, even though I still plan on finding something to do. "Let's buy The Coffee Shop."

If Gabe had still been throwing the baseball, I think it would have hit him in the face again. Maybe rounded out his forehead welt with a nice black eye.

"Buy The Coffee Shop? It's not for sale."

"It can be… I have it on good authority that Ethel and Albert are ready to retire. You know Jules is unhappy in his job. Let's go in on it together. Jules can do the menu—all the frou-frou coffee stuff. I'll run the business side of things."

Gabe looks off put when I don't continue. "What about me?" he questions, displeasure written all over his face.

I raise an eyebrow at him. "What about you? I thought you were happy at work?"

His bottom lip juts out. "I am. But I still want to be involved! I don't like being left out."

"Fine," I concede. "You can be an investor."

He seems to be satisfied with that answer because he flips back over and starts tossing the ball again. "Where are you going to live?"

I hadn't thought that far yet. I don't particularly want to live with Mom and Dad. Jules would probably welcome me out of some made up sense of obligation. I'm sure I could find an apartment fairly quickly but—

"Just move in with me," Gabe continues before I have a chance to answer him. "Like I said, I don't like being left out. No one has lived with me since Anders moved out, and I think I'd like having a roommate again."

Gabe lives in the same apartment he's lived in since he and Anders—his best friend and our sister's husband—were in college. It's right above Louie's, our favorite bar, which makes it an easy yes.

"You sure?" I check.

"Wouldn't want you to be homeless."

"Well, I wouldn't be homeless. I'm sure Mom and—"

"Look at me, saving the day," Gabe interrupts. "You're welcome."

"Thank you, Big Brother. What would I do without you?"

He grins back at me, lopsided and upside down. Looks like I'm officially moving back to Sassafras.

———

The rest of the holiday flies by—full of Christmas decoration competitions, time at the skating rink, and a really scraggly looking Christmas tree. On Christmas morning, my sister Bex and her husband, Anders, announce that they are pregnant with a girl, which means I get another niece. Their oldest daughter, Elodie, is one of my favorite people.

I don't want kids of my own, but damn I love being an uncle to her. Kids are really fucking cute, *and* I really love being able to do whatever the fuck I want all the time.

A few days after Christmas, I head back to Boston to prepare for the move. The sound of my keys hitting the counter echoes through my threadbare apartment. I can honestly say I won't miss the place.

Looking around I see it with a fresh set of eyes. There's nothing wrong with it, per se. I just never bothered to hang much on the walls or pull together any semblance of style when it comes to furniture. The mismatched couch, coffee table, and TV stand were all hand-me-downs from friends or items I found at the thrift store.

Plopping on the couch, I kick my feet up. The city noise filters in through the thin windows, only slightly distracting me from my thoughts.

When I told the family I was moving back to Sassafras, I was greeted with mixed reactions. For the most part, I think everyone is excited. Bex and Anders seemed jealous—they live in New York City now, but it wouldn't surprise me if they eventually moved home, too. Jules immediately got choked up and excused himself from the room. It really is time someone did something for him, and I'm glad it could be me.

But I'd be lying if I said my intentions were purely selfless. Even now, my thumb hovers over my phone, the habit of opening Instagram to check on her is ingrained.

I don't know if it was luck or fate that she never removed me as a follower. It's allowed me the smallest look into her life over the past twelve years. We've crossed paths occasionally—mostly when both of us were home for some holiday or another. It was more often when we were in college and Maya would throw parties when we were all home. But then she stopped showing up to those... so I did too.

Fuck it. I open the app and see if she's posted anything with Finance Bro Ken—the irony is not lost on me that I could also be considered a Finance Bro Ken. But with brown hair. Is there a brown-haired Ken?

Doesn't matter. I navigate to her page, happy to see no evidence of their coffee-shop date having led to anything. Not that she would post it if it had. I check the date of her last post... November fifteenth. A selfie of her and her dog that I've practically memorized. Exasperated and fed up with my obsession, I close out and toss my phone aside. Instead, I pull out a small moleskin from my back pocket and add another tally mark.

That makes four thousand one hundred ninety-seven days since we made our pact.

Only two hundred three more until I finally get to call it in.

Chapter Three
THE FIVE STAGES OF GRIEF
Cole

GOOGLE SEARCH

Starting over at twenty-nine isn't all it's cracked up to be. I feel ancient in my classes full of students that are only about seven years younger than me, but they look like children. They jumped straight from undergrad to this graduate program with zero life experience.

And while I'm about as far removed from my engineering career as possible, I still feel like I have a leg up after working in that field for so long.

I'm scowling at one of the youths—one that happens to be chewing on the end of his pen and playing Candy Crush on his phone—when Dr. Torres says my name as though it's not the first time she's said it.

"Ms. Russell, is everything alright?" Her face displays her disappointment so perfectly, I feel like my view right now should be framed and hung up next to the *Mona Lisa*.

Clearing my throat, I answer her, knowing she won't let me off the hook. "Sorry, Dr. Torres. I might just need to…" I awkwardly gather up all of my things as everyone in the room watches me and move to a front-row seat. There, now nothing can distract me from her lecture.

She nods once, her reading glasses sliding a fraction of an inch down her nose. "Very well. As I was saying, this course will be a continuation of what you learned last semester in Techniques of Psychotherapy. Completion of this course, as well as the other core courses you are taking this semester, will allow you to select a specialization. It is my hope to see many of you in the Marriage and Family Therapy cohort in the fall"—*No, thank you!* Especially since sex therapy falls into that department and is taught by none other than Elaine Bardot—"but I understand that some of you have your sights set on other paths. Perhaps you'll join Dr. Frank over in sports psychology or Dr. Daly in forensic psychology…"

Dr. Torres keeps talking, but my mind starts to race because forensic psychology is what I want, and I cannot wait until our coursework becomes more specialized.

I think they might have to sedate me when we actually get to go into the field. Not that there's a lot of forensic activity happening in Sassafras, but I've heard we are able to partner with the Boston legal system as they work on cases. After the master's degree, I'll go on to get my doctorate, meaning I'll be in academia for the foreseeable future, and honestly?

I can't fucking wait.

School has always been the place where I can succeed. Where I can make sense of the world around me. Where I can be a little weird… a little intense, and it's a *good* thing.

I've just got to make it through this semester of core work, then I get to do the really cool shit.

An hour later, I'm walking back to my apartment when I spot him. He's standing outside of The Coffee Shop with his brothers, and the only thing running through my mind is *What the fuck is he doing here?*

Before I can stop myself, I beeline toward him to ask him that exact question.

"Benjamin!" Three sets of chocolate-brown eyes swing my way. "What the fuck are you doing here? Why are you still in Sassafras?"

The holidays are over, he should be back in Boston by now. This feels like some sort of personal attack. Like when your leg falls asleep and it feels like needles poking into the sole of your foot every time you take a step. It's your body betraying you, and right now it feels like my eyes must be betraying me. Because he matches my intensity, staring right back with a self-satisfied smirk.

And then he drops a bomb.

"I live here, Red."

"No." My immediate response is denial… which vaguely I register to be the first stage of grief. No, he cannot live here. He has to live away from here, where I won't run into him like this… just out! On the street! In broad daylight!

"Yes," he retorts, just as quickly.

"No!" I reply, stomping my foot. "We can't both live here! It… It—" I wave my arms around looking for the right words. "It won't work!"

Behind Ben, Gabe leans over to Jules and stage whispers, "This is feeling very '*This town ain't big enough for the both of us!*'"

My arm stretches out, pointing at Gabe. "Yes! What he said."

"You can't claim an entire town, Colette." Ben raises his brow, crossing his stupidly buff arms across his chest. To him this is a proverbial checkmate, but I've now entered the anger stage of grief.

As predatorial as I can make it, I take a slow step toward him. "Yes, I can," I seethe. "You weren't supposed to be here. I'm supposed to be able to live my life without worrying about your stupid, pretty face scaring me every time I turn a corner."

He places a hand on his chest in mock flattery. "You think my face is pretty?" Said face leans closer to me, so close that his breath coasts across my ear when he says, "I'm flattered, Red."

I can feel my face scrunching up. Feel the heat radiating from my cheeks. I know that if I looked at myself in the mirror right now, I would be the human equivalent of Anger from the *Inside Out* movies.

So I change tactics.

Taking a deep breath, I let my hand come up to rest on his crossed forearms. "Benjamin, Benjamin, Benjamin... What are we going to do?" My finger lazily traces back and forth across the veins lining his arm. When I look into his eyes, I see that he's affected. He's zeroed in on my movements, a combination of amusement and something else dancing across his features.

"Surely we can figure out a solution," I continue. "You get a day, I get a day type of thing? Maybe stay away from the university and we can make that work."

It's actually an insane suggestion, something that is confirmed when Jules mutters, "This is psychological warfare," under his breath. He says tomato, I say I've entered the bargaining stage. *Will it work?* is the question.

Per usual, Ben quickly shuts down all my hopes. "No can do. Would hate for you to miss out on this pretty face. I know it's been rough only seeing me in your dreams."

He punctuates that swift rejection by taking my hand between two fingers, as if it's a dirty tissue or—*gasp!*—a participation trophy, and placing it back down by my side.

Apparently the stages of grief move incredibly fast because I've arrived at depression. All I want is a sweet treat from inside The Coffee Shop but the Bardot brothers are currently blocking my way.

Without dignifying Ben with a response to his comment about my dreams, because, dammit, sometimes I do dream about the bastard, I sidestep him and his pretty-boy brothers in pursuit of a chocolate croissant.

"Colette—" he starts, but I don't care what he has to say. This conversation is over. Not quite acceptance but as close as I'm going to get right now.

Only, when I finally make it through the hulking men to the front door of The Coffee Shop, there's a note on the door.

That's when I realize, it's surprisingly empty inside and no one has come in or out since I walked over here in the first place.

The note is scrawled in the specific brand of cursive that all grandmothers seem to write in and reads:

Closed early today! Meeting with those handsome Bardot brothers. They are taking over the shop! Retirement can't come soon enough.

   - Ethel

"Absolutely not!" I scream, because now I'm right back at denial.

Chapter Four

STILL, MY CABBAGE?

Ben

GOOGLE SEARCH

🔍 does someone see the notification if you unlike a post immediately after liking it?? 

Her anger is the cutest thing I've ever seen. And when she was stroking my arm like that? I almost gave up right there and told her I'd not only leave Sassafras, but leave planet Earth if she wanted me to.

I hear they are almost ready to attempt human settlements on Mars.

She doesn't know it but it takes everything in me *not* to do what she asks. Because as much as I say I'd move to Mars, it's been torture living so far away from her for the last twelve years. A slow, painful torture knowing that she was off doing amazing things, never once thinking about me while I was trying to achieve, succeed, transform—anything for another shred of her attention.

And now that I have it? No fucking way am I giving it up again.

"Absolutely yes, Red," I finally reply. "Aren't you going to properly welcome me home?"

Stepping forward, I open my arms and gesture for her to give me a hug. To my absolute shock, she tentatively takes a step to close the gap between us—and then forcefully shoves me backward into the waiting arms of my brothers.

"Fuck you, Bardot!" Colette shouts before stomping off down the sidewalk. After a moment she calls over her shoulder, "You better have chocolate croissants when you reopen, or else!"

"*Or else?*" Gabe asks. "She's an angry little thing, isn't she?"

I scrub a hand down my face. "Yeah, she is."

"And Ben loves it," Jules chimes in. Before I have a chance to deny it—not that I would—he continues, "I've got to head back to school to finish up a few things. Are we done for today?"

Nodding, I run through the list of things we still need to do. "We should be good for today. It'll be a few more weeks until we can sign all of the paperwork. Let's check in with Colton and make sure he has room in his schedule to start construction after that."

Jules fires off a text, pocketing his phone afterward. "I know I've already told you—"

I hold up my hand to silence him. "Don't. You can't keep thanking us every five minutes for the next however many years we run this coffee shop." Gripping Jules' shoulders, I shake him lightly. "Your dream is our dream, Brother. We're going to make it happen and we are ecstatic—"

"Thrilled!" Gabe adds.

"Elated!" I reply.

"Joyful?" Gabe ponders.

"*Over*joyed to be joining you on this adventure. Got it?"

Jules dips his chin in acknowledgement. "Got it," he murmurs.

"Great. Now, shoo!" I wave him off, satisfied when he seems to relax just a bit before heading back to school.

Gabe and I walk back to the apartment, one of the perks of

living with him instead of with Mom and Dad—I'll literally be able to walk to work every day once we reopen The Coffee Shop.

"Do you think we should keep the name of the shop? The Coffee Shop is a bit on the nose, don't you think?" I ask Gabe. This has all been rather sudden that I don't think any of us have really slowed down to think about how massive of a change this will be for all of us.

"The Coffee Shop is a Sassafras institution. Will people riot if we try to change that?" he muses.

Change is hard, typically uncomfortable, but oftentimes a really good thing. "I don't think it will truly feel like *ours* if we keep operating under the same name…"

He nods, unlocking the door to his apartment—my apartment—and letting us in. It's comfortable. Fairly similar to my place back in Boston. Definitely a bachelor pad but Gabe isn't a complete slob so it's not bad. Honestly, he's been here so long, it wouldn't surprise me if Anders and Bex were the ones who forced him into getting curtains that at least coordinated with the pillows on the couch. It's just enough space for both of us, already feeling much homier than my last place.

Dropping down on the couch, Gabe contemplates for a moment before saying, "I think it should just be the Bardot brothers."

"It is just the Bardot brothers, Gabriel. Remember, Bex and Anders were pissed about it? Bex kept saying how it was anti-feminist to exclude her even though she continued to admit that she didn't actually want to help run the place."

"No, no." He shakes his head. "I'm not talking about *who* is running the shop. I mean that's what we should call it. Bardot Brothers Coffee Shop."

Hmm. Simple but obvious. It's *almost* perfect. "Company," I correct, continuing when Gabe gives me a quizzical look. "Bardot Brothers Coffee Company. Or Coffee Co. really—shortening the word company sounds more official."

"Not too on the nose?" He laughs.

I chuckle, settling in the chair across from him. "It's perfectly on the nose. Pass me my computer, I want to try a few logo mockups."

A few hours later, several logo options have been ordered as T-shirts—Gabe said he "had a guy" for that—and we are digging into one of Gabe's favorite traditions, Margarita Monday.

Various menu items were ordered from his favorite Chinese takeout restaurant and are now scattered across the kitchen island. He pulls out the blender and the tequila for margaritas, pouring with a heavy hand.

"Woah there, are we drinking to forget tonight?" I ask to the glugs of the tequila bottle.

"It's been a rough few weeks," he laments.

That takes me by surprise. Gabe is the happy-go-lucky one. He's never met a stranger, putting everyone around him at ease. There's been a few times I've seen him frustrated, mainly when he steps into his perceived role as the protective older brother, but really he's a big teddy bear.

"Do… you want to talk about it?"

"Girl troubles. But I'll be fine." He turns on the blender to punctuate that statement.

I wait patiently as he blends for what feels like an excessive amount of time. Lucky for him—or not—I'm used to playing the long game. When he finally stops blending and starts pouring our drinks, I ask, "Girl troubles?"

Gabe sighs. "I said I'll be fine," he repeats, taking a sip of his drink.

And I wait him out.

And wait.

Not touching my drink, just waiting.

Finally he says, "You aren't going to quit staring at me until I talk, are you?"

"Bex says you aren't very smart, but you are proving otherwise, Big Brother." I smirk.

He runs his hand through his hair, slightly lighter than the rest of ours, and it flops back down across his forehead. "Do you remember Bex's friend Luci?"

"Gabriel. You mean the one that was just here over Christmas? The one you snuck out of Louie's with when you thought no one was watching? The one you've been obsessed with for years? That Luci?"

"Fuck," he mutters. "Yes, Benoit. That Luci. We—" He pauses, trying to find the words. "Things have... it's complicated," is what he lands on.

"No shit."

He rolls his eyes at me. "Anyway, we saw each other over the holidays obviously, but it didn't... end well." He finishes off his margarita at that.

My eyebrows creep up my forehead the longer I watch him gulp this drink that will one hundred percent be giving him a brain freeze. "Oh, like it really didn't end well," I guess.

The glass lands with a clatter when he clumsily sets it down for a refill. "It's complicated," he states again, a sense of finality in the words. "What about you?"

I freeze. Because as much as I want to dish it out, I don't know that I'm ready to take it. "What about me?"

Oblivious to my inner turmoil, Gabe continues, "I mean obviously you didn't have anyone serious in Boston or you wouldn't have left. Are you going to try to date now that you're back? Should we establish some rules? A sock on the door situation?" He winks, in much better spirits now that the topic of conversation has pivoted.

Or maybe that's because of the tequila hitting his system.

"No one in Boston," I confirm. "And no, we don't need a sock on the door. I'm here to focus on the coffee shop— everything else comes second." The lie tastes bitter on my tongue as a flash of red hair pops to the front of my mind.

Gabe holds his hands up in surrender. "Alright, alright. Well, just know that now that you're back, I'm sure Mom will try to set you up on dates. She already bugs Jules and I about it, but you've had distance to your advantage."

"Noted." What Gabe doesn't know is that Mom is aware of my… uh, infatuation. I've always been close with our mom, and one night I let it slip that I had a crush on my biggest rival. Her response? *The line between love and hate is very thin, my cabbage.* Accompanied by a knowing smirk.

Needless to say, we've both quietly kept up with Cole over the years. Occasionally, Mom will ask, "Still, my cabbage?" and I know exactly what she's talking about without any clarification.

"Still, Mom," has always been my response.

But now I'm here. We're both here. And maybe it doesn't have to be a secret anymore.

Maybe, I can finally confess my feelings for Colette Russell.

When I get in bed that night, I have the unfortunate experience of realizing just how strong Gabe's margaritas were.

Because after years of quietly stalking Cole's Instagram without ever making it weird, I make the fatal mistake that all drunk, lovesick fools make.

I like one of her posts.

From five years ago.

Chapter Five
LOSE MY NUMBER
Cole

GOOGLE SEARCH

Q Snacks for someone who might be pregnant

The next several weeks are blissfully quiet.

Well, except for the morning after I ran into Ben outside of The Coffee Shop and woke up to find that he had liked a picture of me on social media.

And not a recent one either. A picture from when I first got Ernest, my three-legged rescue dog.

Five years ago.

It's not like I post on Instagram often, but it would have taken him approximately seven scrolls to even get down that far on my feed. Seven! Give or take the size of his thumb.

Which I would imagine is large, given the size of… well, *him*.

So maybe it was closer to five Ben-sized scrolls, but still! He was looking.

Strange.

My theory, if I had taken long enough to form one—which I

obviously did not because he does not take up that much space in my brain—would be that after running into me earlier that day, he had to figure out all of the ways he was still better than me.

I'm sure if *he* adopted a dog, he would pick one with all four legs.

Seems like the easy way out, but what do I know?

Said dog chooses that moment to hop onto my lap. I give Ernest a few scratches behind his ears as he burrows deep into the blankets next to me. Ernest accidentally became mine when one of my engineering colleagues had a girlfriend, Cheryl, that ran a pet rescue. Management had allowed her to bring dogs in one day for all of us to cuddle, which really made no sense, but apparently it's a stress reducing technique employed at high-stress jobs nationwide. They were always trying to do things to "boost morale," and I started to wonder why morale was so low to begin with. Why weren't they addressing the fact that maybe we were just overworked and underpaid?

Anyway, at our dog-cuddling-morale-boosting event, Cheryl brought eight puppies and Ernest. One guess on who everyone chose to cuddle with—it wasn't Ernest.

They also posted up right by the coffee station, so every time I walked past to get another cup of coffee, that damn dog just stared at me. He is quite possibly the ugliest dog to ever exist. Truly, I've debated entering him in that World's Ugliest Dog competition. His hair is wiry, his eyes are squinty, and his front right leg had to be amputated due to a bike accident. Both of his ears stick out at odd angles and he has a bald patch near his tail.

Like I said, he's ugly.

The third time I walked by, Cheryl stopped me.

"Want to take a break and play with the puppies?" she asked, gesturing toward the hyper fluff balls circling her feet. "They are all up for adoption!"

And it really pissed me off that she didn't include Ernest in that. "What about the ugly one?" I had asked, pointing right at his lolling tongue.

Cheryl had seemed taken aback by my assessment of Ernest, but she recovered quickly. "Oh! Yes, he's available too. This is Sparkles, we think he's about three years old."

The name would have to change but, "I'll take him," came out of my mouth without a second thought.

Ernest came home with me that night, even though my apartment definitely did not allow pets. He cuddled up on the pillow next to me and looked at the covers expectantly until I pulled them up over his little body.

He is and always has been exactly who he wanted to be, and I really admire him for that. Like right now, he's buried himself so far into the blankets that I can only see his tail and his back left paw. It's really fucking cute, and I swear Ernest is the only man I'll ever love.

I've finally found peace: my ugly dog cuddled next to me, *Dateline* streaming on my laptop, and a cup of peppermint tea helping to sooth my sinuses and my nerves.

That's when my phone buzzes.

BEN

Red. I need your help.

How did you get this number?

BEN

......

You've had the same number since high school.

At least, I'm assuming since you answered the text.

Dammit. He's not wrong.

What do you need?

BEN

Can you bring a pregnancy test over for a
friend? And maybe some mac and cheese for
her kid?

What the actual fuck. A pregnancy test for a "friend"? Did this
asshole get some girl pregnant and now he wants *me* to help?! I
rub my chest, at the weird ache that has formed right there in the
center. I decided a long time ago that I don't want kids, but for
some reason the thought of Benoit Bardot procreating with
someone else has me feeling... things. I let those feelings take
over as I reply.

Are you seriously asking me to help you with
some girl you knocked up? This is a new low
for you, Benjamin.

BEN

Dear God, Colette. You really think I would do
that?

Do I really think he would do that? My anger wants to say yes,
but in reality... No, probably not. Anger wins.

... Yes.

BEN

It's for Jules.

Will you help now?

35

There's going to be rumors that spread like wildfire around Sassafras, but…

Fine.

The next text I get is an address to an apartment above Louie's. Twenty minutes later, I'm knocking on the door of my biggest rival. My sworn enemy. With a fucking pregnancy test in my hand. And several other things because I wasn't sure what you get someone who *might* be pregnant, but still.

When the door swings open, I'm struck by just how *large* he is. I've tried really hard not to look too closely at Ben whenever we've run into each other over the years, but right now I can't help but notice the way he's filled out since we were teenagers. His light wash jeans hug all of the right spots, including thighs that look like they know their way around a squat. A trim waist leads up to an old Hawthorne T-shirt—one that fits snuggly around toned biceps. His clean-shaven face is sporting a smirk and—

"Since when do you wear glasses?" I ask at the same time Ben says, "Finished checking me out, Red?"

I fake a gag. "Blegh, I would never check you out."

I was definitely checking him out.

"You were definitely checking me out."

Narrowing my eyes, I stare him down. It's been less than two minutes back in each other's presence and he's already inside my head. Which is exactly what I was trying to avoid.

Shoving the bags into his chest, I tell him, "I'll be going now. No reason for me to continue cleaning up after Bardot messes today."

"Wait!" Ben's hand—another large part of him—clamps over

mine, holding me hostage against his chest. "Will you… can you take it across the hall?"

He looks behind him and I follow his gaze to a sulking Jules, who keeps sitting down on the couch, jumping to his feet, and pacing back and forth, before repeating the whole thing over again. Lowering his voice, Ben actually looks sincere when he speaks next. "Look, Jules is freaking out. Thea, her daughter, Chloe, and her dad, Hank, all live across the hall. Thea is… also freaking out. She's new in town and needs a friend. Can you—will you take this to her?"

I might be a loner freak who would rather work on jigsaw puzzles while listening to a true crime podcast than go to a cocktail bar to gossip about who wore it better, but I'm not a heartless bitch.

"Lose my number," I seethe as I turn and knock on the door across the hall. In response, I get a chuckle from Ben and the soft click of his apartment door closing. I roll my eyes hard enough that I hope he can feel it, even though he can't see it.

Fifteen seconds later, a gorgeous blonde woman opens the door. *Get it, Jules!* is my first thought because this woman looks like she was created from every man's fantasy. But my arms are falling asleep so my second thought wins out.

"Scoot over, these are heavy."

She moves enough to let me in, so I make my way over to the counter, unceremoniously dumping the paper sacks. After rifling for a minute, I find the smaller paper sack nestled against the Pop-Tarts and the mac and cheese. When I turn around to give it to who I'm assuming is Thea, she's still standing at the front door.

She looks a bit like a deer in headlights. I approach slowly before handing her the bag. "Here."

Thea looks down and then back up at me. "Sorry, who are you?"

"Are you fucking kidding me? Did Benjamin not tell you I was coming over?" I do my very best attempt at the cartoons who are able to shoot lasers out of their eyes as I stare straight into the peephole of Ben's apartment. There's no way he's not watching this go down.

"H-he did! He did not tell me who you were, though. Just that you were 'good people.'" She uses air quotes on that last part.

Skeptically, I ask, "He said that?" Thea just stares at me, and I remember why I'm not very good at making friends. "Whatever. I'm Cole. Colette, but people call me Cole. Do you want to…" I glance down at the package she currently has a death grip on.

She takes one look inside before shoving it back toward me. "Nope."

Alright. I did my part, I can't force her to pee on the thing. "Okay." I shrug.

At that exact moment, a miniature version of Thea runs in. I like kids—they are usually much more straightforward than adults—and this one seems like fun.

"I'm Chloe!" she shrieks. "I already have a best friend, but I like your hair so maybe you can replace him."

"Is it Jules? He's a pretty cool best friend."

"I like Jules…" Chloe concedes. "But Ben is my best friend."

Ew. We'll need to fix that. I get down on her level before saying, "Oh, love bug, not for long if I have anything to say about it."

"Any mac and cheese in that bag? Chloe is pretty easily bought," Thea chimes in, stopping me from going on a tirade about Benjamin.

The great news is that I definitely brought all of the good food. I've always wanted to be the cool aunt, but I don't have any siblings so I was out of luck on that front. I rub my hands together, beginning to unpack the grocery sacks. "Not only do I have mac and cheese… I have the best kind of mac and cheese—shapes!"

Chloe's jaw drops. "Mama never lets us get the shapes!" She drags a chair over to the counter to help me unpack. I rummage around until I find a pot to start boiling the water, not stopping when I hear Thea clear her throat.

"Cole, um… Sorry this has just been a very overwhelming day. You really don't have to do this."

"Listen, Sassafras is a weird-ass place—"

"Language!" Chloe interrupts. Guess I'll need to be careful about that.

"Right… a weird—" I cannot think of another word to replace ass. "'Bleep' place, and the Bardots tend to be fairly persistent, but they are also some of the best people in the world. Benjamin excluded, of course. Chloe and I are going to make our Frozen-shaped, cheesy-pasta deliciousness. You go… do whatever you need to do."

I look meaningfully at the test still lying on the counter. Thea contemplates it for a moment, finally giving in. "Fine," she growls before walking out of the room.

Satisfied, Chloe and I continue making dinner. When Thea comes back out, her face is ashen. I don't ask, but I don't need to. We eat, I distract Chloe long enough for Thea to pull herself together, and by the time I leave, I think I've successfully made two new friends.

Chapter Six
LOOKING FOR A PARTNER IN CRIME
Cole

GOOGLE SEARCH

Q What should you put in your dating app bio? 🎤

The problem with attempting to date in a small town—especially when I stupidly chose to go on a date with someone in my master's program—is that there's a one hundred percent guarantee that you will see them again. Sure enough, Brody and I not only have several classes together, but we also seem to run into each other every time I leave my apartment.

So far, I've successfully avoided speaking to him, but unfortunately that ended today when Dr. Torres paired us up for the midterm project.

It has been over two months since our coffee date… honestly, thank God we didn't sleep together. That would have made this ten thousand times worse.

Our partnership, however, along with Ben's stupid ability to infiltrate my thoughts at the absolute worst moments, is serving as a reminder that I need to stay the course in my quest.

The quest to find a partner before my birthday, that is.

Because after twelve years of leaving me the fuck alone, of course he's becoming a regular annoyance right when he's decided that he *does* remember the pact we made as teenagers.

And clearly, I am a grown-ass adult and, as much as I loathe him, I know Ben would never hold me to something that I don't want.

It's just that… maybe I do want it.

Not with Ben, obviously. But, maybe having a partner again would be nice.

Brody chooses that moment to plop down in the seat next to me. "Hi, partner."

I can't help my cringe, hearing him use the word I was just thinking about in a different context.

"Cole." Brody sighs. "We went to coffee once. It was a really bizarre experience, but this doesn't have to be weird. We can be partners in this project. I can be cool—can you be cool?" he asks, giving me a wink that I think is intended to soothe my nerves.

The problem is I am the opposite of cool. I mean, I work my ass off to present as cool—aloof even—but I'm like an iceberg. Well, not the cold part of the iceberg but the fact that it looks approachable on the outside, but if you get too close it will destroy you.

That's not even speculation. That's a cold, hard fact.

Instead of going down that rabbit hole with Brody, however, I just give him the answer he wants. "Yeah, I can be cool."

And I'm probably not lying to him. I don't particularly care about Brody, so I can be cool. Cool as an iceberg.

Brody nods, and I can see his shoulders relax a fraction of an inch. "Great. Let's set a time next week to get started."

We do just that, and I'm so proud of how totally and completely normal I acted around a man that I went on one date with, that I make the decision to download a dating app when I get back to my apartment. I've never used a dating app before. Both of my previous relationships have been friends of friends—

the type where you're around each other so frequently that one day you look at the other person and think, *Hmm, I guess I tolerate you.* So using an app is… foreign.

Ernest snuggles next to me as I scroll through my camera looking for a profile picture. It needs to show that I'm hot, but approachable. The hot part is easy. My college roommate, Jess, let me know that I'm conventionally attractive. Symmetrical, unique hair, full lips. Things I didn't realize made me pretty but that's what Jess said, and it didn't occur to me to question her insight. I also learned that other girls don't like you when you are pretty. Which might be part of the reason I'm not great at making friends… I haven't quite figured that part out yet.

It's the approachable part that is more difficult to capture in a photograph. Or in real life.

I settle on the picture of Ernest and me that Ben liked on Instagram. Dogs, I've heard, make someone appear more approachable. Not sure if that logic applies to dogs like Ernest, but he's the only one I've got.

Okay, picture is done. I think I've managed the perfect mix of approachable and hot. Up next… hobbies.

Hmm. I look around my apartment, the jigsaw puzzle three quarters of the way done spread across the coffee table. My small TV that I really only use to stream *Dateline*. A stack of text books mixed with my favorite fantasy novels.

My thumb hovers over my phone. Next to hobbies, I type: Puzzles. Television shows. Reading.

Done.

Now for the lifestyle questions…

Drink? *Socially.*

Exercise? *Occasionally.*

Night owl or early bird? Why isn't middle of the day pigeon an option?

Interested in? *Anyone.*

Age range? 25+. Hopefully that will weed out any of the undergrads that I might accidentally match with.

About me… Ugh. Isn't the point of this so people can learn more about me? Why do I need to write it down in a witty way that will most likely still be judged by half of the people on the app?

After staring at the screen for over a minute, I finally type: *Former engineer, current psych student. Takes me a while to warm up.*

Oof. Nope, delete that last part. *Enjoys some light kink?* That's sure to bring out some overconfident men with small dicks. *Trying to teach myself how to cook?* No.

Wait!

Former engineer, current forensic psych student. Looking for a partner in crime.

Perfect. Albeit a little creepy, but I'm not mad about that.

I publish my dating profile and immediately set my phone down to process what I've just done. Instead of thinking too hard about it, I pour myself a glass of wine. Taking a sip, I work to ground myself. Stockinged toes feeling the firmness of the faux hardwood against my feet, the cool press of the countertop against my hand, the tart glide of the bottom-shelf Malbec down the back of my throat.

Groaning, I lay my forehead against the counter. I feel overheated after the events of the last several days… several months. There's been a lack of control looming over me, something I haven't felt to this degree since high school.

Since the days when Benoit Bardot would catch my eye after a track meet and wink as if we were in on some joke together. Though, I'm not sure what he found so funny about running.

Or that time in biology class when we had to create Punnett squares and Ben kept looking at my hair and telling me how rare I was. It caused a weird swooping low in my belly, one that I definitely—probably—didn't like.

He has that infuriating effect on me. Scrambling my thoughts in a way that makes it hard to focus on anything else.

I need a bath. That will help.

Piling my hair on top of my head, I pad to the bathroom and

let the water run until it's boiling hot. I don't like the feel of bubble bath so I skip that, instead lighting three of my favorite Irish-coffee-scented candles to give the room a relaxing aroma. Yes, three of the exact same candle. Because when I find something that doesn't irritate me I have to hoard it like some pre-winter squirrel gathering nuts.

I sink into the water and watch as my fair skin turns splotchy red.

The next thirty minutes are spent contemplating what the fuck I'm going to do about Benoit Bardot. By the time I get out of the tub, I have a match on the dating app. Here's to hoping *that* will finally reset my brain.

Chapter Seven
PROMISED TO ANOTHER
Ben

GOOGLE SEARCH

Q best pastas for carbonara

I've committed to playing the long game with Cole. I mean, obviously twelve years is quite possibly the longest game I could play, but I kind of figured once I moved back here things would escalate quickly.

I was wrong.

Despite reaching out to her for help with Thea, despite revealing my stalker-ish tendencies on her Instagram, Cole continues to pretend like I don't exist every time we cross paths. Which is frequently. This is a small town, after all.

We ran into each other at the grocery store last week. My eye caught hers as soon as she turned down the pasta aisle. She was wearing sweatpants and a matching sweatshirt that said "I could be meaner" across the front. I, however, could not help the quirk of my lips at that. Cole immediately clocked it, scowled, abandoned her cart, and walked straight out of the store.

That's when I realized she wasn't kidding about her hatred of me. My hands tingled, my blood rushed, and my heart literally skipped a beat—finally, a challenge. Finally someone who actually makes me *feel* something.

Walking over to her cart, I looked in to see the ingredients for carbonara. Not surprising, Cole would pick one of the most complicated pasta dishes to perfect. Because there was no doubt in my mind that she makes a phenomenal carbonara. I paced the pasta aisle before picking out a fusilli noodle, buying her entire abandoned cart, and dropping the bags at her apartment door.

The last part was the most difficult part of my plan. I ended up asking Ethel if she knew where Cole lived, which, of course, she did. Ethel knows everything. I knew I'd probably have to answer her probing questions later, but it was worth it.

Cole and I have had several similar interactions over the past few months, as winter is slowly melting into spring. Which is why I'm not surprised to see her when I'm walking to check-in on progress at the coffee shop. What is surprising is that she's with someone.

She's never with someone. Cole is a loner, through and through. She had one friend throughout middle and high school, Maya, who come to think of it, I haven't ever seen in any of Cole's social media posts. But right now she's with a tall, tan brunette woman, standing outside of Harriet's flower shop.

And she's *laughing*.

An insane flare of jealousy hits me square in the chest. She's so beautiful when she laughs, her red hair practically glows in the afternoon sun, ponytail shaking back and forth as she nods at whatever the woman is saying.

The woman's hand slides around Cole's waist, pulling her in to whisper something in her ear, and I see red, literally.

My feet are moving before my brain has a conscious thought about what the fuck I'm doing. All I know is this is wrong, Cole is supposed to be *mine*.

Casually, I grab a red carnation as I sidle up to Cole and her new friend. I use the term "friend" loosely because Cole is now whispering back in her ear in a decidedly not-friendly way. As nonchalantly as possible, I accidentally bump into Cole while reaching for another flower that just happens to be right in front of where she's standing.

"Hey!" she snaps, whipping her head around to glare at me before growling, "Benjamin."

There she is. That's the Cole I know and—"Colette! I didn't see you there. What a coincidence that we would both be getting flowers at Harriet's right this very moment. The smallest world!"

Her eyes narrow, something I choose to ignore, and instead I pretend to only just notice the woman beside her, who is almost eye level with me. Sticking my hand out to shake, she clasps it with a surprisingly firm grip. "Hi there, I'm Ben. Are you Colette's friend? I honestly didn't know she had friends. Good for you, Red. We've all been rooting for you." I wink to piss her off even more.

It works. She straightens up to her full height, still a good head below me, and points her thumb behind her. "This is Heather. We are on a date, so if you could just…" She waves me off.

"A date?" I ask, feigning shock. I lean in close and whisper, loud enough for Heather to hear, "Does she know?"

"Do I know what?" Heather asks, looking confused as hell.

Cole ignores her, instead attempting to incinerate me on the spot with the heat of her gaze. "There's nothing for her to know, Benjamin."

"You wound me, Red. I think it's imperative for her to know that you are promised to another," I retort.

"'Promised to another'? Was I involved in some nobleman's trade that I'm unaware of? Have I been dropped into an episode of *Punk'd*? Where's Gabe? Is he filming?" She's breathless by the time she finishes her rant.

And Heather is—blissfully—backing away slowly from the red-faced Cole.

Shrugging, I answer her first question. "Something like that."

"What the fuck, Benjamin?" She starts to take a step toward me but she miscalculates her surroundings, her elbow knocking into one of the buckets of flowers. It tips, dumping all of the orange lilies onto Cole's tights-clad legs. We both try to stop the bucket from completely emptying, unfortunately causing a collision of both of our heads.

In an attempt to steady herself, Cole's hand clasps onto another bucket of flowers, completely emptying its contents as well.

"Fucking hell, Colette. Stop moving."

She does just that, literally freezing in her place on the sidewalk. She's surrounded by a sea of orange lilies and yellow carnations. Her bottom half is soaked with flower water, and Heather is nowhere to be seen.

"Let me go pay Harriet for these. Stay here." My hand wraps around the front door to the small flower shop before I pause to add, "Please."

Harriet is confused as to what happened, and honestly, so am I. While I will admit that my intentions were to run off anyone who felt like they could touch Cole, I do feel a small bit of remorse about how it was done.

Turns out, leaving Cole alone was a bad idea though, because by the time I make it back outside, there's a look of pure determination on her face. She watches as I pick up all of the flowers around her, not bothering to help. She just stands there, arms folded and hip cocked to the side.

And I'm down here. On my knees for her. A place I'd be pretty content to stay.

So I do. While I'm still down on one knee, I look up at her and smirk, presenting the bouquet in my hands as an offering.

"Colette Russell, will you—" The smallest flash of surprise crosses her face, as if she doesn't quite know how I'm going to finish that sentence. "Take these flowers home with you? Think of me every time you look at them." I bite my lip, holding back my grin.

"Yes, I will," she responds, matter-of-factly. "And I hope you didn't have any plans this afternoon because you will also be coming home with me. You've ruined two of my attempts to fuck someone, so congratulations. You'll be the one getting me off today. Get up, let's go."

She doesn't wait for my response, she simply starts walking. And I'll be damned if I don't scramble after her like a lovesick puppy.

Chapter Eight
SAFE WORD: FOUDROYANT

Ben

GOOGLE SEARCH

I follow a good six feet behind Cole all the way back to her apartment. There is no fucking way I am going to speak for fear of saying something that will make Cole change her mind.

A fleeting thought passes through my lust-addled brain that maybe we should slow down. That this is too good to be true. But this is Cole, and fuck if I'm not a desperate, pathetic man that has repressed just how much I've been pining after this woman since middle school. Even when I've acted like I hated her, it was just that—an act.

I dig my hands into my jean pockets as I watch her unlock her apartment door. We are immediately greeted by Ernest, her three-legged dog. The one I obviously know about even though I'm not supposed to.

The bastard growls at me.

"Good boy," she coos, sending a jolt straight to my dick. *The dog. She's talking to the dog, Benoit.*

She stands and begins stripping off her boots, socks, and tights, leaving her legs bare beneath her plaid skirt. She mutters something about "gross, sticky tights," kicking them away from her with a flick of her toe. Not a single glance has been thrown in my direction.

"Colette…" I venture, testing my luck.

"Benjamin…" she replies, stripping her sweater off.

"Fuck." I turn around because it is incredibly difficult to focus when Cole's tits are popping out of the top of her lacey bra. "I—Is this real?"

"Here's the deal, Benjamin. I've been… frustrated. And that is partially your fault, so now I need your help remedying that situation." I can hear her sigh, but I still refuse to look. I need to be able to think straight, even as my dick is pressing uncomfortably against the zipper of my pants.

"Something I've learned since the last time we lived in the same city," she continues, "is that I like things a particular way when it comes to sex. I get the feeling you'll be okay with that, but if you're not, that's completely fine, too."

I clear my throat, hand scrubbing over my face. The problem with that is when my eyes close, Cole's perfect breasts are burned into my mind. My eyes pop open, and I focus on the peeling paint making an unintentional pattern across the back side of her front door. "What, uh… what exactly does that mean?"

"I prefer to be in charge," she states plainly. A new image has popped into my head, one I've conjured completely on my own. Cole in full leather, my hands bound above my head. She's climbing on top of—"I know it's not for everyone but I've done a lot of research, some trial and error, and that's what I prefer. We can come up with a safe word, you can be out at any moment, no questions asked. Most men are more apprehensive—"

"I'm in," I interrupt, turning back toward her. I've surprised her with how quickly I agreed, but she recovers instantly.

"Great. Safe word?"

"Foudroyant." Her mouth pops open in a surprised "O"—probably because that was the word she spelled correctly in our junior year spelling bee, beating me to win. She went all the way to the state level that year.

"Foudroyant," she repeats. "O-okay." It's the first time I've seen her stumble since I walked out of Harriet's. Good. She can be in charge in the bedroom but I don't want her to confuse what this means to me. The fact that she even let me into her space—I don't take that for granted.

"One more thing." She steps closer to me, her eyes bouncing back and forth between mine. "This doesn't mean we are friends."

"Excellent," I reply. "I don't want to be friends with you anyway." Which is a partial truth. The part she's ready to hear.

"My bedroom is the second door on the right. Clothes off. I expect you to be waiting for me."

My returning grin is wicked. "Yes, ma'am."

"Good boy." She smirks, and this time it *is* directed at me.

Biting my knuckles, I turn and follow her commands. When I open the door to her room, I immediately see that it screams *Cole*. The walls are a dark charcoal color, the white sheets pop against the wooden accents and moody vintage art on the walls. There's a psychology textbook on her bedside table and an ornate rug covers most of the floor.

It's very… serious. In a deep, sensual way.

As I start to strip, I notice a snake plant on the window sill that is in desperate need of some water. Looking around, there's a half-empty water glass abandoned next to Cole's bed that has just enough water left in it. That's how Cole finds me: in nothing but my boxers, watering her dying plant.

"You aren't very good at listening," she admonishes.

"Your plant is dying."

She quirks a brow. "Maybe I wanted it to."

"You didn't."

"No," she admits, "I didn't."

She watches as I finish and then looks meaningfully at the bed. "Oh! Right, let me just… should I keep the boxers on?"

Cole's hand comes up, massaging her temple as if I'm causing her great distress. Her other hand is firmly planted on her hip. She's still only wearing a pleated plaid skirt and a deep green lace bra, her creamy skin is on full display, speckled with freckles. I take a moment to admire her, aware that she's now staring right back at me.

One particular area of me.

"What if I said boxers off?" she asks.

"Then the boxers would come off, Colette. I meant what I said. You're in charge here."

"Keep them on… for now. And get on the bed, Benjamin."

"Are you ever going to call me by my real name?"

"No," she says, opening the top drawer of her dresser and pulling out a long silk cloth. "How do you feel about being restrained? I'd love to gag you but that might be too much for your first time."

"This isn't my first time!"

Her *mhmm* is non-committal.

"Red, when did you become such a freak?"

"I always was a freak," she starts, holding up a hand when she sees me begin to protest. "But I know that's not really what you meant. I started exploring kink in college. Nothing intense… Kink-lite, if you will. I had one serious girlfriend… Eventually she also had a boyfriend. I learned a lot from them, specifically that that wasn't really the type of relationship I wanted. But it was a safe space to explore my sexuality. And—" Her spine snaps straight as if she just registered something. "I'm realizing now that I just gave you a long-winded explanation that you probably did not want or need."

"I did," I reply simply. Then, in what I hope will be a peace offering, I hold out my wrists. "Tie me up, Red."

"Patience, Benjamin. I have an IUD and I've been tested since my last partner. There are also condoms in the dresser." As she's speaking, she steps up to me, her hand coming to my shoulder and guiding me down to the bed. It puts me eye level with her tits, and I have to fist the sheets to stop myself from reaching toward her.

"I had a vasectomy," I admit, my entire focus on how easy it would be to lean forward and lick the spot where her bra meets her skin.

I'm about to do just that when I realize she's stopped moving. "Everything okay?" I ask.

Her eyes are narrowed again, trying to read something on my face.

"You had a vasectomy?" she asks.

"It's reversible, if you want kids. But I don't think I do. Do you?" Suddenly her answer means everything to me.

"Why would it matter to you whether or not I want kids?" That non-answer makes my skin crawl.

"It does matter to me." *Everything you do matters to me.*

Cole's lips rub together, contemplating whether she's going to answer my question. Ultimately, she shakes her head. "I don't want kids."

I can't help myself any longer.

Finally—*fucking finally*—I kiss Colette Russell.

Chapter Nine
I BARELY TOUCHED YOU!
Cole

GOOGLE SEARCH

Meditation for when you accidentally sleep with your nemesis.

Somewhere between picking out flowers with Heather and the sight of Ben kneeling at my feet, I lost my mind. Ben showing back up in my life, reminding me of the pact, being there at every fucking turn… I made a rash decision. Something I almost never do.

And now, he's kissing me. With his lips. His extremely luscious lips. Because I said I don't want kids.

I. Am. So. Confused.

Also, turned on.

I'm confused and turned on. And confused about being turned on by Benoit Bardot. Someone who has been firmly planted in the "nemesis" portion of my brain for over half of my life. I knew that moving him to the "fuck buddy" portion of my brain would be difficult, but he's doing it all wrong.

We aren't supposed to be kissing.

Control. I need to take back control.

Ben's hands start roaming up my naked thigh, underneath my skirt, with firm touches—exactly how I fucking like it—and my control slips even further out of my grasp.

No.

No!

I will not allow this man to take over. Wrenching myself away, I smack Ben's hand off my thigh. His lips are kiss stung, his eyes hazy. When I tell him to give me his hands, he complies. I knot his wrists together, leaning in to whisper, "Remember the safe word?"

I watch as his Adam's apple bobs up and down with his gulp. "Yes."

"Good." Taking a step back, I unzip my skirt, allowing it to pool at my feet. Ben's eyes bounce down to the matching lace panties I just revealed to him. "You have a choice, Benjamin. I liked seeing you on your knees for me earlier, but I would be open to riding your face if that's what you prefer."

The heated gaze that was tracing my body snaps back up to meet my eyes. His reply is instant. "Ride my face. Please," he adds.

"Needy, needy." I *tsk*. "Lie back. Hands above your head."

He awkwardly—desperately—scoots himself across the bed so his lean body can stretch out. He easily overtakes most of my king bed, and I admire his erection, visibly tenting his boxers. And there's a *lot* to admire.

Moving to the foot of the bed, I bare myself completely to Benoit Bardot. What a bizarre world I'm living in. Obviously the matrix has glitched. Good thing this means absolutely nothing. It's just sex. A carnal need—an itch to be scratched.

Climbing onto all fours, I slowly make my way up Ben's body to a chorus of "Fuck, fuck, holy hell, Colette." He continues his incoherent mumbling, even attempting to take my nipple in his mouth when my breast is eye level with him. When I move just out of his reach, this grown-ass man gives me an honest-to-God pout.

"I'm in charge, Benjamin. Be a good boy and I might let you come."

Ben swallows, his head hitting the pillow in defeat. "Last chance to back out, Ben," I continue, making eye contact with him so he can see that I truly want him to make the choice.

"Hands on the headboard, Colette."

I allow him this one opportunity to tell me what to do. Moving further up until my thighs bracket his face, I steady myself on the headboard, Ben moaning underneath me. He turns his head enough to nip at my inner thigh, sending a shiver up my spine and heat exploding low in my belly.

"Reach up and tap me if you can't breathe," I tell him as I lower myself.

"Don't need to breathe," he murmurs. "Sit." When I don't immediately do as he said, he adds, "Please."

"Much bet—*oh!*" I temporarily lose all coherent thought as Ben gives me one long lick from my core to my clit. I cant my hips, rolling them in time with the stroke of Ben's very capable tongue. "Fuck," I whisper, because of course he's good at this.

He expertly swirls and flicks, working me into a tizzy. Not like that would have been too difficult after how hot and bothered I've been lately. But Ben... I should have known this would be world-tiltingly good.

Not only do we both have experience, I'm assuming, but Ben and I have always had a connection. Albeit, not a positive one. Apparently that doesn't matter to my traitorous body. A connection is a connection and something that it yearns for.

Ben's hips buck involuntarily behind me. "Enjoying yourself?" I ask.

He can't answer me, but his nod is enthusiastic and partnered with a guttural moan that vibrates through me. He hasn't been at it too long, but already I can feel the telltale signs that my body is going to tip over the edge. Something I haven't done with a partner in… quite a while.

"Yes, Ben," I encourage. "Right there!"

He doubles down, continuing to flick in that exact spot until my legs clamp around his head like a vise. It's an effort to keep myself up, my grip on the headboard the only thing stopping me from crumpling in satisfaction.

My hips continue to rock, riding out the waves of pleasure that crash and crash *and crash*. Somewhere the hazy realization that I'm literally and figuratively fucked passes through my brain.

When I'm able to somewhat compose myself, I turn around, leaving my cunt in Ben's face and bending forward toward his boxer-clad dick.

My turn.

I allow my tongue to brush lazily across his dick, over the fabric. I wonder how long I can tease him like this before he's begging for me to strip him bare and take his cock in my mouth…

Turns out it's not long because after a few strokes, I can feel him whimper, his abs tightening underneath my tits.

"Colette, Cole… I—" My hand wraps around his length, cutting off his words. "I'm—wait, I—"

And then the motherfucker comes in his pants.

"Fuck, fuck. No, shit, Cole." His string of curses fill the room, and I can't help the surprised laugh that pops out.

Maneuvering my body off of his, I find a towel in the linen closet, wetting it with warm water before bringing it back to the bedroom. Ben is looking like a man who had his cake and ate it too—not even slightly bashful. "I cannot believe you just came. I barely touched you!"

He just shrugs. A small smile dancing across his lips. "That was the hottest thing I've ever done. I was barely hanging by a thread when you turned around, as it was."

I hum in response, not truly believing *that* was the hottest thing Ben Bardot has ever done. "I'm taking a bath. You can let yourself out once you've cleaned up."

"Wha—wait." He scrambles off the bed, not without difficulty since his hands are still bound together. "Can't we... I don't know, hang out?"

Now he has the audacity to look bashful.

Carefully, I untie his hands, only replying with, "No," when he's free.

"No?" Is he... sad?

"No. We aren't going to be friends, remember? You agreed to that." I pull my green silk robe off the hook, wrapping it snugly around my exposed body.

"But... but I just made you come! I know it was good, don't try to tell me it wasn't."

I pat him a few times on his stupidly chiseled pec. "Yes, it was very good. Thank you for that orgasm. If you are still in my apartment when I get out of the bathtub, it will never happen again." I give him a condescending grin and he sticks his tongue out at me.

"Fine," he concedes, taking his dirty boxers off and wiping himself down with the washcloth. There's a small tattoo on his hip, something I hadn't previously noticed, but he turns away before I'm able to get a good look. "But this discussion isn't over, Colette."

It is, but I'll let him believe that.

"Whatever you say, Bardot. See you around." With that, I step into the bathroom, shutting the door in his beautiful, barely tolerable face.

Chapter Ten

PICK A DIFFERENT PATH
Ben

GOOGLE SEARCH

🔍 best books to read to preschoolers 🎤

"You okay, Benny boo?" Gabe teases from where he's lounging on the couch. Jules and I are tackling dinner tonight, and it appears that Gabe is content to leave us to it.

"I'm fine," I drawl, not sounding fine even to my own ears. "Why?"

Jules eyes me suspiciously. "I think the onions are small enough, Brother."

Looking down I realize he's right. I've pulverized what were supposed to be chunks of onions for our salsa. "Shit, sorry," I mutter, placing the knife gently on the counter.

"I'm going to ask you again, you okay?" Gabe sits up this time, actually listening.

I'm not sure if I'm ready to talk about whatever the fuck happened with Cole, but I also trust my brothers implicitly. "Yes." I pause. "No. I don't know."

"Would you like to talk about it?" Jules asks. He's always so matter-of-fact in everything he does.

"Have you ever miscommunicated with a… partner?"

"Yes," both of my brothers answer at the same time. Then Gabe clarifies, "We're talking about like relationship type partners, right? You aren't having issues with a business partner, are you?"

"You both are my business partners," I deadpan. "Yes, it's an… intimate partner."

"So, Colette Russell finally paid you a modicum of attention?" Jules smirks knowingly at my reaction to that question. "C'mon, Ben. There's a fine line between love and hate. You and Cole have always been at each other's throats. It was only a matter of time before you were *at each other's throats*." He winks to emphasize the distinction.

"That's why you really moved back, isn't it?" Gabe asks.

Yes.

"No, I came back for the shop."

"You came back because you were unhappy in Boston," Jules corrects. "And that was partially because your people weren't there, right?"

Scooping the onions into a nearby bowl, I debate how much I really want to dive into this. If I'm being honest with myself, even after pretending I was fine with Cole asking me to leave, I feel… *vulnerable.* I don't think my brothers will judge me for jumping into bed with Cole, but I'm not sure they won't.

"Of course. But you are my people. Cole is… Cole isn't even a friend."

I can sense Gabe and Jules exchanging a look, so I cut this conversation off before they can respond. "How are things with Thea?"

My twin tenses up, casting a glance toward the front door of Gabe and my apartment, and I can't say I'm sorry for turning the spotlight on his love life instead of mine. He takes his bun out, running his hands through his hair, then quickly reties it—his nervous tic. Thea, our across-the-hall neighbor, turned out to also be Jules' "one that got away" after they spent a night together in Boston. She didn't get too far, though, because they reconnected when she unexpectedly moved to Sassafras, and now she's pregnant with Jules' baby.

"Things are fine," Jules replies.

Gabe answers by throwing a pillow at him. "I'm having déjà vu. You know, because of the whole twin thing. And the whole pretending-like-nothing-is-happening-in-your-personal-lives thing."

Jules sighs, tossing the pillow back toward our oldest brother. "I'm not pretending like nothing is happening. Things are… complicated with Thea. I want to be involved. I'm ecstatic about being a dad, but she needs time and space. I'm trying to give that to her."

Alright, Jules' situation seems a lot more complicated than mine. There's a fucking kid involved. Well, two because of Thea's daughter Chloe. Clasping Jules on the shoulder, I squeeze a few times in reassurance. "You're going to be a great dad, Julien. I'm being serious because I used your full name, see?"

He cracks a smile at that. Gabe hops off the couch, finally making himself useful. "Benoit is right. You'll be a great dad. Margaritas, anyone?"

Conversation continues, wading into shallower waters. We talk about construction on the coffee shop, Jules has a few ideas for menu items, and I'm appointed the job of managing the social media.

It's good. It gives me a purpose in a world where I am still feeling aimless. I thought moving back to Sassafras would be an immediate fix for that, but it appears that I was wrong.

Honestly, I kind of thought maybe Cole would become my purpose—it appears I was wrong about that, as well.

———

"Ethel! Do you want to be in a TikTok?"

We were at the shop checking in on progress when I spotted Ethel walking by. I know she was just being nosy about the changes that are going on both inside our shop and inside of the dance studio next door that Thea is renovating.

"Oh, I didn't notice you there Ben-o-it!" She's a terrible actress *and* loves to give me grief about the spelling of my name. It's a deadly combo.

"Well now that you have noticed me, come film a video with me. We can do one about the transition from The Coffee Shop to Bardot Brothers Coffee Co."

She gives me an appraising look. "Is this what you're doing with your life now? Making videos?"

Ethel is one to talk. "Ethel, darling. You have fifty-thousand followers on TikTok. You know as well as anyone how important a social media presence is."

"It's actually sixty thousand," she corrects. "And my followers like me because I add value to their lives. I give advice to the young ones, share my OOTD—that stands for outfit of the day—and teach them how to garden. What value are you adding to your followers, Benoit?"

Wow, way to call me out, Ethel.

"I—Well, I mean the goal is to get people to come to the coffee shop…"

She rolls her eyes at me. "Duh."

Ethel has to be in her mid-seventies, so hearing her say duh is jarring. She takes my silence for what it is—disbelief—finally patting my cheek and telling me she'll be in a video once I've found my value.

"You mean the shop's value?" I ask.

"No, Ben. Your value." She pauses, assessing. "I'm volunteering at the library later today, why don't you come with me?"

Volunteering? It's not like I can do much at the shop while the contractor is working… "Sure, Ethel. What time?"

That's how I find myself conducting a pre-school storytime at the Sassafras Public Library. Acting out the conversations between an illustrated pig and elephant. The kids are eating it up, Chloe included. I had no idea she would be here, but we've become fast friends, living across the hall from each other. She's loud and sassy, and throws an amazing tea party. I really lean into the different voices for her benefit.

Afterward, she bounds up to me with excitement written across her little face. "Ben! You are so good at stories! I can't wait until I can read."

I ruffle her hair. "You'll get there soon, Chlo."

"You have to do all of the stories at the library now!" She leans in conspiratorily, attempting to whisper in the way all young kids do. "The person who usually does it is so boring!"

"I'm sure they are trying their best," I reply, trying to hide my laugh.

She scowls at that. "They should probably pick a different path. That's what mommy says when someone isn't very good at something."

I can't hold my laugh in at that. I can totally see Thea attempting to frame it in a kind way and Chloe seeing straight through that. "Well, I think this might be part of my path. I'll be back to do storytime next week, okay?"

She nods, satisfied with my compliance. And I really do think Ethel might have been right about volunteering. Sassafras has given so much to me… it might be time to give back to the town that raised me.

Keeping my mind off Cole will be an added bonus.

Chapter Eleven
COLE TALKS ABOUT ME?
Ben

GOOGLE SEARCH

The entire Bardot crew—well, those of us in Sassafras—has assembled to move Thea, Chloe, and Hank out of their apartment. I will admit, I'm pretty sad to lose my little buddy across the hall. But when a pipe burst in their apartment, Jules went all caveman on everyone, insisting that they move into his house.

Honestly, it made me wonder if he orchestrated the entire thing just to have Thea closer to him on a daily basis.

We're all waiting outside of Louie's when Jules and Thea pull up. Jules looks downright giddy, causing me to be even more skeptical of his intentions. I'm also not sure how much is actually salvageable inside the apartment, but there's an unspoken Bardot family rule that when one of us calls, all of us answer. So here we are, on a lovely spring day, doing everyone's favorite activity: moving.

Jules introduces Thea and her family to Mom and Dad. To absolutely no one's surprise, our mom, Elaine, has zero chill when meeting Thea. I think she's so glad that one of us boys has brought *someone* home, it wouldn't matter if that person was actually a blow-up doll at this point.

Not that Thea is like a blow-up doll. She's actually really great and I'm happy for my twin. Happy and... jealous? Yeah, I'm fucking jealous of him too.

I watch, trying to shake that feeling off, as Mom gives Thea a giant bear hug, telling her, "I always wanted a daughter."

"I'm telling Bex you said that," Gabe shouts.

Mom lets go of Thea, turning to wag a finger in Gabe's face. "Gabriel. You will say nothing unless you want me to dethrone you as my favorite son."

Everyone knows Anders is her favorite son.

"Everyone knows Anders is your favorite son," Jules chimes in, apparently drawing upon our twin telepathy.

Mom faces me. "I think Benoit is my favorite son right now," she says with a wink.

"Benoit?" Thea questions. "Your name isn't Benjamin?"

I give my parents a pointed look because this is a question I've answered most of my life. I was the child they decided to give the uber-French name to—it's my burden to bear. "No," I answer. "But that's a very common assumption."

"It's not an assumption," Thea replies. "That's what Cole calls you."

My head immediately snaps to Thea at that. "Cole talks about me?"

I hear it. I hear the desperation as soon as the words fall from my lips. *And* so does everyone else because they are all currently staring at me with varying degrees of interest. Mom looks absolutely feral.

"I mean, ha! Yeah, that Cole. She always calls me the wrong name. Silly really..." I trail off, shoving my hands in my pockets and praying to the universe that someone, anyone, will take pity on me and end this conversation.

I'd even take an unexplained natural phenomena at this point.

A freak tornado. An on-land shark attack. A sharknado!

Instead, I get Chloe. The most honest, vocal four-year-old I've ever met.

"You kind of look like Kristoff when he realizes Anna went on an adventure without him," she helpfully points out.

"Enough of that, Princess Chloe!" I scoop her up, heading inside the building in an attempt to get away from this conversation. "Let's get your things, shall we? I heard you get to stay at JuJu's house." I throw a wink over my shoulder to a blushing Thea.

She hasn't quite accepted it yet, but I already know that she and Jules are inevitable.

———

After a long day of moving, I've stopped by the coffee shop to check in on progress. The more I think about it, the more I'm glad that Cole is talking to Thea. Not only because she's talking about me, but also because both of them need a friend. They are opposites in so many ways.

Thea is mild-mannered but protective. She's been through a lot and that makes her nervous, skittish.

Cole is… unapologetic. Intimidating. Beautiful. A force to be reckoned with.

Both tend to hold the world at arm's length, so it's encouraging to see them open up to one another.

Not for the first time, I think about Cole's friendship with Maya —or lack thereof—and how lonely it must be to not have anyone. I imagine Cole putting her delicate hands on her hips, telling me she doesn't *need* anyone. But that doesn't mean she doesn't *want*…

And, as I hoped it would when I moved back, luck is on my side because the menace herself just walked by the coffee shop.

Cole looks adorable, per usual. She's got an oversized Hawthorne University sweatshirt on over loose fitting jeans. Her typical "fuck off" boots are laced up halfway, as if she just didn't have it in her to finish the job. A haphazard braid curls over her shoulder. She looks tired, though I would never tell her that.

All of the lights are off, so I'm sure she doesn't realize I'm in here when she stops to read the flyer on the front door. It's got all of the typical *Coming Soon* information on it. Soon is relative because this renovation has taken much longer than any of us anticipated. She scowls, hiking her backpack up onto her shoulders.

I inch closer to the door but she doesn't see me until I'm right on the other side of the glass. When she finally realizes I'm there, she lets out a string of expletives, doubling over as she catches her breath. "For fuck's sake, Benjamin. Warn a girl next time!"

Her voice is muffled through the glass, and I can't help but crack a smile at her distraught state.

"Quit laughing at me!" She doesn't miss a thing. Never has. I unlock the door to let her in and then hold up my hands in surrender.

"Sorry, didn't mean to scare you."

"So you regularly stare at unsuspecting women through a window." She narrows her eyes. "Why are you wearing those glasses again?"

"To see…"

She rolls her eyes, cocking that damn hip out to the side. "Honestly, Benjamin. I am aware of the general purpose of glasses. However, I did not realize you were… how should I put it? Visually lacking. You never answered my question about it the other day."

"We are getting older." I step to the side, holding my arm out for her to enter. To my surprise, she doesn't argue.

"My vision is still 20/20," she brags as she passes. It takes everything in me not to inhale her heady scent—a sweet mix of vanilla and caramel.

"Not all of us can be perfect, Colette."

She huffs a laugh, taking a look around. "The place looks…"

"It's a mess," I finish for her. There's a pile of hardwood flooring in the corner, ready to be put down. A stack of chairs lines one wall with one singular long table in the center of the dining space. I've been working from there most days, so I can supervise and make decisions while Jules is still at school. He'll be done any day now, and I know he's itching to be in the shop full time.

My steps are hurried as I place a few chairs around the table. I had just stacked them up for the day when Cole walked by, but now that she's here I'm not eager to let her leave. "You can study here if you'd like," I offer. "I can grab something for you to drink? Diet cherry cola?"

Her eyes narrow at me. "Why do you have diet cherry cola?" I know it's her favorite, but I shrug instead of answering her.

She sighs, mumbling to herself but sets her backpack down, though, I can tell she's wrestling with herself about it. I leave before she can say anything else, getting the drink I promised her.

Popping the top on her can, I hand it to her as she plops down into the chair. "I have some more emails to answer, so you're welcome to stay here and work for as long as you'd like."

That's a lie. I have zero emails to answer. It's a stark contrast from my life in Boston where I felt like I was always working.

She yanks a psychology textbook out of her bag, followed by a laptop, a planner, and a pencil bag, ignoring me completely the entire time. I take a few sips from the soda I got for myself and pretend to be doing something of great importance on my computer.

What I'm actually doing is sneaking glances at the gorgeous

redhead across the table from me. She flips to a marked chapter in her book, her finger slowly tracing across the page. An involuntary shiver runs through my body at the thought of that finger tracing… other places. Her brow furrows when she gets to a particular line, and she glances at her laptop screen as if she's cross-referencing something.

I admire the light dusting of freckles, almost too faint to notice, that covers the tip of her nose and cheeks. She's illuminated by the bluelight glow, her brown eyes looking practically black as they reflect her screen.

It's so quiet in here, I'm about to ask if she wants me to turn on some music when she says, "We aren't having sex again."

Choking on my spit, I erupt into a coughing fit at that statement. "I—" I don't even know what to say to that. Cole hasn't even looked up from her schoolwork after dropping that metaphorical bomb.

"Not even one more time?" I try. "I can be good."

That gets her attention. She levels me with a stonefaced glare. "You could barely follow directions last time."

"You caught me by surprise," I counter. "I wasn't expecting to go from interrupting your date to being tied up in your bed."

"Aha!" She jumps up. "So you admit, you were sabotaging my date!"

Shit.

"No. I said I was interrupting. Very different from intentional sabotage."

She deflates slightly. "You *are* up to something. I know you are. And I will find out what it is."

"Your determination is admirable, Red." I smirk and she lets out a growl of frustration that I can feel all the way in my dick.

As if she can sense her loss of control coming, Cole hastily shoves everything back in her bag. She honestly lasted longer than I expected her to.

It still hurts, though. I'm trying to bridge that gap between hate and… being able to spend an adequate amount of time in the same room together. I'm obviously fucking failing.

That much is clear as Cole flips me the middle finger, storming out of the shop just as quickly as she arrived.

And maybe I'm a masochist because there are a whole lot of things I'd like to do with that finger.

Chapter Twelve
MY SPECIAL INTEREST IS YOUR HAIR
Cole

GOOGLE SEARCH

Q Witchy spell to deter men who wear glasses. 🎤

When faced with an entire day with zero plans, my choice is usually to cuddle up with Ernest and find the latest true crime documentary. I survived my project with Brody, coming out relatively unscathed because of his ability to act like a grown-ass adult and not make things weird.

I definitely made things weird. Especially when he was over at my apartment late one night and went in for a perfectly platonic high five. I misinterpreted his arm movements, going in for a hug instead. I'm not even a hugger! I have no idea what possessed me to do that, and I've been waking up around two in the morning every night to overthink it.

But, we passed our midterms and I'm on the way to passing the entire course—no, *acing* the entire course. I should be hearing back about placements for next semester any day now, as well.

So, yes. I decided to take a day off. No studying, no working on projects, no agonizing over the way Ben looks in glasses.

It was going to be a great day.

Then I matched with a guy named Garrett on the dating app. And, well… my Ben-in-glasses dilemma needed a solution, so I set a date with Garrett for this evening.

Fine, it will be a partial day off. I'm getting ready to settle down on the couch with popcorn and a diet cherry cola—though, even that has now been ruined by Ben—when my phone dings.

Maybe it's Garrett canceling the date. I really don't want to go out tonight.

THEA

Hey Cole! It's Thea!

> Yes, Thea. We've been texting. I even saved
> your number in my phone.

THEA

Wow! What a compliment.

That really is so great. Are we friends?

I feel like we're friends now.

> I don't have friends.

THEA

Right… I do remember you saying that. But
saving my number feels awfully friend-like

> Do you need something, Thea? It's my day off

THEA

Shoot. Any chance you'd like to help out at the
studio on your day off?

Help a pregnant woman out?

It's not my fault you didn't use a condom

THEA

We did!

What the fuck?!

THEA

Well... it broke. But the intention was there!

Oh thank God. I was getting ready to sue the condom company on her behalf.

That is...

THEA

Incredibly unfortunate? Yes, I'm aware.

But we are moving on! The studio needs to be finished so I can actually teach students.

I eye Ernest. I'd like to think he'll be mad at me for leaving him today, but I think he prefers when he can have the couch to himself.

Fine, be there soon.

———

"This place really does look great. Not going to lie, it was giving a little more crack den than ballet studio before you took over."

Thea is standing in the middle of the dance studio—conveniently located next door to the soon-to-be Bardot Brothers Coffee Co. She takes a moment to look around the entire space, as if she's seeing it for the first time. The walls are a soothing shade of green, the floors have been cleaned and re-stained, and we are currently almost done adding a translucent film to the giant front windows that face the street. Thea explained the need to let some light in while also preventing dancers from getting distracted by the passersby.

She absentmindedly rubs her belly, which looks like she just had a really large lunch, biting her lip as a blush runs up her neck and fills her cheeks. After a few moments of silence, I wave my hand in front of her. "Earth to Thea."

"Hmm? Oh! Sorry, what's up?"

"You were thinking about sex, weren't you?" Or maybe that's just me. Sex with Ben. Because of course he was working at the coffee shop when I arrived today.

Thea looks as if I've offended her sensibilities. "What?! No! Sex? What's that? I—"

"Mhmm, very convincing." I cut her off. "So are you and Jules…?"

She stares at me. "Are me and Jules what?"

Thea is either an idiot or *really* doesn't want to talk about this. Too bad. Ben is making me feel destructive, and unfortunately Thea is in the line of fire. "Fucking, Thea. Are you and Jules fucking?"

Thea spins around, searching the area for… an answer maybe? She finds nothing to help her in the empty studio. "So, that's a no. But you want to be."

She proceeds to explain to me how Jules is *too* perfect, so obviously she can't sleep with him. Again.

I watch as she lays herself across the floor in exasperation. It's hard for me to relate to this exact scenario, but I do feel bad for her, and Jules is a good guy. Taking a seat on the ground next to her, I do my best attempt at friendship. "Just because Chloe's sperm donor is a douche canoe that wouldn't own up to his part in her creation, doesn't mean all guys are like that."

From what Thea has told me, Chloe's dad essentially groomed Thea and then left her as soon as she got pregnant. "I've known Jules since high school. Middle school actually. He's always been a good one." *Unlike his brother.*

"It's annoying. The man should have at least one flaw. And even if it didn't work out romantically between the two of you, he would never let that affect his relationship with his child." I'm absolutely certain of that. The Bardots—minus Benjamin— are good people.

Tentatively, I pat Thea's leg because it feels like the comforting thing to do. "Better now?" She grunts in response. "Great. I've got to go, I have a date tonight."

"With Ben?" she asks.

I can feel the look of disgust painted across my face. "Ew. No. Why would you ask that?"

She grins at me. "He seems to seek your approval like a puppy dog looking for scratches."

Gag. "He can scratch his own ass."

"This feels like a 'you're not fucking but you want to be' type situation," she says, throwing my own words back at me. If only she knew.

"Bye, Thea! Off to go get ready for my date with Garrett—not Benjamin. See if I come back to help again after that sass."

The door shuts behind me as Thea shouts, "Bye, Colette! Good luck!"

"Good luck with what?"

I stop dead in my tracks, knowing exactly who will be standing there if I turn around.

"Leave her alone, Ben." Ah, thank fuck. Jules is here too.

Turning to face the twins, I address Jules while completely

ignoring Ben's question. "You should go talk to her," I tell him, nodding toward the studio door. "She… she wants you, so for fuck's sake put us all out of our misery and do something about it, okay?"

Jules' answering smirk is sheepish. "Okay," he simply replies before walking into the studio.

"Wow, that was easy." I turn toward Ben. "Does it work on you as well? Go away!" I shoo him, but he doesn't budge.

"You can't get rid of me that easily, Red." He chuckles.

"I'm aware."

"So what do you need luck with?"

I debate not answering but maybe he'll leave me alone if I do. "I have a date."

"Of course you do. That birthday deadline is coming up, isn't it?"

"We are not getting married," I seethe, taking a step toward him.

He matches me as he asks, "Why not?"

Why not? Why not! Because… because… "You don't even know me!" I splutter. "Just because we knew each other over a decade ago does not mean we should get married!"

He hums, as if I didn't just make an excellent point. But then he opens his mouth again. "I don't? I know that you like to tie people up."

Now he's standing entirely too close. "People don't base a marriage off of that information."

Ben tips his head side to side. "I suppose not. But I also know that you're a hard worker—that hasn't changed. You smell delicious—" He holds his hand up to stop me from interrupting. "Also not something people base a marriage off of, I know. You are kind to animals, even the really ugly ones."

"Stalking my Instagram again?"

"You have an obsession with *Dateline*," he continues.

"It's called a special interest."

"And…" He steps in so close, I can feel the heat of his breath coasting across my nose. His hand lifts, and my eyes drift shut on their own volition. He's going to kiss me again.

I think I'm going to let him.

My body sways toward his, but instead of the kiss I'm expecting, his hand wraps around my ponytail and *tugs*. My eyes snap open to see his chocolate-brown irises dancing with mirth. "My special interest is your hair," he whispers.

Then all of a sudden, he's gone. My body is cold in his absence, but my stomach is on fire.

"Have fun on your date tonight, Red," Ben calls over his shoulder, not once looking back as he heads up the street toward Louie's.

Chapter Thirteen
THE HAIR THING
Cole

GOOGLE SEARCH

I, in fact, do not have fun on my date. Garrett takes me to Louie's, so of course all I think about is how Ben could walk in at any moment. Louie's is also known for its karaoke nights.

I fucking hate karaoke.

Excusing myself from the table, I make my way over to the bar simply so I can have a break from Garrett's incessant droning about which All American Rejects song he wants to sing. He was debating between "Swing, Swing" and "Dirty Little Secret." When he suggested the latter, he gave an exaggerated wink and elbowed me awkwardly in the side.

That is when I excused myself.

Louie and another young bartender are serving drinks to the mostly college-aged crowd. When Louie spots me, he waves me over to his end of the bar, already pouring me a glass of red wine by the time I get there.

"You are a saint," I yell over the noise. It's so, so loud in here, my skin has started crawling.

Taking a sip of my wine, I try to recenter myself, but I'm failing miserably. "Louie! Can I get an ice cube?"

He wraps one in a paper towel before handing it to me. I place it on my wrist in an attempt to ground myself. "Who is that guy you're with?" Louie asks, leaning forward on the bar so he's not having to yell. "He looks…"

A chuckle escapes as I watch Louie search for the appropriate word to describe Garrett. He's tall but all pale, gangly skin and bone. It appears as if his hair has been straightened, and there's enough product in it to create another hole in the ozone.

"That's not what his picture looked like," I say in defense. "Listen, I really don't want to stay in here—no offense—so can I pay for our tab and sneak out?"

I don't think I can stomach listening to Garrett sing. There's absolutely no way I will be able to pretend that it's good.

Louie waves me off. "It's on the house! Get out of here."

This is not the first time Louie has, lovingly, kicked me out of his establishment, and I'm even more grateful for it tonight. "Thank you," I mouth, draining my glass.

When I finally make it out onto the quiet street, I'm so relieved I could cry. I lean against the wall outside of Louie's, taking a few deep breaths. I feel the smallest inkling of guilt until it's quickly washed away by two things happening simultaneously.

First: The opening chords of "Dirty Little Secret" drift out from behind the door to Louie's.

Second: A door on the other side of me swings open, revealing Benoit Bardot.

"You!" I point my finger at a confused looking Ben. "You ruined my date."

"Me?" His reply is indignant. "I've been in my apartment all night. How could I have possibly ruined your date?"

"It was the—the hair thing!"

Ben doesn't feign confusion. He knows exactly what I'm talking about. "The hair thing?" He saunters toward me, so much more muscular than Garrett—taking up so much *space*.

"Yes! The hair thing!" I'm mad that I liked it so much. I'm mad that I can't find someone who makes me feel the things that Ben makes me feel. I wave toward my ponytail in emphasis. "The hair thing!" I repeat.

"I heard you, Red. You liked the hair thing. Where's your date? Is it over?"

"It is for me," I reply. The wind leaves my sails, and I slump back against the exterior wall. Ben misreads my frustration with myself as something else because his demeanor immediately changes.

"Did he do something to make you uncomfortable?" His voice is low, serious.

"Does bringing me to karaoke count?"

"I'm serious, Colette. What happened?"

I wave him off. "Nothing, Benjamin. I'm just overstimulated. That's why I left. I was not expecting to run into *you* out here."

He's quiet for a moment. "Come upstairs with me."

"No."

"C'mon, Red. I'll let you tie me to anything you want."

Groaning, I lightly bang my head against the wall. "I shouldn't have ever let you into my bedroom. I'm not even a big restraint person! I just want to go home and take a bath."

"I have a bath upstairs."

"I don't like bubbles."

"I'll throw the bubble bath away," he counters.

"There are specific candles I like."

"Hmm. Well, since I don't know you, there's no reason I should have Irish coffee scented candles upstairs in my bathroom."

My head snaps toward him. "What the fuck?"

His body tips back, head nodding toward the door he just came out of. "Let's go, Red."

Against my better judgement, I follow him.

I'm telling myself I have no idea why—that's not really true though, is it? Ben, whether I want to acknowledge it or not, has been one of the most constant things in my life. After my parents divorce, I was never able to form a secure, stable relationship with them—hell, even before the divorce. My parents didn't understand my quirks. Neither did Maya, apparently. But Ben…

We climb the stairs to the apartments above Louie's. I knew Ben lived here, but I've never been inside. I'm expecting it to be loud up here but it's surprisingly quiet. I look down at the floor, wondering if I'm just so overwhelmed, I've detached myself from the world around me.

It doesn't look like a bachelor pad, either. The furniture is semi-coordinated, and there are pictures of the various Bardot family members hung up on the walls. Ben reaches back, linking his pinky with mine in a surprisingly sweet gesture, while leading me down the hall. He pushes open the door to a bedroom and guides me to the bed.

I stop short. "I was serious—no sex."

"We aren't having sex, Red. I respect you, as much as you'd like to think I don't."

He walks through another door, and after a moment I hear the water start to run. "Extra hot," I call.

"Boiling lobster, got it!"

Rolling my eyes, I stand and wander around Ben's room. There's a queen bed with a plaid comforter, a nightstand holding a variety of knickknacks—including an extra pair of glasses even though he's currently wearing a pair—and a small desk pushed up against the wall. Might as well be nosy while I'm here, not sure I'll get the chance again. I inch closer to his desk, looking over my shoulder to make sure Ben is occupied.

A drawing catches my eye, of… is that a princess? And a knight that is hiding behind a bush? "Chloe" is written in all caps across the bottom. There's also a moleskin journal open on the other end of the desk. I didn't take Ben as a journaler, but I can't say I'm not curious. Slowly, I creep sideways, trying to get a peek. My brow furrows as I realize it's just full of tally marks. Is Ben a serial killer?

"Water's ready," Ben calls from the other room. Sure enough, when I walk into the bathroom there's an Irish coffee candle lit on the counter and steaming, bubble-less water in the bathtub. "Strip, Red."

"Help me?"

I'm pretty sure he mutters a *fucking hell* before standing from where he was kneeling next to the tub. He taps my elbows, urging my arms up. I feel his hands slide under my sweater, across my stomach. I've kept up running since high school, but not even a run gets my heart rate up the way Ben's hands roaming my body does.

Soon my clothes are on the floor and I'm dipping my toes into Ben Bardot's bathtub.

The warm water immediately soothes me. Ben watches with rapt attention as my ivory skin begins to splotch red all over. I sigh, in contented silence, pulling my legs in toward my chest, feeling suddenly exposed and vulnerable even with this man who has already seen me naked.

"Why did you leave your date tonight?" Ben asks.

I choose defensiveness as a response. "I already told you about the hair thing," I say, sliding further into the water.

The corner of his mouth tips up. "Yes, we've established that you like the hair thing, Red. But that's not really why you left Louie's, is it? You said something about being overstimulated?"

Oh. That's what he means. "Have you been to Louie's?" I deadpan. "It's loud. It's hot. People are making poor choices. And I really didn't want to listen to Garrett sing and… Pretend. Pretending is so fucking exhausting."

"Do you—Do you get overstimulated often?" he asks, genuine curiosity in his tone.

I debate how much I actually want to open up to… Well, I'm not sure if I can actually call him my nemesis anymore. I close my eyes and lean my head back against the cool tile. He's already seen me naked, physically. Might as well strip down emotionally too.

"I was diagnosed with autism in college. I—Well, I'm not sure if it's a surprise to anyone. I've always been 'quirky.'" I add air quotes for emphasis. "Always been a 'bitch.' But I wasn't doing it on purpose, not that anyone believes me when I say that."

"I believe you."

So simple. Just immediate belief, no need for me to convince him. No additional questions. He says he believes me and I want to believe *him*.

"Hey, Ben?"

"Yeah, Cole?"

"Come do the hair thing."

Chapter Fourteen

I SUCKED ALL OF YOUR BRAIN CELLS OUT

Ben

GOOGLE SEARCH

Q how can I be a good partner to someone with autism? 🎤

"Come do the hair thing." Cole rolls her head across the tile, dark eyes finally meeting mine after her confession.

She was nervous telling me about her diagnosis, but it changes nothing about the way I see her. The only thing it'll change is the research I'm about to do on supporting a partner with autism. Not that she's my partner.

Yet.

But she *is* asking me to do the hair thing. Moving from my perch on the counter, I sit on the edge of the tub next to Cole, spending a delicious moment staring down at her naked body. She curves in all of the right places, and the hot water is turning her skin my favorite color: red.

My eyes skim from her cherry-red toenails, up her lightly freckled calves, all the way to her pert tits and rosy nipples that will have me hard for days after this. When I meet her eyes, there's uncertainty there. Like she's waiting for my final assessment of her body.

"Perfect," I murmur, leaning in to untrap the hair that she's currently using to cushion her head against the tile. Her mouth parts as I wrap her ponytail around my fist, tugging slightly. Testing. Teasing.

A groan falls from those open lips, her eyes falling closed in pleasure. "Take your pants off," she rasps.

I freeze. "You said no sex tonight," I remind her, fully planning on sticking to that promise.

She contemplates a moment. "No penetrative sex," she clarifies. Her mouth tips up in a wicked grin. "I didn't say anything about oral, though."

For fuck's sake, this woman.

"Excuse me for being under the impression that 'no sex' meant no sex of any kind, Colette." I give an extra tug on her hair to emphasize my point.

"Well." She bites her lip. "What a happy surprise for you."

A happy surprise indeed. As long as I don't come in two seconds like I did last time.

Cole taps the leg nearest her where I'm sitting on the edge of the tub, urging me to stand. When I do, she follows, rising onto her knees, the water sloshing a bit over the edge of the tub. Eager hands find the waistband of my jeans, unbuttoning the row of buttons with fervor. Her melodic laugh echoes through the bathroom when she realizes I'm not wearing anything underneath.

"Really, Ben? Going commando now?" She smirks, eyes meeting mine, and damn this view is… *unforgettable.*

"I…" I've temporarily forgotten how to communicate. Staring down at Colette Russell, on her knees for *me*. It feels wrong. I should be the one on my knees worshipping her like the goddess she is. "I was just running down to the shop. Wasn't expecting to have anyone else taking my pants off," I explain lamely, my mouth still dry from simply looking at her.

My dick springs out from between the buttons as soon as she's undone all of them. Then, this vixen *licks her lips* at the sight. Her hand wraps around my cock, the same way my fist is wrapped around her hair. She doesn't even bother pulling the jeans all the way down before her tongue darts out to catch the precum already dripping out.

I use that hand in her hair to guide her toward me. My hips are eager to meet her lips, pulsing forward on their own volition. Cole looks at me and sticks her tongue out, flat and ready. Pulling slightly, I angle her head, positioning my dick with the other hand.

In the back of my mind, I know she's avoiding deep conversation with me. She opened up and now she's closing herself off to me mentally by opening those pretty, plump lips. I care, I do. And at the same time, I'm a pathetic man who will take any crumb this woman offers me.

So I thrust, eliciting a deep moan that vibrates through my very soul as Cole wraps around me. She's needy, squeezing my thighs in encouragement as she bobs enthusiastically. Tears leak from the corners of her eyes, running down her flushed cheeks. The sound of splashing water is what I concentrate on as I try not to come down Cole's throat. Yet.

Yet—the word that is sustaining me right now.

She whimpers, and I watch, enraptured, as her hand slides down her own body. She pinches one of her nipples before allowing her hand to disappear between her thighs. It moves rapidly, dragging her own pleasure out even while she still has me wrapped in the wet heat of her mouth. She's so fucking good at anything she does, always has been.

It's one of the first things I noticed about her all those years ago, and I'm happy to see that drive hasn't changed even as her, *ahem*, focus has shifted.

Cole continues to work us both up, and I'm doing my damndest to hold out for her. *She comes first*, plays like a mantra in my head, and I'm about to lose that battle when I feel a sharp pinch to my ass. Refocusing on Cole, her pleading eyes send me careening over the edge, my hand still fisted firmly around her ponytail. Involuntarily I tug as I search for some way to ground myself, my orgasm spilling thickly down Cole's throat. She swallows and swallows and swallows until I pull her off of me with a lewd *pop*. Half a second later, she's coming too. Her lips are swollen as they part, fingers working fervently, chasing her ecstasy wave after wave.

"Look at me," I rasp, tugging her ponytail until her lust-riddled eyes meet mine. The caramel swirl of her irises mesmerizes me, a thick sheen of tears glistening in the candlelight. My thumb swipes across her cheek, collecting any fallen tears—the result of having my cock in her mouth for an extended period of time. "You're beautiful," I mutter.

It's the wrong thing to say. Cole tenses, immediately sliding on her mask of indifference. "Hey," I whisper. "Don't do that."

"Do what?" she asks, not meeting my eyes.

"Run away."

A scoff is all I get in reply as she sinks back into what has to be lukewarm water. She lifts the drain, quietly watching the water as it lowers. I tuck my dick back into my pants, buttoning them back up. Waiting to see what Cole will do next. Both of us are silent, but I know better than to rush her.

When the tub is almost completely empty, she does something that surprises me. She turns the hot water back on. "I'm not running anywhere," she says, still not looking at me.

My shoulders instantly sag in relief. I eye the detachable showerhead, an idea springing into my head. "Can I wash your hair?" I ask.

Finally, she looks back up at me, a smirk dancing across her pretty lips. "You really are obsessed, Benjamin."

I shrug, not bothering to correct her.

"Fine." She works to undo the tie holding her hair up. "But no stealing pieces of my hair to keep on some secret altar you have hiding in your closet."

"I knew you were going to snoop," I quip. She guffaws, but I ignore her, opting to switch the faucet so it's streaming from the showerhead now. "I don't have any fancy hair products."

"It's fine. I'll wash it again after my run in the morning." She pauses, smile turning mischievous. "This is more for you than it is for me anyway."

"I believe it's called aftercare, Red."

"You been reading up since our last encounter?" she jokes.

I roll my eyes. "You aren't my first partner, Cole. I knew what aftercare was before our 'last encounter.'" I use the showerhead to help me form air quotes, getting dangerously close to spraying her in the face.

Cole narrows her eyes at me. "No funny business," she scolds.

"That part already happened. Now lean forward."

She rolls her eyes and maneuvers herself so I have room to wet the hair that is now cascading down her bare back. I relish watching as it turns from a bright auburn to a dark, almost-brunette shade everywhere the water hits. Slowly, deliberately, I let the water soak all the way down to her scalp. Once it's time for shampoo, I realize this is going to be a bit more complicated than I anticipated.

"Just a sec," I say before handing her the showerhead. As quickly as possible, I change out of my jeans and into a pair of boxers. When I walk back in the bathroom, I angle my leg with my foot in the tub so Cole can lean back against me. I fan her hair over my thigh, enjoying how easily she's complying with my nonverbal requests.

She starts to hum as I massage shampoo into her scalp. I don't think she even realizes she's doing it, but the sound wraps around me, burying itself beneath my ribs. Cole Russell is making me crave her. I've had a sip of this side of her and now I'm a lush.

And I'm so royally fucked.

We sit in companionable silence—minus the occasional

humming from Cole—as I finish shampooing and rinsing. I want to invite her to stay. I want—fuck, I want to *cuddle* with Colette. While I work up the courage to ask, she lazily gets out of the tub, wrapping the nearby towel around her body. I miss seeing the creamy expanse instantly.

Cole twists her hair back into a wet bun, securing it with her hair tie. I'm about to open my mouth, about to just spit out my request, when she sighs.

"I need to get home." She's back to not making eye contact.

I dry my leg off, trying, and failing, not to make things awkward. "Right. Of course. I-I could get you a drink or something though." We both pause. "If you want," I rush to add.

"I need to get home to Ernest."

Ernest? No, there's no way she has someone waiting for her at home. That would be fucking diabolical, it would be—

"My dog," she says slowly, as if explaining what a dog is to a very small child. "You met him when you came over."

Right. I knew that. The ugly dog. Thank God. "Yeah, no… yeah. You definitely should get back to him. Good point."

"Okaaaay, Benjamin. And maybe you should go ahead and go to bed. It seems like I sucked all of your brain cells out." She smirks, pulling her clothes back on before seeing herself out of the bedroom while I'm still standing there like a goddamn fool.

She's all the way to the front door by the time I come to my senses. "Wait! When will I… when can we see each other again?" I ask.

"We see each other far too often for my liking," she snarks. "Bye, Benjamin. Thank you for the orgasm."

She waves her fingers over her shoulder as the door to my apartment closes behind her. I can't be sure, but I'm pretty sure I hear maniacal laughter coming from the other side of the door as she leaves.

And, dammit, I can't help my grin at this infuriating, gorgeous, amazing woman.

Chapter Fifteen
COLETTE RUSSELL IS SITTING HERE!
Cole

GOOGLE SEARCH

I am absolutely not analyzing the fact that I gave Benoit Bardot a blow job before allowing him to wash my motherfucking hair.

Obviously, I do asinine things when I'm overstimulated.

With finals coming up, what I don't need is a distraction. Especially not one with chocolate-colored eyes, cute little reading glasses, and a nice—

No. Focus, Cole.

I have an appointment with my advisor later this afternoon. She sent an ominous email yesterday that I've been agonizing over ever since. I swear, there's a special place in hell for people who set a meeting with no explanation or—even worse—text you saying, "Call me." My stomach has been in knots for multiple reasons, this meeting is just the icing on the cake.

I need to distract myself and use my time wisely because my favorite table was available as soon as I walked into the university library today. This almost never happens, and usually I end up sitting across the room, with the sunlight blazing into my eyes, as I watch a table of undergrads fuck around at *my* table.

But today, I arrived in time to grab it and I'm taking it as a good omen. It really is the perfect spot. Slightly separated from the main library seating area, there are half-shelves that form a wall between me and the entrance to the cafe. I can get up, refill my coffee, and also keep an eye on my things. I'm not sure who would steal a stack of psychology textbooks, but those things are expensive and I can't afford to replace them. Between that and my banged up laptop, the logical side of me knows that I'm not really taking a risk by leaving such valuable items out while I go in pursuit of more caffeine, but I still feel better being nearby.

My finals include two written exams and a presentation. The written exams should be fine, it's the presentation I'm worried about. I'd rather pluck my toenails out one at a time than speak in front of a group of people that I know will be judging the quality of my work. I know it's unavoidable, especially in academia, but my body goes red with all of the attention, truly helping me live up to Ben's nickname for me.

Shit. *Don't think about Ben.*

And I don't. For the next hour and a half I do a great job of outlining my presentation, filling in a few lingering gaps. My phone dings, reminding me that I have an appointment with my advisor in thirty minutes.

It doesn't take long to get across campus, so I find a seat outside of her office and use the extra time to squeeze in a little more studying. I'm almost immediately distracted, however, by a laugh that sounds strangely familiar. I eye the end of the hallway, watching as Elaine Bardot rounds the corner. Despite the fact that we are technically housed in the same building, we don't see each other very often.

The waging *Don't-Think-About-Ben* internal battle comes to a screeching halt as I try to hide myself behind my open textbook.

I like Elaine, actually. She's a badass sex therapist, and even with four kids, was somehow at all of the important events when we were in school. Something my own mother wasn't able to do with one child. I'm baffled by how she spawned such a rage-inducing human. A strange feeling unfurls in my chest at the thought.

Jealousy, that's what this is. Now I'm fucking jealous of Ben.

I roll my eyes, sliding deeper into my chair, forgetting that my bright red ponytail acts like a flashing neon sign above my head saying *Colette Russell is sitting here!*

"Studying hard, dear?" Elaine asks, sitting casually in the chair next to me.

"Oh! Hi, Dr. Bardot. I didn't see you there." I lower my textbook, still not making eye contact.

"Elaine, darling," she scolds. "Dr. Bardot is so formal."

Sitting in the psychology building—her place of work—I can't help but think that our relationship *is* formal. She *is* a professor, albeit not mine. As if she can read my thoughts, she interjects, "It's also a rule of mine that if I've known you since before you hit puberty, any formalities are out the window."

"That… seems like a reasonable rule," I concede.

Elaine's hands hit her knees with a resounding *smack*. "I thought so! Now, I'm glad I ran into you. I've been meaning to invite you to family dinner, it happens every Sunday, and I think it's past time that you made an appearance."

Blinking rapidly, I peek over to find a beaming Elaine. As if she didn't just throw out a *family* dinner invitation to a relative stranger. "You want me at family dinner? A dinner that is with your family? And me?"

She purses her lips, but there's a lingering twinkle in her eye. Something that tells me there's more to this request than she's letting on. "Obviously," she says.

Obviously?

"Does—uh, does Ben know that you're asking me?" I can't

imagine he would be thrilled for me to show up to his family's home—his safe space. Only, sometimes I think…

"Ben would be elated to have you!"

I quirk my eyebrow, searching Elaine's face for the lie.

"Right, I will—"

"Ms. Russell, are you ready?" My advisor, Dr. Winthrop, pokes her head out of her office, surprise flashing across her face when she sees Elaine sitting next to me. "Dr. Bardot! I apologize for interrupting."

"Not at all, Vivienne. Colette and I were just finishing up. She's all yours!" She stands, patting me on the shoulder. "See you Sunday, dear."

She's gone before I have time to formulate a response.

"Ms. Russell, come on in." Dr. Winthrop pushes the door open, holding her arm out to welcome me into her office. It's creepily clean, the books seemingly organized by height versus by topic or author. There's a singular family photo on her desk that I have to tear my eyes away from because all three of her doll-like kids are eerily similar looking. Same bright blonde hair clipped back with a seersucker bow, same shit-eating grins, same rosy-red cheeks. Do they have blush on? They can't be older than seven?

"Aren't they sweet? Triplets. Blair, Darcy, and Sutton. They are the light of my life." Dr. Winthrop's sickly sweet tone has always thrown me off, and it's positively dripping now. There's a false sincerity that underlies everything that comes out of her mouth.

When I don't respond, she continues, getting straight to the point. "Well, I bet you are wondering why I called a meeting today."

Duh, Vivienne.

"The good news: you were approved to pursue an emphasis in forensic psychology next year." She taps her pencil three times in rapid succession. "An interesting choice. A loss for the Marriage and Family Therapy department, for sure."

Dr. Winthrop pauses, as if she's expecting me to change my mind. When I don't, she clears her throat. "Right. Unfortunately, there is some bad news."

My stomach clenches painfully. The seconds feel like they stretch into hours as I wait for her to get on with it.

"Currently, half of your tuition is covered under a scholarship that will no longer be available next semester. The donor planned for it to be an annual donation, but, well, these things change."

Fuck. *Fuck!*

There's a loud buzzing in my brain as I register what Dr. Winthrop just said to me. I had a plan when I moved. Money saved. Enough money to cover my apartment and half of my tuition, the other half covered by this scholarship. *That* was supposed to carry me through this degree. I can make one more semester work at full tuition, but then what? I'm spiraling quickly, my breaths shortening.

"I am happy to set up an appointment at the Financial Aid Office for you," Dr. Winthrop continues, seemingly oblivious to my approaching panic attack.

All I can do is nod. Words no longer exist.

"Okay, let me look at their schedule…" She turns toward her desktop, the screen illuminating her face with a blueish glow. "Does next Tuesday work for you? They have an 11:30 appointment available."

"O-okay." My voice is feeble and I hate how affected I sound. But this is my life. My future. And it feels like it's crumbling around me inside of this sterile office, creepy children mocking me from inside the frame.

"Great, it's booked. You should be getting an email shortly." She turns back toward me, bright white smile broadening as her eyes dart toward the doorway. "Anything else you need from me, Ms. Russell?"

I suppose that's my cue. In a haze, I stand, leaving the office without another word. It may be considered rude, but I could not form a coherent sentence if I tried.

I make it exactly twenty-seven steps away when my phone dings. Opening up my email, I see two unread messages. The first is from the financial aid office. The second is from Elaine Bardot.

To: Colette Russell (colette.russell@hu.edu)
  Subject: Meeting Confirmation

This email is to confirm your appointment at the HU Financial Aid Office on...

Swiping out of the message I move on to Elaine's email.

To: Colette Russell (colette.russell@hu.edu)
  Subject: Family Dinner!!

Hi Colette!

I realized I don't have your phone number. See below for information about family dinner and I'm also including my cell number. Text me so I have yours or I will be forced to get it from my son. Don't make me do that, dear.

The rest of the email included an address, a phone number, and little room for argument.

I ignore both emails.

It takes me a month before I eventually make it to a Bardot family dinner.

Chapter Sixteen
ORAL SEX LECTURES
Ben

GOOGLE SEARCH

Q why won't she text me back?

Red, am I allowed to text you?

Two hours later

I'm feeling like that's a no...

One day later.

Okay I know I'm not supposed to text you but I just wanted to offer my services for the hair thing if you need or want that again.

One week later.

Mom keeps asking about you which seems a little weird? Everything alright?

Two weeks later.

Red…

I miss you…
I'm here if you ever need anything…

Hope you're okay

Opening Bardot Brothers Coffee Co. has been more difficult than any of us anticipated. We open in two days and we still have a to-do list a mile long. Though Jules would never outwardly show it, I can tell that he's nervous. I watch as he fiddles with the espresso machine, inching it over so there's enough room for stir sticks and cup sleeves to fit next to it.

When he's adjusted it for the third time, I decide it's time to step in.

"Placement looks good, Brother."

He glances up, surprise flitting across his features, as if he forgot Gabe and I were in the room with him.

"Oh. Yeah? I wasn't sure if we should move it to a different part of the counter," he replies.

"It's perfect," Gabe jumps in. "And everyone is on their way for dinner. Let's take a break and we can pick back up afterward."

Our typical Sunday night dinner is being moved to the shop tonight. The work here is a bit overwhelming, and knowing Jules would never outwardly ask for help, Gabe and I intervened. If we invite everyone here, there's no way Jules will refuse when Dad inevitably suggests that he does some paint touch ups.

The youngest Bardot—now technically a Bardot-Olsson—will also be in attendance. Bex, Anders, and their two kids are in town from New York for the shop opening. It's nice when all of us are together—there's a sense of peace, completeness.

Jules feels it too. Even more so when Thea, Chloe, and Hank Rose arrive. Thea's baby bump is evident, and I catch Jules staring at it on more than one occasion.

He's obsessed, and I get it. At least the person he's obsessed with will actually spend time around him.

When everyone arrives, we sit down for dinner at tables that have been pushed haphazardly together, pizza boxes scattered where everyone can reach. Not our typical, home-cooked family dinner, but perfect all the same.

I'm about to pop the first box open when the front door bangs open and Colette Russell walks in. "Sorry I'm late!" she exclaims, as if it's perfectly normal and acceptable for her to be here.

The speed at which I burst from my seat has me knocking my knee against the table. "We aren't open, Colette. What are you doing here?"

In my tone, you can hear my anger. I think about how I haven't seen her in a month. I think about the string of unread text messages and how her social media has been nothing but crickets.

Over the years, I've gone so much longer between seeing Cole. A month shouldn't bother me. But things have changed. I thought… I thought things were changing.

"I invited her," my mom—the traitor—responds.

Before I can process that proverbial bomb drop, Chloe jumps up from her seat. "Cole! Come sit by me!"

Et tu, Brute?

"Really, Princess Chloe? I thought we were closer than that." Chloe and I have been spending time together at the weekly library story time and whenever Hank needs a break. Thea is busy now that her dance classes are up and running and, the truth is, I really enjoy Chloe's company. Except for right now, while she's befriending the enemy.

Chloe narrows her eyes at me, scolding in a way that only

kids can. "Don't be mean to Princess Cole and maybe we can be friends again."

Ouch.

I turn my attention back to the infuriating red head. "Hear that *princess*? We can't be mean to each other."

Instead of responding, Cole stares at me. And stares.

And stares.

Whispered conversations move on around us, but two can play the game that Cole has started, and I'm determined to win this time. After several moments, I can't hold it any longer, blinking with a muttered *fuck*.

Cole smirks. "How does it feel always coming in second place?"

"I love coming second." My reply is instant. "Especially if you're the one coming first."

Now it's her turn to blink. She looks at me, stunned, until Chloe tugs at her hand in an attempt to get Cole to sit down.

Tentatively, she slinks into the open seat. I notice the small shake of her head as she joins in a conversation with Thea.

As hard as I try, I can't help but sneak glances at her throughout the evening. She mostly sticks to conversation with Chloe and Thea and, after seeing her interact with a new friend, it crosses my mind that I still don't know what happened with Maya. I want to ask her about it.

I want to know everything about Cole.

My anger is still there, though. Simmering below the surface. Frustration that she's avoiding me, holding me at arms length.

"Take a breath, *mon chou*." Mom's voice cuts through my thoughts.

Scowling at my mom, I do as she says, inhaling a mix of fresh-baked pizza and lingering bits of Cole's Irish coffee scent. "This is your fault," I mumble, the petulant teenager in me rearing its ugly head. "You at least could have warned me."

Mom's sigh is heavy. "She was supposed to join us a while ago. I think she's had a hard few weeks."

That catches my attention. Why does Mom have this knowledge but I don't? "Who did you hear that from?" I ask, turning toward her.

She glances over my shoulder to where I know Cole and Thea are conversing. Mom's lips purse together, contemplatively. I search her eyes, waiting for an answer. Seconds tick by before she returns her gaze to me, hand gently patting my cheek. "You should ask her."

Huffing, I drop my head into my hands and gently massage my temples. "She doesn't talk to me. She barely even looks at me." I pause. "You know this," I whisper.

"Keep trying, my cabbage." She rubs soothing circles up and down my back, and I really do feel like I'm back in high school when I first confessed to my… obsession with Colette Russell. "And don't forget, oral sex is the best sex."

"No, oh God!" Mom has notoriously told us that oral sex is the best sex since we were all in high school. Growing up with a sex therapist for a mom was certainly… interesting. Her initial reasoning for the unconventional lecture was that no one could get pregnant via oral sex, but now I think she just likes to fuck with us. "Please, no more talking about sex tonight."

"I cannot guarantee that, *mon chou*." Her twinkling laugh is a comfort amidst my swirling emotions. "Talk to her," she repeats, patting me once more on the back before abandoning me to join the other women.

Talk to her. If only it was that simple.

Turns out, it is fairly simple to get Cole alone later that evening. Part of me is sure that this is my mother's doing, but I can't say that I mind her meddling—this time. After we scarfed our pizza, the women continued to talk, someone eventually saying something that spooked Thea. She hightailed it out of here followed by an uncharacteristically angry Jules.

We all get started working on little projects around the shop, and eventually I find Cole alone in the storage closet. Ironically, it's the same closet that Ethel and I were in all those months ago when I told her that I wanted to take over The Coffee Shop. We had stumbled out of this very closet and bumped right into Colette Russell. At the time I was still pretending that I had zero positive feelings for Cole, but after coffee that day…

We've always been inevitable. Even if she doesn't realize it.

"So," I whisper conspiratorially, "were you the one who freaked Thea out? I thought you two were becoming friends."

Cole bristles, looking toward me out of the corner of her eye, but not turning to fully face me. "It's not my fault she isn't comfortable talking about sex."

"And you are?" I question, my eyebrow quirking.

"You aren't?" She matches my expression, a batter waiting for the pitcher to throw the next pitch.

"Of course I am. You can't grow up in the Bardot house and *not* be comfortable talking about sex."

She makes a gesture with her hand as if to say, *See!* "I'm just trying to get her used to it," Cole replies. "Seems like she'll be around for a while."

I hum in agreement. Because Thea will be around for a while. Jules has never shown interest in anyone the way he does with her. And there's the whole baby thing. But I get the feeling Jules wouldn't have cared whether she was pregnant or not, he wanted Thea from day one.

That, I can understand.

"Don't just stand there," Cole cuts in. "Make yourself useful, Benjamin."

"Yes, ma'am." I wink, earning an eyeroll and a swish of her ponytail as she shakes her head.

We unpack supply boxes in companionable silence. She seems to already have a place for everything to go so I follow her lead. The entire time though, I keep coming back to Cole's friendship with Thea and, in turn, her former friendship with Maya. That and Mom's insinuation that Cole has had some difficulty in the last few weeks. I'm desperate for her to open up to me.

"Spit it out."

I stop unloading various paper cups from the box in front of me. "Excuse me?"

"You are thinking very loud over there," Cole clarifies. "What is it?"

My stomach does an idiotic flip over the fact that she noticed me, the smallest seed of hope that she *cares*.

I shove it down.

"Well, I was thinking about friendships."

"We aren't friends, Benjamin."

Yup, shoving that hope down deeper.

"I wasn't talking about us, Red. Don't get your panties in a twist." I pause. "Or do—I'm happy to help." I smirk.

"Fucking hell," she mutters, head hitting the shelf in front of her. "Fine, what friendships were you thinking about?"

"You and Maya." It's as if I dropped a bomb inside this storage closet. Cole pauses for a heartbeat, and I can see the look of pain that crosses her face. And then just as quickly she rebuilds her mask of indifference.

"We aren't friends, either."

"But you were." I let that linger. My tone softens before asking, "What happened?"

She's quiet for a long time, so long that I think she's not going to answer my question. I wait, my pinky finger finding hers. To my complete and utter shock, she doesn't withdraw when I tangle my finger with hers.

When I'm just about to change the subject, she starts talking. "Maya and I... struggled when we left for college." Cole's opposite hand comes up to fiddle with the bulk box of napkins, twisting it so it's lined up perfectly with the front of the shelf. "I'm not a good friend—" She holds her hand up when she sees that I'm about to protest. "Let me rephrase. I'm not good at being a friend.

"Maya and I were more so friends out of convenience than anything else. I didn't know anyone when I moved here in middle school. Maya knew everyone, as you probably remember. She was my opposite in so many ways, but"—she shrugs—"it was easy because I didn't have to put in a lot of effort. She was an extrovert so she did most of the talking, planning, socializing, and so on."

I listen, slowly weaving more of our fingers together. She doesn't stop me.

"When I went to California and she went to Chicago, it became even more work for her. I didn't initiate calls because I just didn't think about it. I missed Maya, sure. And it was never a matter of whether I loved her or not, because I did. I really did value our friendship. But I think Maya grew tired of being the only one who was keeping us together. Which is fair. I couldn't figure out how to navigate things when she wasn't right in front of me."

With a squeeze of her hand, I encourage her to continue. I'm too nervous to say anything, worried that I'll accidentally fuck this up. Colette Russell is not an outwardly vulnerable person, and it is not lost on me that she's chosen me to share this with.

"One day we had a really big fight and she said something along the lines of 'Why can't you be like a normal person and pick up the phone?'" She sighs heavily at this, and my heart aches for the version of Cole that had to hear her best friend— her only friend—insinuate that she wasn't normal.

"It got me thinking... maybe I'm not normal. Maybe something is wrong with me."

"Nothing is wrong with you." My voice is firm, because fuck that.

She gives me a sad smile. "I know that now. But that fight was the catalyst for finally getting my autism diagnosis. I scheduled an appointment with a therapist the next day. To

Maya maybe I wasn't 'normal,' but she did help me get a better understanding of myself. Ultimately, I am grateful for that. I love who I am now. I know having autism doesn't make me abnormal."

Cole glances down with a shrug. Then, she does a double take as if she's just realized that our hands are intertwined. She yanks her hand out of my grasp, effectively bursting our intimate bubble.

"It's okay to be vulnerable, Colette."

"I know that." She turns her back to me, adjusting something else on the shelf. "By the way, do you guys need any additional help around the shop? I'm looking for a job."

That's one way to derail me. "Looking for a job? What are you talking about? You're in school. That should be your focus."

"Thank you, Captain Obvious." She glares at me. "It's just that I—" She starts obnoxiously crinkling a roll of packing paper, lowering her voice so I can't hear the end of her sentence.

My hands firmly grasp both of hers. "Try again."

With a slump of her shoulders, she admits, "I lost my scholarship."

"Lost your… did you fail the semester?"

She looks irate. "Fuck no, asshole. They thought it would be a multi-year scholarship but the donor pulled out. I haven't been working because I had enough saved up but now… I will have to figure something else out."

Not if I have anything to say about it.

"We can find some shifts for you," I say instead. "But I will not allow it to interfere with your classes."

She gives me a mischievous grin, and I realize I've stepped closer to her, forcing her head back so she can meet my gaze. "Oh, you won't allow it? You under the impression that you're in charge here?"

"I can be."

My breathing is heavy as Cole lifts onto her toes, her breasts brushing against my chest. She leans in, her breath sending a shiver down my spine as it coasts across my ear. "Fuck. You," she whispers, before deftly sliding around me and walking out of the closet.

I don't allow her to get too far before I catch her wrist. The sudden movement sends her careening back into me, her entire body pressed against mine. I tuck a piece of hair behind her ear before leaning down to whisper my own parting blow.

"Thirty-four days, Colette."

Chapter Seventeen

BARGAIN BASEMENT BENOIT

Cole

GOOGLE SEARCH

Q My date is a podcast listener - red flag?

A mistake was made when I allowed myself to be vulnerable in front of Benoit Bardot.

I keep making mistakes with that man, keep allowing him access to me in a way that I've never allowed anyone else.

It's infuriating.

It's… intoxicating.

It cannot happen again.

Which is why after coming home from Bardot family dinner the other night, I immediately got on my dating app and found someone to go to the Bardot Brothers Coffee Co. grand opening with.

Because things with Ben make sense to me. Well, they used to make sense to me. I had him in this box in my brain labeled "NEMESIS" in all caps. He was tucked onto a shelf with all of the other boxes with labels like "WORK IDIOT" and "GYM

GIRL." Everyone fit nicely inside of their box, and I knew what to expect of them.

Until he fucked it up. He doesn't feel so nemesis-y anymore, and that's messing up my boxes. So, naturally, I'm going to do my best to get him firmly back where he belongs. Keep his identity as the high school rival that I was always competing with.

Was I, though?

Looking back, I'm even more confused. Was I the only one actually competing?

The thought irks me.

That feeling like I'm missing something, some big, important thing that everyone else is in on, but I don't have the ability to put it together the same way.

It's one of the reasons I did mourn my friendship with Maya when it ended. At least I could always count on her to be straightforward with me. To catch me up on whatever social cues I was missing, even if she didn't realize that's what she was doing.

There's a large jigsaw puzzle in pieces on my coffee table. It's an apt metaphor for my life, which is currently *also* in pieces. I've gotten the edges put together when there's a knock on my door. Ernest hops off the couch, scrambling over to the door to greet my date.

Connor technically lives in the next town over, but I had to adjust my radius after my last date. The pool of eligible, and age appropriate, people in Sassafras is miniscule. He was a good sport when I suggested trying out a new coffee shop for our date.

I open the door to reveal an aesthetically attractive man. He's about a head taller than me with light brown hair and glasses. His voice is a deep timbre when he greets me before turning his attention to Ernest. "Cute dog," he comments, bending down to scratch under his chin. "When did he have his leg amputated?"

"Before I got him," I reply. "Wait right here, let me grab my shoes and then we can go."

They should have already finished the ribbon cutting ceremony by now. I didn't feel like I should be there for that part of the day. I don't think I could handle feeling like an intrusion on such an important event.

Turning off the episode of *Dateline* I had on as background noise, I slip into my Doc Martens that take me three times to put on properly so the sock line doesn't bunch against my toes. Today I've paired them with cutoff jean shorts and a crop tank top. The midsummer heat wave has been rough on someone as chronically overheated as I am.

When I get back to the front door, Connor is standing there awkwardly staring into the space. "It's kind of dark in here."

I have no idea how to respond to that, so I just say, "Yup," before moving past him out of the apartment.

"Does your dog just roam free while you're gone?" he asks.

"Ernest is a good boy," I reply. "He won't get into any trouble."

Connor shoves his hands into his pockets, nodding. "I've always heard it's better for them to be in a crate during the day."

Again, I don't know what to say. It's not like I'm going to take advice from this man that I've only just met. "Do you have any pets?" I ask. Maybe he's a secret dog trainer and that's why he feels the need to comment on mine.

"No pets. I'm a lifelong learner though, so I was listening to a podcast the other day about how to best train your dog."

I'm proud of the restraint I'm exercising in *not* rolling my eyes. "Yeah, but it's a little different listening to a podcast about something versus actually doing the thing."

He doesn't take my hint to shut up, instead launching into a spiel about how many different things he's learned from podcasts. I bet he's one of those men that feels confident that he would be able to pilot a plane without any actual training.

The good news is his podcast diatribe lasts until we park in front of the brand new Bardot Brothers Coffee Co., preventing me from having to make small talk. Really, he should start his own podcast about how much he loves podcasts.

Getting out of the car, I see there's a line out the door and a group of people crowded outside with branded coffee cups already in their hands.

I feel a sense of pride looking around at the grand opening hoopla.

For Jules, obviously.

Not for Ben.

"There's no way this coffee is good enough to wait in that line," Connor says, setting me on the defensive.

"It's really good, actually," I reply, walking to the end of the line, mad that this man just made me give a compliment in Ben's general direction.

We wait in line, Connor making small talk while I add in the occasional "mhmm," "for sure," and "yeah" so he thinks I'm listening.

What I'm actually doing is watching Benoit—in his slutty glasses—be stupidly competent at running a bustling business. It's hot. It's pissing me off.

He's taking orders while Jules is making the coffee. Ben is effortless as he interacts with each person, chatting with them just long enough to keep drinks moving at a steady pace for Jules. It's impressive, watching how well they work together. If you really pay attention, you see the signs of their twin telepathy. A small nod from Jules has Ben wrapping up a conversation or Ben's hands grip the register which prompts Jules to take over with a certain customer. It would be fascinating to have that kind of connection with someone.

I'm so caught up in their back and forth, it takes me a moment to realize that Ben is staring back at me through the window. He has a stupid grin on his face, and I'm fighting hard to make sure mine isn't sporting a matching one. We stand there like that for one breath... two.

And then Ben's face contorts. I'm confused for a moment before I catch my reflection in the window. Before I see that Connor's hand has come to the small of my back and is urging me forward in line. For the first time, I think I might have fucked up by bringing a date.

Ben flags down Gabe to take over the register, right as we walk into the shop. He explains a few things to Gabe and then rounds the corner, heading straight in our direction.

"Red." He dips his head in greeting. "Glad you could make it."

"The place looks great," I reply, watching as Ben eyes Connor. "Oh, this is—"

"Connor Page. Nice to meet you." Connor sticks out his hand for a shake, Ben grasping it a little too hard.

He doesn't reply to Connor, instead turning to face me, and I ready myself for whatever he's about to say. "Odd choice."

Odd choice?

"I—" Connor starts, pausing when Ben lifts a hand in his direction.

"Don't be rude, Benjamin," I snap.

He shrugs his shoulders. "I'm just saying." He turns and gives Connor another once over. "Looks a bit like the bargain version."

"The bargain version of what?" Connor asks, obviously having a hard time keeping up with our conversation.

"Of me." Ben winks.

"Oh for fuck's—"

Connor looks between the two of us, interrupting with, "Am I missing something?"

Ben claps Connor on the shoulder. "You, I'm assuming, are missing a lot of things, Conrad."

"It's Connor," he replies, peeling Ben's hand off of him.

"Doesn't matter." Ben rubs his hands together. "I won't ever see you again, anyway. Gotta get back to work." He points his finger at me as he slowly backs up.

"Don't say it," I plead.

He opens his mouth, closing it just as quickly with a flex of his jaw. "Once he's run off, you stay," Ben commands.

"No," I retort.

But I do.

Connor stays long enough to get a cup of coffee and then makes up some excuse about how he completely forgot he was meeting his grandma this afternoon. I don't look at Ben when Connor leaves, but I can feel him watching me.

I find a seat by the window, continuing to observe the shop operations. Thea and Chloe come over and sit with me for a while before they both decide it's time for a nap. Gabe brings his computer by at some point so we can get my first few shifts scheduled in the coming weeks. Elaine even sits with me for a while, talking all-things psychology and my shift from the engineering world.

The entire time I feel Ben's gaze. Every time I look up, he's watching. He's not even a little bit subtle about it.

I hate that it's comforting.

I hate that it's familiar.

And, most of all, I hate that I don't hate his attention on me.

Eventually, though, I realize I need to go home and let Ernest out. Maybe take a bath. Maybe make sure my vibrator is charged.

Or maybe...

As if he can sense my impending departure, Ben takes another break from behind the counter, dropping into the seat across from me.

His long legs take up so much space. The veins on his forearms are bulging as he folds his arms together and leans toward me. "Thanks for coming today." The sincerity in his voice has me looking up to meet his eyes. "Even though you brought Bargain Basement Benoit with you."

"He likes podcasts," I groan, knowing he'll understand my lament.

"Gross." Ben wrinkles his nose. "At least listen to an audiobook."

That makes me laugh. A real, deep belly laugh. Something I didn't even know I was capable of. And fuck, Ben's face lights up.

"Come over tonight," he says, eyes searching mine. Back and forth, back and forth.

"I can't," I reply.

His shoulders slump so minutely I barely notice it happen. "Another date?"

"Yeah..." I watch Ben tense—maybe it's a little bit fun torturing him. "With Ernest," I finish.

"Ernest," Ben repeats. "Your dog."

"Mhmm," I nod. "But... you could come over to mine?"

Ben responds in a similar manner to when Ernest is offered a treat. He instantly perks up, his head notching to the side. "Yes," he replies, planting his large hands on the table and pushing himself up. "I'll... I'll text you. After I'm done. But I'm walking away now before you change your mind."

I chuckle to myself. "Goodbye, Benjamin. See you later."

His goofy smile is back. "See you later, Red."

Chapter Eighteen

EROTIC PUZZLING
Ben

GOOGLE SEARCH

🔍 tips for speed jigsaw puzzling   🎤

Closing up, be there soon.

Do you need anything? I can grab some dinner.

Or if Ernest wants treats.

I want him to like me.

RED

I'm already regretting this.

You won't regret it later *wink emoji*

IF that's where the night is going

Totally fine if not. No expectations.

RED

God, you don't shut up even in text form.

I'm out of diet cherry cola, Ernest loves the
expensive treats that are in the bakery section,
and I wouldn't say no to a burger from Louie's.

Damn, Red.

RED

YOU OFFERED.

Yes, I did. See you in thirty.

Twenty-nine minutes later I arrive at Cole's apartment. The last time I was here, I didn't really get a chance to look around, but I get that chance now when Cole throws open the door, wearing the same mouthwatering cutoff jean shorts and crop top that she had on earlier. The only difference is the fuzzy polka dot socks now covering her feet.

I smirk.

She scowls.

"Come in, Bardot."

Kicking my shoes off, I make my way to the kitchen. "I've been demoted to my last name now?"

I can't help but watch as she moves around the oversized emerald couch, searching for the remote in the cushions. "I never know what to call you. Benjamin when you're being annoying. Bardot... when you're being annoying. Ben when you're being less annoying."

"Never Benoit, though." I find the bag of bougie dog treats right as Ernest hobbles into the kitchen. He jumps a few times on his back legs before I bend down to offer him one.

Cole finally locates the remote amidst the piles of pillows, pausing the true crime documentary that was streaming. "Sometimes Benoit," she replies, and fuck if I don't love the sound of my name on her lips.

"When I'm being annoying?" I joke, offering her a diet cherry cola and her dinner from Louie's.

She sits down at the counter, wagging a finger at me. "See! Now you're catching on. I always knew you were smart."

"Did you? I seem to remember you thinking I was quite the idiot."

"You are an idiot. But a smart idiot, which is a dangerous combination." She lifts her eyebrow as if she's inviting me to argue. I don't. "So what do you prefer to be called, then?"

I prop my elbows on the counter and lean toward her, pretending to ponder her question. "What about 'husband'?"

"For fuck's sake, Benjamin. I'm not marrying you," she says around a bite of burger.

"Why not? We had a deal," I reply.

She scoffs. "A 'deal'"—she adds air quotes for emphasis—"that we made twelve years ago when I was drunk for the first time in my life. It would not hold up in a court of law on this planet or any other."

"I'm fine with a courtroom wedding, it doesn't need to be fancy."

"What? That's not what I said!"

I continue, pretending I didn't hear her. "Though, I did always picture something a little more formal. Not necessarily black tie, but I could be persuaded if that was what you wanted."

"Benjamin," she growls. "Stop planning our fake wedding."

"But it's so fun to rile you up," I say, booping her on the nose. Her glare is murderous, so I walk away, taking the opportunity to explore the rest of her apartment.

She's on the first floor with a nice little green space that I can see through the sliding glass doors. The rest of the room is painted a deep purple and there are several lamps that cast a comforting glow throughout the space. Similar to her bedroom, there's vintage artwork arranged on the walls in between several floating bookshelves. Cole obviously does not have a green thumb because the two plants on the windowsill are dying, just like the snake plant in her bedroom was.

I ignore the way she is fuming, passing back into the kitchen to find a glass of water for the plants. *Tsking* lightly, I admonish her plant growing abilities. "You need to give these some attention," I say, gesturing to the dying fern.

"For some reason, I have never been able to keep a plant alive. It doesn't bark at me like Ernest does when he needs something."

"Fair. I can help you with that." I don't wait for her response, immediately jumping into a new topic so she can't protest. "I noticed you have a puzzle going. Can I add pieces or is it like a sacred ritual?"

"You like to puzzle?" she asks instead of answering my question.

Shrugging, I finish watering the plants and then walk around the coffee table until I can see how she has things laid out. "My grandmother always used to have a puzzle she was working on. It was something we could do together when I visited. It's so satisfying when you find that perfect piece of puzzle and it snaps into place."

Cole hums, her mouth full of burger. When she's done with her last bite, she delicately licks her fingers before taking a swig of cola to wash it all down. I watch as her crop top lifts, exposing a creamy expanse of skin.

I want to lick it.

"It is satisfying," she finally says, causing my eyes to jump back to her face. "You can add pieces, but if you pick one up and it doesn't fit, put it back where you found it."

"Yes, ma'am." I wink, plopping onto the ground so I have a good view of the puzzle. When Cole doesn't move, I pat the couch right behind me. "Come sit. You can turn your murder show back on if you want."

She hesitates. I can see it when I look back up at her. "Something wrong?"

Her eyes narrow, hearing the challenge in my question. She can talk about what's going on here or she can keep pretending it's nothing.

Turns out, she's fine with the latter. I hide my grin as Cole marches over to the couch, sitting right behind me so her thighs bracket my shoulders.

I reach back and pat the inside of her leg. "See. Not that hard. We can sit here, do a puzzle together, so domest—what are you doing, Red?"

"Taking my shorts off."

When I turn to look, my throat dries up at the sight of Cole planting her feet on either side of me, unbuttoning her cutoff jeans, and lifting her hips so she can slide them down over her ass.

"I—I see that." I gulp.

"Don't let me stop you from puzzling." She smirks. She's now lifting her legs so her shorts can come all of the way off, leaving her in the crop top, black underwear, and polka-dot socks.

She's a vision, a dream, a bombshell.

There's no way I'm going to be able to focus on anything else besides her. Cole slides her finger in the top of her panties, back and forth, hypnotizing my very being. I'm a dog, begging for more treats. She's the fucking treat.

My hand reaches toward her before I can stop it. "*Tut-tut,* Benoit. Be a good boy and work on the puzzle."

"Work on the..." I can't wrap my mind around what she's saying right now. She angles her chin to the table behind me, the one I've completely forgotten about.

"The puzzle, Benoit."

My heart's racing as I turn away from her and back to the task she's asked me to work on. I'm sweating already, my glasses slipping down my nose as I try to concentrate on finding an edge piece. The entire time, I'm hypersensitive to the sound of skin against fabric, the light snap of elastic, and… she's wet. I can hear it.

Cole whimpers and it takes everything in me not to turn around and watch her. I know she's probably flushed, her head thrown back in pleasure as she fingers herself while I'm sitting right the fuck here. My entire body tenses up, waiting.

Then, one hand slides over my shoulder while the other comes around to tap on my mouth. "Open up," she commands, so I do. "Suck."

So, of course, I do. I suck her sweet taste off of her own finger, my eyes rolling to the back of my head at the flavor of her. "Fuck," I mutter around her finger. "More."

She pops her finger out of my mouth, then stands in one swift motion. "You haven't done anything."

Haven't done anything? Confused, I look up and see that she's staring at the puzzle in front of me.

"Do you need more of an incentive?" She quirks her eyebrow but doesn't wait for my answer. Her ass swings from side to side as she walks across the room, positioning herself on a chaise lounge directly across from me.

Giving me the perfect view.

Her hand slides back into the top of her underwear. And then she waits.

Tearing my eyes away from her, I stare at the puzzle in front of me, not really seeing the pieces. It's a mountain scene of some sort, I've gathered that much from the box that's been propped up as a guide. Cole has most of the edges done, but the right side sits mostly incomplete.

She's neatly laid out the remaining edge pieces, so I pick one up and catch movement in my peripheral vision. Cole has dipped her hand further, her legs falling open as she moves her fingers in slow circles. I can feel her eyes on me, watching to make sure I'm following her rules.

This is her way of taking charge, taking control back. And,

fuck, I'm not mad about it. I don't think anyone on planet Earth has ever been this turned on while doing a puzzle.

I pick up a piece, attempting to place it in the correct spot but my gaze keeps wandering to this perfect woman touching herself right in front of me.

She moans, her eyes drifting shut. "C'mon, Bardot. Finish that edge so you can come over here." Her words are breathy, desperate—as close to a plea as I'm going to get from her.

But they get the job done, because now I have the motivation I need to fit the rest of these pieces together. I get five pieces connected in quick succession. There are eleven left, so I push my glasses up again and get to work.

The sound of Cole's arousal is lewd, spurring me on.

Three pieces left…

Two pieces.

One.

"Done!" I practically shout, jumping to my feet.

Cole sits up, holding her hand out to stop me from moving toward her. The whine I let out would be embarrassing if I wasn't so fucking hard just thinking about how much control she has over me.

"Shirt off," she demands. My Bardot Brothers Coffee Co. T-shirt is immediately on the floor. She smirks, enjoying how eager I am. "Now crawl."

I'm on all fours before she finishes her sentence. The area rug bites into my palms as I slowly crawl toward Colette Russell. Her bottom lip comes between her teeth as she watches, hand returning to her pussy to slowly circle.

A piece of hair flops down in front of my face, and she leans forward to push it back. Her hand tangles, pulling just slightly as she tips my head up. "You were a good boy following directions. Now you get to make me come."

Nodding my head as much as I can, I beg. "Please, Cole. Please let me."

With one more light tug, she lets go, allowing me to rise onto my knees. My hands slide up her bare legs, squeezing incrementally as I go. When I reach the spot where her hips meet her thighs, I press my thumb into that crease, slipping under her underwear toward her clit.

She arches back, anticipation painted over every part of her body. But before I put my finger where she wants it, I hook her panties and pull them off so I can have a full view of her perfect cunt.

I contemplate taking my glasses off, reaching up to adjust them, but Cole's breathy, "Leave them on," has me stopping in my tracks.

"I will only wear glasses from now on if that's what you like, Colette."

"It's what I like," she moans, pushing her chest toward me.

One of my hands moves under her shirt while the other begins firm circles around her clit. "I'd like to use my mouth now, if you're okay with that."

"I—" She cuts off with a moan. "I'm okay with that."

Leaning toward her, I replace my fingers with my tongue, doing my best to keep up the pace I'd set. She tastes exquisite, and now it's my turn to moan. I lightly tweak her nipple before circling her areola several times, mimicking the movement on her clit. She bows back, mouth popping open in ecstasy as her thighs slam around my face, knocking my glasses askew.

"Fuck," she cries. Her body is shaking as she rides the waves of her orgasm. Slowly, I press one finger, and then two into her center, hooking them to increase her pleasure. "Why—" She gasps. "Why are you so good at this?"

"Research," I reply between strokes of my tongue. I want her to keep coming. I want to make her come again and again for the rest of my life.

"Research?" She laughs. "You did research on how to have sex?"

She's slowly coming down now, her chest still heaving, her legs lazily draped over my shoulders. I run my hands through my hair with a shrug. "I looked up some tips on sexual pleasure when your partner is autistic."

When she just stares at me, I continue, "Everyone is different, obviously. And if there's anything you like or don't like, please tell me. But firm touch and predictability seemed to be a common theme."

"You did research on how to be a better partner to someone with autism... for me."

"Yeah, Colette. For you. And for me," I joke. "I would very much like to keep having sex with you so I had to make sure it was enjoyable."

A beat passes and I'm worried I royally fucked up. And then she springs forward, pinning me to the ground, her legs on either side of my hips.

"Stop being nice to me," she says before kissing me senseless.

I don't know how to tell her that if she wants me to stop, she can't keep kissing me like this.

Chapter Nineteen
MY DATE WITH GABRIEL BARDOT
Cole

GOOGLE SEARCH

Ben Bardot has got to stop being nice to me.

I tell him as much right before I kiss him. I'm pretty sure he mutters "no" but I'm choosing to ignore that. Because I'm not done with him tonight.

He's laid back against the floor, hands pinned above his head. Ben is much larger than I am and could obviously change our position at any time. But he doesn't. He continues to allow me to control the situation, even as my emotions are secretly unraveling with each passing moment.

Grinding down, I enjoy the press of his thick cock through his jeans. Relish that I'm making a mess of them as my bare pussy gyrates. The mess he's making of me is internal, but the mess I'm going to make of him? I want visual evidence.

After a moment, I pull away, laughing as his mouth attempts to follow me up. I tease him, yanking my top off over my head to reveal the sheer bralette I'm wearing underneath. His hips buck up involuntarily, seeking more friction. I circle my hips, but his strong hands are instantly there to stop me.

"If you keep doing that, I'm going to come in my pants. Again. I would really, *really* like to be inside of you when that happens."

Acquiescing, I stop my movements. He inhales deeply, trying to regain composure. I'm mesmerized by the flex of his jaw, the squeeze of his hands, the way his breathing remains labored.

My patience runs out rather quickly so I scoot myself down, maneuvering to where I can unbutton his pants, dragging the zipper down slowly until I can reach my hand into his boxers. When I wrap my hand around his dick, Ben sucks in a ragged breath. "Colette," he warns.

"Sorry, sorry," I reply, lifting my hands up in surrender.

"No, you're not," he laughs, slipping his legs out of his jeans before kicking them off to the side.

"No," I agree. "I'm not."

The boxers are next to go, and I finally get a look at the small tattoo that sits low on his hip. It's tally marks. Five of them… four in a row and then one slashing across, just like all of the marks filling the page of his journal. The journal I was definitely not supposed to see, I'm sure of that now, but I don't know why that's what my gut is telling me.

My finger grazes across the ink, head tilting to the side and mind racing. "Interesting tattoo."

Ben freezes for the briefest second. I wouldn't have noticed if I wasn't sitting right next to him. "Lost a bet in college," he replies, focused on pulling my leg back over him.

I drop it because honestly, I don't feel like I have the right to pry. I might be fucking this man on my living room floor, but he doesn't owe me anything.

"Still okay with not using a condom?" I ask, my mask slipping back into place.

He nods, biting his lip. His gaze is zeroed in on where I have the tip of his dick positioned at my entrance. His hips jump, right as I lower. I'm still so wet, I glide right down to the hilt. Ben's cock fills me deliciously, and I pause to adjust to the feel of him inside me.

All thoughts of his mysterious tattoo disappear the second he bucks his hips into me. His hands come back to my waist, holding me down as he plants his feet on the floor behind us and thrusts. I waste no time stripping the last bit of clothing that remains between us. My bralette discarded, I cup my breasts in my hands as Ben continues to push into me. "Fuck, Red. You're perfect. Look at those tits bouncing for me."

I tweak my nipple in one hand and reach between us with my other. My clit is swollen and ready, quickly sending me over the edge again. Ben is fast to follow, his entire body flexes, face scrunching in an admittedly adorable way as he pumps in and out a few more times.

When he slows to a stop, his hands come up to grasp mine, gently tugging me toward him. "What are you doing?"

"Shh. Just come lay on top of me for a minute." He pulls down a little more firmly this time, sending me careening toward him. Ben catches me, his arms snaking around my back. My head rests in the crook of his neck, and we stay like that for several minutes, simply existing together.

"Are we… cuddling?" I ask, breaking the silence.

"Depends. Are you enjoying it?" Ben murmurs.

"No."

"Liar."

I am a liar. And that's enough of this *feelings* shit. Pushing away from Ben, I hear his deep sigh. "I'm going to—"

"Take a bath, I know," he interrupts. "I'll see myself out?"

Seems like our best course of action. "Yeah. Thanks for dinner and, uh, the sex."

Ben props himself onto his elbows, his full naked body splayed out before me. "One day you'll let me stay after the sex."

"Probably not."

Several minutes later I hear the apartment door shut as Ben lets himself out. I remind myself that it's easier this way, less of an opportunity to get hurt. With the loss of my scholarship, my life feels out of control. But here, I can control the narrative. A voice in the back of my mind tells me that's not fair to Ben.

I tell that voice to fuck off.

———

Two surprising things happen in the next couple of weeks.

Actually, make that three.

First, Ben leaves me alone. He doesn't text. He's not at my shifts at the coffee shop. Shockingly, I don't see him around town.

It's freaky.

It's like he's… intentionally avoiding me? Or maybe he's out of town. I think it's the longest I've gone without seeing or talking to him since he moved back to town.

Second, Dr. Winthrop, my advisor, called me to let me know that a new grant opportunity became available. She said this grant was specifically for second year grad students going into forensic psychology. The grant would not only cover the amount I needed after losing my scholarship, but also is meant to completely cover full tuition. Meaning I can keep the money I was saving up for school costs as a fallback and quit my job at the coffee shop.

The relief I felt after that call rivaled the orgasmic high I was on after my last encounter with Ben. I almost cried. Almost.

Finally, since Ben has disappeared off the face of the planet, out of boredom one night I swiped through my dating app until I happened upon a different Bardot brother. I instantly opened up a chat with him, my curiosity getting the best of me.

Gabriel Bardot. Fancy seeing you here.

GABE

Oh God, Cole. PLEASE don't tell anyone you
saw me on here.

I mean... you also saw me here.

GABE

I know. It's just... I'm trying to forget someone.

I can understand that.

GABE

What are you doing on a dating app anyway? I
thought you and Ben were...

Were what, Gabriel?

GABE

Who the fuck knows with you two.

Where is he? I haven't seen him in a while.

GABE

He's been holed up in his room working on
something. He's being very secretive about it.

I think I know what could get him out though...

What?

GABE

Hear me out.

And that's how I end up on a date with Gabriel Bardot.

––––––

"This is a bad idea."

Gabe sits across the table from me at Louie's and shrugs. *Shrugs!*

"Gabriel. What if he doesn't come? This is a small town! People talk!"

He chuckles. "Yes, Cole. That's the point. There's no way at least five people in here haven't already told someone they know that we are here together. It will get back to Ben. I give it twenty minutes, tops."

I groan, my head flopping down until it's almost hitting the table. I slide a napkin in front of me and then proceed with the headbanging minus the gross table germs. Why am I doing this? Why do I care if Ben sees me on another date?

Other than being nervous that Gabe's plan will backfire, I'm actually having a good time. There's no karaoke tonight so I don't have to worry about listening to mediocre singers while I eat my plain burger and fries. And conversation with Gabe is easy. Probably because this isn't a real date so I don't feel like I have to pretend to be having fun.

"Fine. But you have to distract me. Who are you trying to forget?"

Gabe's eyes narrow. "I can't tell you that."

"Why not? Is it someone I know?"

He thinks for a moment. "I don't think so...? I'm not sure when your paths would have crossed."

"Then I think you can tell me. It's not like I have anyone that I'm going to tell."

"What about Ben?"

"What about Ben?" I repeat.

"You won't tell him?" Gabe clarifies.

I scoff. "Ben's on my shit list. I won't tell him."

Gabe takes a slow sip of his beer. I can see the moment he decides he's going to let me in on his secret. "She's one of Bex's friends."

"I see." I don't see. "And Bex wouldn't want you to date her?"

"It's not that. I don't think? I've never really asked Bex, if I'm being honest." He fiddles with his glass, rolling it between his hands. "We almost—"

Just then, the door to Louie's slams open. Benoit Bardot stands there, backlit in the dim bar. I try not to smile when Gabe mutters, "That was quick."

Ben storms over to our table, grabs Gabe by the collar and utters a sentence I am simultaneously turned on and mortified by. "What the fuck are you doing here with my wife?"

"Your what?!" Gabe and I ask at the same time. Well, Gabe kind of chokes it out because Ben has such a tight grip on his shirt.

I jump out of the booth and start smacking Ben on the arm. "Let him go, you lunatic! It was a joke!"

Gabe's hands are up in surrender as Ben continues to stare at him. His grip slowly loosens until Gabe shoves him the rest of the way off. "A joke?" he asks in a daze.

Gabe looks at Ben as if he has three heads. "Yes, Brother. A joke."

"I told you this was a bad idea," I say to Gabe.

Ben stands there for a beat, looking between the two of us. Finally, he turns toward Gabe. "We'll talk at home. Sorry about your shirt."

Then, he turns toward me. His eyes are full of mischief as he closes the gap between us. "If you wanted my attention, Red, all you had to do was ask."

Before I can respond, Ben bends down, throwing me over his shoulder. He lands a smack on my ass that I'm one hundred percent sure everyone in the bar sees.

But Ben doesn't give a single fuck. And he carries me that way all the way up to his apartment.

We both enjoy my punishment.

Chapter Twenty
BROTHERLY INTERVENTIONS
Ben

GOOGLE SEARCH

My attempt at avoiding Gabe over the next few days is unsuccessful when he corners me early one morning as I'm coming out of the bathroom.

"Can't a man shower in private?" I ask, attempting to squeeze past Gabe and head to the kitchen.

"Negative, Brother. We need to chat."

"As, uh… ominous as that sounds, can I at least put some clothes on?" I nod down at my bare torso, towel slung low across my hips.

"Fine, but I'm coming with you."

I scoff. "I'm not going to climb out the window while you're waiting."

In lieu of a response, Gabe follows me into my room, making himself comfortable when he plops onto my bed.

"Gabriel, shoes off the bed."

He shuffles so his feet hang haphazardly over the edge and then props his head up in the palm of his hand. I stand there staring at him, waiting for him to—I don't know—avert his eyes? "Do you mind?" I ask.

"Nope," he replies, popping the *P* obnoxiously. "You aren't escaping me, Benny boo."

"I'm not trying to escape you!" I sigh, dropping my towel and quickly hopping into some boxers. "I'm just trying to get dressed in private."

"Don't worry, I'm not looking at your dick. I'm too busy trying to figure out what that tattoo is. Do Mom and Dad know about that?"

"As a thirty-year-old man, I didn't think I had to update my parents on everything new that happens with my body," I retort.

"What about Jules? Does he know?"

Gabe is cruel for bringing up my twin. Mainly because I feel guilty that Jules does not know about my tattoo.

"Fuck," Gabe mutters. "I'm calling him. He needs to be here for this."

Scrubbing my hand down my face, I ask, "Be here for what?" But it's too late, Gabe has already FaceTimed Jules.

"Everything okay?" Jules asks as soon as he answers. Always the worrier.

"Everything is fine," Gabe says at the same time I yell, "I'm being held hostage!"

Jules' low chuckle comes through the phone. "Do I need to come over there?"

"Yes," Gabe replies.

"No," I counter.

"Be there in ten," Jules says before hanging up.

Gabe tosses the phone onto the bed next to him, appearing to have no care in the world. After a moment, the motherfucker starts *whistling*. I finish getting dressed, leaving the room without another look his way.

The plus side of working at the coffee shop with Jules is that he's taught me how to make a phenomenal cup of coffee at home. I grind the beans, measuring out just enough for myself when Gabe joins me in the kitchen. The island chair scrapes across the floor as he pulls it out and takes a seat. "Will you make me some too?" he has the audacity to ask.

"No, asshole. Make your own coffee."

"Touchy, touchy this morning."

I smash the button on the kettle a little too hard, effectively proving Gabe's point. "You would be touchy too if you woke up to an intervention."

Gabe laughs at me. "This isn't an intervention. Jules and I just want to know what's going on in your life."

"Yeah, because you are both so forthcoming," I huff.

He considers me for a moment. "Fine, I can be forthcoming. I have… had a thing for Luci Ramirez for… a while. And I just found out she's been dating someone since January."

"Luci Ramirez… as in Bex's Luci?" Damn, we've all been keeping secrets it seems.

He nods, a crease forming between his brows. "Yeah. So I downloaded a dating app and guess who else I saw on the app?"

I groan because I bet I know exactly who he saw. "Colette."

"Mhmm."

The sound of the door unlocking halts our conversation. Jules lets himself in, untying and retying his man bun before he sits down next to Gabe. "I don't want to rush this, but I do need to go help Cole at the shop this morning."

My head snaps toward him. "What's Cole doing at the shop?"

Jules looks at me like I'm an idiot. "Working… You're the one who got her the job," he replies.

"But, she shouldn't have to—she shouldn't need another job anymore." Did they fuck something up? I thought she would have—

"Is that why she said we need to talk today? Is she already quitting?"

I immediately feel defensive over Cole. "She's not quitting. Well, I mean hopefully she is, but she's not a quitter. She's an extremely hard worker."

Jules holds his hands up in supplication. "I'm not implying that she's not."

"See what I mean?" Gabe directs the question to Jules.

"What are you talking about?" The kettle beeps indicating that the water is ready. I turn away from my brothers to finish making my coffee—I have a feeling I'm going to need it for this conversation.

In a rare moment of silence for Gabe, they don't answer my question until I have completed my task. Once they have my attention again, Jules starts talking. "Gabriel is slightly concerned about you." I start to protest but Jules gives me a look that says, *shut up*. "Would you like to hear what we have to say or would you like to explain what's going on with you and Cole?"

It's on the tip of my tongue to say, *Nothing's going on with me and Cole!* But that would be a lie. I'm just not quite sure how to answer that question truthfully. "Go on," I reply instead.

Jules looks momentarily disappointed but continues anyway. "We just want to make sure you aren't going to get hurt. Obviously you two have a history. What was once an academic rivalry seems to have turned into some sort of mind game. And we want to make sure that you're not getting too wrapped up in something that she's not putting the same effort into."

"Just because her effort looks different, doesn't mean she's not putting in effort."

Gabe quirks his eyebrow at me. "Is she?"

I turn to Jules. "I know that you get it. You're going through the same thing with Thea."

"It's different," he immediately replies.

"Is it? To me it just looks like the Bardot brothers are attracted to partners that are scared of commitment." I look meaningfully at Gabe, who gives me the smallest shake of his head.

"Thea's been through a lot." Jules' hackles are raised and I get it.

"So has Cole."

My twin takes a deep breath, centering himself before he continues. "I believe you. And you know that I've always liked Cole. She kept you on your toes all through school and it seems like that hasn't changed. Just... don't do anything impulsive, alright?"

I ignore the very impulsive purchase that is sitting in my nightstand drawer. "I won't."

"He got a tattoo!" Gabe snitches, seemingly upset that he hasn't been able to contribute anything to this conversation.

"What the fuck, Gabriel?"

Jules, who has more tattoos than I can count snaking up and down both of his arms, looks betrayed. "I'm the tattooed brother," he states.

"It's one tattoo! Don't worry, I'm not about to get matching sleeves to yours."

"Good, that would be extremely creepy." He smirks, which is Jules' version of a full on belly laugh. "What's the tattoo?"

"It's a bunch of lines," Gabe answers. "Does it stand for something? Is it like how many people you've...?" He bounces his eyebrows suggestively.

I roll my eyes. "That would make me a world-class jackass if I got a tally mark for every person I'd fucked."

"They're tally marks?" Jules questions in a way that makes me think he sees way more than I want him to.

"Yeah..."

I wait a few beats to see if he asks anything else. After he's stared at me long enough that my temples have started perspiring, he abruptly stands from his chair and claps Gabe on the back. "Well, I think that went well. I've got to head to the shop. See both of you later?"

Gabe looks incredibly confused, but he doesn't argue as we watch Jules leave.

Finally he shrugs, also getting up so he can move to the couch. I sit next to him with my hot cup of coffee, watching as he finds the ESPN app and turns on SportsCenter. Several minutes go by before he says, "I'm always here if you want to talk, you know that?"

"Me, too. Okay?"

"Okay."

And that's the end of my brotherly intervention.

Chapter Twenty-One
HBD RED!
Cole

GOOGLE SEARCH

I hate birthdays.

Why do we feel the need to celebrate being born? We didn't even do anything to make it happen. I had no part in the fact that someone, well, two someones, decided to procreate and deliver me into this world.

And the singing? I hate singing. I can't think of anything more mortifying than a group of people singing *at me* while I sit in front of a cake. And opening presents? In front of people? What if I don't have the correct reaction and then someone thinks that I hate their gift? And what if I do hate their gift and I have to pretend that I don't?

It's one terrible cultural tradition after another.

Thank God there's only one person in this town who knows that today is my birthday. If I stay home, I can avoid him completely and only have to worry about the obligatory "Happy birthday!" texts from my parents.

In fact, my phone buzzes with one of them now. A little earlier than usual… I wasn't expecting to hear from them until dinnertime.

BEN

Happy birthday, Red *red heart emoji*

Fuck off, Benjamin.

BEN

Thirty.

Big birthday.

Anyone to celebrate with?

You are an asshole.

BEN

I love when you're mean to me.

There is something seriously wrong with you.

BEN

Stop with the dirty talk, Colette.

I'm blocking your number.

BEN

That's fine, I'll be by in a bit to help you
celebrate. *wink emoji*

What?

NO.

I won't let you in.

Why aren't you responding?!

"Ugh!" I scream, startling Ernest where he was napping on his dog bed. "Fuck."

I don't want to see Ben. I don't want to think about our pact. I don't want to celebrate my birthday!

As if he was standing right outside of my door when he texted, I hear a knock less than thirty seconds after I send my last text. Begrudgingly, I shuffle over the door and peek through the peep hole.

Benoit Bardot is standing there, his slutty little glasses sitting high on his nose. His arms are full of gift bags, and he has a fucking cake in his hands.

"Go away!" I yell through the door.

He smirks, looking directly into the peep hole. "Open the door, Colette."

"No," I reply, turning the lock anyway.

Annoyingly, he looks like the perfect gift when I finally do pull the door open. His hair is effortlessly tousled and he's wearing a striped button-down and khaki shorts. The cake in his hands is covered in red icing with "HBD Red!" in white icing across the top.

"That cake looks like blood," I remark, scowling.

"You like blood, murder, crime, et cetera, et cetera." His lips tip up at the corner, knowing he caught me.

"No, I don't."

"Yes, you do. Are you going to let me in?" he asks, cocky as ever.

"Do I have to?"

"No." His reply is quick and I actually believe him. If I turned him away right now, he'd leave.

My eye roll is overdramatic as I move out of his way.

He walks in like he owns the place, setting the cake on the counter and arranging the presents just so. "Come sit in front of your cake," he commands, pulling a candle and a lighter out of his pocket.

I narrow my eyes, walking toward him. I don't know why

I'm letting him boss me around. Why I'm letting him acknowledge a day that I rarely ever acknowledge. He pulls out the chair for me, nodding in satisfaction when I take a seat.

He steps back and holds up his phone for a picture. "Smile and say, 'Thirty'!" Instead, I scowl and flip him off. "Perfect," he mutters, and when he sets the phone down on the counter beside me, I see that he's set it as his background.

"I won't sing to you," he promises, leaning down to whisper in my ear. "But I do want you to make a wish."

"I wish that you'd leave me alone," I reply, blowing out the candle.

"Bummer. You told me so now it won't come true. Oh, well." He smirks. "Guess I'll have to stick around."

Ben takes it upon himself to locate a knife and two plates in my kitchen. When he slices the cake, I see that it's red velvet inside.

"What's your obsession with red?" I ask.

He pauses, eyes darting up to my hair. "I would think it's obvious."

I scoff. "Red... What an unoriginal nickname, too."

Ben considers me for a moment. "Maybe for some. But when I look at you, all I see is red. The color of your hair, sure. But also the flush that runs up your neck when you feel anything—and you feel so deeply, though you don't let many people see that—excitement, frustration... desire. It's the color of your toes when you allow yourself the frivolity of painting them. The color of your tongue when you drink diet cherry cola. It's your hair, yes... but it's so much more than that."

I'm momentarily stunned, speechless. Where the fuck did that come from?

"I've been paying attention, Red." He winks, pushing a slice of cake toward me.

I take a bite because I don't know what else to do. "Mmm, damn that's good," I mutter, unable to control my reaction.

"Great. Have as much as you want. Then I'm going to go to

the grocery store and pick up something to make for dinner tonight. Any preferences?"

"You're making me dinner?" I ask, surprised.

"I figured you wouldn't want to go out in public, so I'll bring dinner to you. And you need to open your presents."

Eyeing the bags he's arranged on the counter with trepidation, I tell him, "You didn't have to get me anything."

"I know." He punctuates the statement by taking his own bite of cake. "Fuck, this *is* good."

"Did you think I was lying?"

He doesn't respond, instead pushing the first present toward me. I slowly remove the tissue paper to reveal new Irish coffee candles. The exact same brand that I already own and love. "Figured you'd need some replacements soon, all the baths you've been taking."

"That's… that's really thoughtful. Thank you."

He nods before nudging the second present my way. This one is a little bigger which makes me nervous. I unwrap it and find a sweatshirt. It's light purple, but other than that, pretty unremarkable. "A sweatshirt… in July. Thank you?" I can't help the way my voice goes up at the end so it sounds more like a question than a statement.

This is exactly why I don't like opening presents with people.

"It's a sensory sweatshirt," Ben explains. "It's a heavier weight material and there are built in stress balls in the sleeves. I may or may not have been targeted by an ad on social media."

Underneath his cocky exterior, Ben looks almost… shy. Like he's not sure how to interpret my reaction. Honestly, I'm not sure how to handle these feelings either. I can feel the telltale flush creeping up my neck and my eyes feel oddly prickly. No one has ever bothered to accommodate me the way Ben has ever since he learned of my diagnosis.

Popping up from my seat, I start to pace the floor. Ernest senses my agitation and hobbles over to press against my legs.

"Cole?" Ben questions.

"I'm fine. I just need a second." I bend down so I'm eye level with Ernest. He pops up onto his hind legs, his one front leg pressing into my shoulder in a way that grounds me. Emotion, even a positive one, can be overwhelming sometimes and, even though he isn't actually trained to be, Ernest has proven to be an excellent form of therapy.

"I'm sorry if I was overstepping," Ben whispers.

I take a few deep breaths before I respond. "I'm not used to people… knowing me. Caring enough to take the time."

"That's really shitty, Cole. I'm sorry that's been your experience." He comes around the counter and sits next to me on the floor, both elbows propped on his knees.

"I'm not under the illusion that I'm an easy person to be around. It takes a lot of work to have any sort of relationship with me."

He shrugs. "I think you're the easiest person in the world to be around. Everyone else can fuck off, that's completely fine with me." When I look up at him, he's smiling. "I'd rather keep you all to myself anyway."

"Don't say shit like that."

"Why?" he asks.

"Because I don't want to like you."

He hums in response. "Ready for another present?"

"No."

"I think I'll give you one anyway. Stand up?" he pleads, so sincerely I actually listen instead of arguing with him.

I start to stand and he follows, but he stays down on his knee instead of getting all of the way up. Then he's reaching into his back pocket and pulling out a small, square box. *Then* he's opening the box to reveal a ring. It's set on a delicate gold band, but the stone in the middle is an obscenely large black gem with three triangular diamonds framing it on either side. I watch this all happen as if I'm an outside observer, completely detached from the situation.

Because there's no fucking way Benoit Bardot is proposing to me right now.

Chapter Twenty-Two

I'M NOT RETURNING IT
Cole

GOOGLE SEARCH

🔍 Pawn shops near Sassafras, Massachusetts. 🎤

Except, it appears that he is. Proposing, that is.

"Colette Russell—"

"No."

"You're thirty, Colette. I'm thirty. We made a pact, and I've waited four-thousand-four-hundred days until I was able to call it in."

My mind short circuits. "You've… I—No."

"Why not?" he asks, and I laugh. Laugh!

I take the box out of his hand, closing it so I don't have to see the most perfect fucking ring staring at me—mocking me. "People don't get married because of a pact they made at eighteen, Benoit! Are you insane? And how much was that ring?! You should return it."

"I'm not returning it." His hand slides up my leg, stroking

my thigh under my skirt. I bat it away because damn him for distracting me.

"Well, I'm not taking it. Get up! You need to leave." I can hear the panic in my voice. Feel it in the way my heart is beating out of my chest.

Blessedly, he listens to me, getting slowly to his feet. "Five dates."

"What?"

"Go on five dates with me. Then you can decide if I should return the ring," he clarifies.

"No!"

"Five dates… please?" His brown eyes meet mine, flecks of gold dancing throughout his irises. He's serious. I can tell just by looking that this isn't a joke to him.

"Maybe. If I agree, we go on five dates," I repeat. "And then you take the ring back."

His grin is panty melting, and I really, really need him to leave before I do anything stupid. "Deal," he mutters, handing me the box.

I pull my hand away from his. "You keep it until then. I don't want it."

"Wear it?" he asks, head dipping toward me. He's a breath away when he whispers, "Please?"

I shake my head because that is ludicrous. I can't wear this ring. It's huge! People will notice!

"Please?" he asks again, lips brushing mine. The barest touch that sends an electric shock through me.

"Maybe," I reply, because I'm no longer operating out of my prefrontal cortex. That one word is all it takes, and then he's kissing me fully. His arms wrap around my waist, drawing me flush against his strong body. I kiss him back until I remember what the fuck he just talked me into. Then I put my hands between us and shove, hard.

"Out!" I gasp, but my heaving chest betrays me.

The motherfucker grins, leaning in to plant one more kiss on my forehead. He drops the ring box on the counter and then he's gone. Leaving me reeling over whatever the fuck just happened.

————

Hey Thea. It's Cole. Any chance you are free for coffee this week? Or I'm not sure if you can drink coffee when you're pregnant...

Just googled it and there are mixed opinions but I'm happy to meet somewhere else too. Maybe Louie's?

Fuck, why is this so awkward. I haven't tried to make a new friend in... I actually don't recall ever intentionally trying to make a friend. Thea and I have seen each other a few times and texted here and there but we haven't really "bonded" yet. So here I am, trying.

And resenting the fact that it's incredibly humiliating to put yourself out there like this.

THEA

lol yes I can drink coffee! But I'm also craving fried pickles from Louie's so I'm happy to meet there!

How about tomorrow night?

Perfect.

Thea is already in a booth when I walk into Louie's the next night. Her baby bump has grown since the last time I saw her. *Obviously, Colette. That's how it works!* My palms are a bit sweaty as I make my way toward the table. Thea spots me and waves me over.

She moves to get up but I stop her. "No, no. Don't get up for me."

She smiles warmly at me, rubbing her belly absentmindedly. "How are you feeling?"

"Good," she sighs. "Everything looks good with the baby, and I'm not huge yet so it's pretty much smooth sailing right now."

"That's good. I know nothing about pregnancy. You're the first pregnant person I've ever spent much time around," I admit.

"Really? No other friends having babies yet?"

I wince because she accidentally hit a nerve. Trying to school my features, I reply, "I don't have a ton of friends. None, actually."

Her lips tilt up in a sad smile, and my stomach drops. I don't want pity. I've never wanted pity. The thought of her feeling sorry for me almost propels me out of my seat and straight back home. She surprises me though when she says, "Me either. Unless you count Chloe." Thea lifts one shoulder in a resigned shrug.

Relief crashes over me. "Oh my God, that's so great." Her face twists, and I play what I just said back in my head. *Shit.* "Not like that! Sorry. It's not great that you don't have friends. It's just… really nice to find someone else who has had a similar experience."

"Yeah, I get that," she sighs. "My mom died when I was young so I never really saw a good example of female friendships. I was close with my cousins growing up—still am— but I was so focused on ballet for most of my youth that I didn't have time to cultivate friendships."

I nod, because in a way we have a lot in common. "Both of my parents are still alive but I don't talk with them often. After they divorced, I think my mom saw an opportunity to 're-do' her early twenties. I moved here with my dad in middle school, but he retired to Florida a few years back."

"That would be hard." Thea's tone is sympathetic. "I can't imagine not having my dad around to help with Chloe."

"I don't think either of them ever wanted to be parents. They haven't said outright but I think I was a failed attempt to save the marriage." I pause, considering how much I want to divulge. "It's part of the reason I don't want kids of my own."

Most people try to talk you into having kids when you admit you don't want them. I especially expected that from Thea, who is on the way to having two kids of her own. Yet, Thea continues to surprise me. "That makes a lot of sense," she simply states. "People need to listen to their gut when it comes to a lot of things, but especially whether or not they want to have kids."

My mind flashes to Ben… to his flippant admission to having a vasectomy. Then again to the ring that is hidden in my underwear drawer. For the first time, I start to visualize what a life with Ben could look like. Start to unpack the box I've put him in, questioning whether or not he actually fits the idea of him I've had in my mind all these years.

"Earth to Cole." Thea waves her hand in front of my face, interrupting my thought spiral. When I refocus on her, I can see the worry lining her features. "I thought I lost you there for a minute. Did I offend you with my comment about having kids?"

"Not at all," I reply. "It is refreshing to not have someone try to convince me that 'kids are a gift' and 'what if I change my mind,' yada yada."

Louie brings over an order of fried pickles and a plain burger for me. "It's on the house ladies, so make sure you order dessert." He winks.

"On the house?" I ask.

"Jules?" Thea guesses.

"Close," Louie replies, looking pointedly at me. Then he turns around and walks away, not ever giving us an answer.

Thea pops a pickle in her mouth and then leans forward on

the table. "So… Ben is buying our dinner? That's what Louie was implying, right?"

I take a page out of Louie's book and also avoid answering that question. "How are things with you and Jules?"

Thea raises a single eyebrow. "I'll allow you to redirect for now, but if we're going to be friends, I expect you to come back to that at some point." When I nod, she continues. "Jules and I are… complicated. Actually, Jules is perfect. I'm the complicated one."

"Felt," I reply.

"My ex—Chloe's dad—was a complete asshole. Something I probably need to dive deeper into in therapy. And I feel bad that Jules is dealing with the fallout of that, in a way. But he's so patient, so kind to me."

"And the sex?" I ask, pumping my eyebrows a few times.

Thea slams her palms down on the table, sending a pickle flying. "Don't even get me started on the sex." She winks.

Laughing at her dramatics, I reply, "Good for you, Thea."

"Could be good for you, too…" she sing-songs.

"Maybe."

Maybe.

The rest of dinner is an absolute joy. I forgot how nice it is to open up to someone, to joke and tell stories.

I was sufficiently distracted, but when I get home later in the evening, I beeline to my underwear drawer and pull out the small velvet box that's hidden there. Popping it open, I take the ring out, admiring how it sparkles even in the low light glowing from my lamps. Slowly, I slide it onto my left ring finger.

It fits perfectly.

Of course it does.

Maybe I can just wear it around the house. It's too pretty to sit, untouched, in my drawer. Wearing it when no one is around can't hurt, right?

Right.

Chapter Twenty-Three
AN INTERESTING DEVELOPMENT
Ben

GOOGLE SEARCH

Q where should I take my sort of fiancée on a date?

It's been two weeks and I have yet to hear from Cole after she kicked me out of her apartment on her birthday. Was it bold to propose when we technically aren't even dating?

Honestly, I don't think it was bold *enough*. My preference would have been to take her to the courthouse right then and there. But it's probably good to take baby steps.

Though I don't think Cole would consider buying a ring "baby steps."

I wonder if she's wearing it.

Regardless of the fact that I never got a firm yes, I've already started planning our first date. If five is all I get, I want to make sure I leave a lasting impression. I want her to see how good we are together. That all of the reasons we were rivals in high school are actually the reasons we could work as a couple.

We could challenge each other, push each other, and like I always have been, I'm perfectly content letting her shine.

I just need to get her to go on a date with me.

Date one should be lowkey. She's already mad at me, I don't want to piss her off even more.

Opening my laptop, I do a quick check on inventory at the coffee shop, look through my investment portfolio that I've not been paying enough attention to, and then I start googling. Surely there's a serial killer museum or something that Cole would enjoy. On the other hand, maybe that's not lowkey.

A spa? A bathhouse? She enjoys her baths, but I can't imagine she would want to enjoy it in the presence of other people. Maybe I could rent one out for the day, so it's just the two of us...

Actually, that's an excellent idea. An hour and several phone calls later, I've got a spa secured near Boston next week. If I can get Cole on board.

I have the day off from the coffee shop so I decide to go see Cole in person instead of texting her, hoping she can't resist me in my glasses and short shorts.

After showering and changing, I run over to Bardot Brothers Coffee Co. so I don't show up to Cole's empty handed. Taking a deep breath, I knock on her door, smiling to myself when I hear Ernest's loud barking.

"Down boy!" Colette calls from the other side of the door. She flings it open, looking frazzled and not entirely pleased to see me.

"Yes, ma'am." I smirk. When she stands there staring at me, I lift the drink carrier in my hand. "I have a peace offering?"

"It's going to take way more than a cup of coffee to bring peace to our relationship." Cole rolls her eyes moving to wave me in, and that's when I notice it. A big onyx stone framed with diamonds sparkling on Cole's left hand.

Shifting the drinks, I take Cole's hand, holding it up in front of my face. Her eyes widen as she desperately tries to pry herself out of my grasp. "Hmm, what an interesting development, Red."

"Fuck off," she gasps, squirming as I back her into the wall.

"I don't think I will." Her chest heaves, breasts grazing me as she shakes her head. "I like seeing my ring on your finger, Colette."

Her eyes flash up to mine from under her full lashes. They flip back and forth between blazing anger and fiery lust. I drag her knuckles slowly across my lips, kissing right under where the ring sits on her finger. When Cole whimpers, I nip lightly before finally letting her go to walk into the kitchen.

She doesn't immediately follow me, and a glance back shows her leaning back against the wall, eyes closed. She fiddles with her ring, and my stomach clenches when she starts to pull it off.

"Don't," I plead. Cole freezes, her hazel eyes meeting mine again. I can't decipher the look she gives me—I'm really hoping that's not regret that flashes there.

She sighs, pushing off the wall and following me into the kitchen. "What are you doing here, Ben?"

I consider her. She's as beautiful as ever, creamy skin dotted with freckles and auburn hair that has lightened in the summer sun. It frames her face, and I smile when she tucks a piece behind her ear. "You haven't given me an answer about our deal."

"Pardon me for being a little weary of entering into another deal with you," she snarks. "Last time you ghosted me for twelve years before calling it in."

"I didn't ghost you."

She levels me with a stare. "A drunken pact that was never supposed to be serious and then nothing."

"It was always serious. To me, at least."

A little crease forms between Cole's brows. She looks at me like I'm a problem to be solved. "I don't understand you."

"Yet," I amend.

She sips her coffee and, fuck, I can't help that my eyes keep going back to her ring. It's ignited something unexpectedly primal in me, and there's no fucking way I'm letting her give it back to me.

"I've planned our first date for next week," I continue, prying my eyes away from her delicate hands. "I'm assuming you'd like to know what we are doing so you can prepare? I can keep it a surprise, if you want. It's completely up to you."

She bites her bottom lip, contemplating my question. "Part of me wants to keep it a surprise. I'm already in way over my head here, maybe I should just fully embrace it?"

"I'm loving this can-do spirit, Red." I wink. "How about a compromise? I can give you a few of the important bits, yeah?"

"Okay... what are the important bits?" She scrunches her nose, and I can tell she's holding back from asking me to tell her all about it. "It's nothing fussy, right? I-I don't like to be around a lot of people or—"

"I know, Colette." I interrupt. "There won't be anyone else there."

She cocks her hip, one hand holding coffee and the other coming to settle on her waist. "No one else there? That sounds a little creepy."

"Alright, there will be a few people there," I correct. "But it won't be open to the general public."

"What should I wear?" she asks.

"Doesn't matter." I shrug. "We won't be wearing clothes for very long."

Cole sets her coffee down on the counter so she can begin massaging her temples. "You are not inspiring much confidence, Benjamin. Where the fuck would we go where we won't be wearing clothes?"

I walk toward her, gently prying her hands off of her face. Wrapping both of her hands in one of mine, I tip her chin up to look at me. "Do you trust me?" I ask.

"No," she quips, not missing a beat.

"Liar," I laugh, the pad of my thumb running across her

bottom lip. Her eyes flutter closed and that simply won't do. "Eyes on me, Colette."

Popping open, they bore into me. It's fine with me because I want her attention for the next thing I say. "I will work my ass off making sure I prove myself to you. Making sure I do everything in my power for you to trust me. I might have waited twelve years until it was time to call in our pact, but I was just waiting twelve years for *you*. To be a man who deserved your attention. Your devotion. And I would wait another twelve years, if I had to. But I really, really don't want to. Please don't make me wait anymore. Go on a date with me?"

Her eyes dart back and forth, assessing. Eventually, she pushes away from me, putting space between us again. "Fine. I'll see you next week."

Chapter Twenty-Four

NO RING, NO DATE
Cole

GOOGLE SEARCH

What's the meaning of a dream where you are naked and everyone else is wearing clothes? 

I've been nervous all week about my date with Ben. He was one hundred percent correct in assuming that I would want to know where we were going. I like to know what the expectation is so I can prepare, walk through all possible scenarios in my head in the hopes that nothing catches me by surprise.

Reluctantly, I will admit that it was very kind of Ben to offer to prepare me. It was not kind, however, to tell me that wherever we're going doesn't require clothing.

Every night this week I've had a nightmare about being on very public dates with some faceless man. We are at a bar or a hockey game or a movie, having a great time until I look down and realize that I'm completely naked. As soon as I notice, everyone else in the dream world begins to notice too, pointing and laughing at me until I wake myself up, completely soaked in sweat.

It's really fun to be me.

I don't really have time to go on dates—or to be losing sleep —either because classes start back up in a few weeks and I should be preparing. I need to purchase my textbooks, print out the syllabi, check in with my advisor about—

A knock startles me out of my thoughts and my heart skips a beat knowing who is on the other side of that door. It's midmorning and I have no idea how long we are going to be gone. I should text Thea and ask if she can come let Ernest out if I'm gone too long.

I'm drafting the text when I open the door to let Ben in. His eyes instinctively dip down to my ring finger, but the engagement ring is tucked back in my drawer after he caught me wearing it last week. "Hold on, I need to text Thea about letting Ernest out and then we can go. Does this outfit work, by the way?"

I'm wearing my denim shorts, a black lace-trimmed tank top, and my Doc Marten's. My hair is tied up in my signature ponytail, and I can feel Ben's eyes as he takes his time looking me up and down before giving me a nod and a boyish grin. "You look great. Do you have a swimsuit? Also, we're going to drop Ernest off at my parents' house so don't worry about texting Thea."

"That is—I don't want to inconvenience anyone."

He shrugs. "You won't. My dad loves dogs, and they have a big backyard he can run around in. We have a bit of a drive so I figured that was better than Ernest being alone all day."

I inhale, shaking my head. "That's really thoughtful. Thank you."

"Of course." He holds his hand in front of him, two fingers raised. "Two things, though. One, I'd grab a bathing suit. Just in case you're worried about the no clothes thing. Two, we aren't leaving until you have a ring on your finger."

"Benjamin," I scoff.

"Redddd," Ben sing-songs, dragging the nickname out into two syllables.

"I'm not wearing that ring in public."

"No ring, no date," he replies, noncommittally. I hate how he always seems so unaffected. "Plus, I already told you we won't be in public."

"Are we breaking in somewhere? Doing something illegal? I can't do illegal things or they won't let me finish my degree." I'm rambling. I know I'm rambling, but I cannot fathom putting that ring on and walking out of my apartment.

"Bathing suit. Ring." He shoos me away from him, both of his hands flicking toward me.

I look at his hands in disgust—I cannot believe he's shooing me!—but that disgust quickly dissipates as I remember how large and veiny his hands are. They are very nice hands... I deflate, knowing I'm going to do what he's asked of me.

Shuffling back into my bedroom, I pull a red bikini out of my dresser before reluctantly finding the ring and slipping it on my finger. When I get back to the kitchen, Ben has leashed Ernest and is packing a grocery tote with dog toys, Ernest's water bowl, and the remaining fancy treats that Ben previously bought.

"Anything else you think he might need today?" he asks.

Looking around the living room, I locate Ernest's raggedy stuffed rabbit that he's had ever since I adopted him. It's only got one eye, and I've sewn the tail back on multiple times, but it's his favorite and I can't bring myself to replace it. "That should be everything," I say, stuffing the rabbit into Ben's bag.

"Excellent." Ben grins, not being discrete about checking my hand. "Let's head out."

We load into Ben's car, which is surprisingly nice. Leather seats, a large screen that automatically connects to his phone without any sort of cord, and... "Is that air conditioning cooling my seat?"

Ben just laughs, his arm coming to rest on the seat behind me as he skillfully maneuvers out of his parallel parking spot. "Why do you have such a nice car?" I push. "I don't want Ernest to fuck anything up in here."

Ernest perks up, hearing his name, but then quickly smooshes his face back against the window—his favorite way to ride in a car.

"There's nothing to mess up," Ben shrugs. "It's just a car, nothing fancy."

"Nothing fancy? My temp-controlled ass would beg to differ," I joke. "I've had the same car since high school though, so anything with working windows really feels like a luxury."

"Yeah, I noticed you were still driving that piece of shit. Did they not pay you anything in your engineering job?"

"They paid me!" I can hear the defensiveness in my tone. "But it was expensive to live in California, and then when I realized I wanted to go back to school, I saved all of my money for that."

"Fiscally responsible? Are you trying to turn me on?"

"Oh yeah, I almost forgot you were a Finance Bro. Seems so… counter to who you are."

He laughs at that. "Really? How so?"

I shrug, jostling Ernest, who gives me a scathing look. "I'm pretty sure the definition of Finance Bro is a douche canoe that thinks too highly of himself." I pause. "Actually, now that I'm saying it out loud, it's a pretty accurate description of you."

Ben's hand clutches his chest dramatically. "Colette, you wound me."

Before I can respond, we pull up in front of the Bardot family home. It's a house that would be the perfect setting of any early aught primetime comedy, practically screaming that a functional, loving, and communicative family lives here. No shoving things under the proverbial rug in this house.

Wonder what that's like. Quickly, I twist my ring around so it's not as obvious on my finger. Ben clocks the movement, frown lines forming between his brows. In an extremely cowardly move, I hop out of the car before he has a chance to protest.

Elaine and Hugo are out on the porch as soon as my car door closes. "Hello, my cabbages!" Elaine calls, huge grin flashing from beneath her riot of curly gray hair.

"Did she just use a cruciferous vegetable as a pet name?" I ask a smirking Ben.

"It's a French endearment," Ben replies, but I don't register anything other than the tingling sensation at the base of my spine where his hand now gently rests, urging me forward.

We've touched each other in downright indecent ways, but this, this small sign of affection, might be my undoing. I'm momentarily paralyzed until the tug of Ernest's leash brings me back to the present.

He hops up the steps and into Elaine's waiting arms. "Aren't you the cutest boy I've ever seen?" she coos.

"Mom, not in front of Cole," Ben teases.

She rolls her eyes. "You know full well I'm talking to the dog, Benoit Francis."

My eyes widen, and I do my damndest to keep my mouth tightly clamped, not wanting to offend the elder Bardots. Ben sighs, turning to me. "You can laugh."

I shake my head emphatically, not daring to open my mouth. But the feeling of bubbled up laughter is hard to ignore. He gives me a look that says he knows how much shit he's going to get later, and then he puts that infuriating hand back on the small of my back. With a quick "Bye, be back later!" called over his shoulder, we are back in the car and on the road again.

"Say it."

"Say what?" I know exactly what.

"Go on," he presses. "Make fun of my name."

"Francis is a perfectly acceptable middle name," I reply. "Does kind of ruin the Finance Bro image, though."

The corner of his mouth lifts. "Wouldn't want that."

"Absolutely not."

The rest of the ride goes by in companionable silence, only

broken up by my occasional, "Are we there yet?" Asked only to piss Ben off just a little bit.

Ben, annoyingly, rolls with any and all punches thrown his way and just laughs every time I ask him how much longer. We leave Sassafras and drive into the neighboring town that's just slightly bigger. After driving all the way through to the other side of town, I'm about to bug Ben about our ETA when he pulls to a stop in front of a building I can only describe as *zen*.

There's an abundance of lush vegetation, a stream of water that trickles through gardens, and a stone path that leads up to a red-brick building with a black-tile sloped roof. *Bay State Bathhouse* is written across a large plaque that's nearly hidden amongst the foliage.

Panic gnaws at me because, "I can't bathe with other people!"

Ben's hand wraps around my clinched fist, prying it open and massaging gently. "Red, remember to trust me."

His rhythmic circles across my palm have the intended effect. Taking a deep breath, I murmur "Fine," and then open the car door to meet my fate.

"Trust," Ben reminds me when he circles the car.

If only he knew how much I was trying.

Chapter Twenty-Five
MR. AND MRS. RUSSELL

Ben

GOOGLE SEARCH

Q what is the process for changing your last name?

Cole is wound so tightly, I swear if she were to let go of some of that tension she would spring straight into the atmosphere.

Sliding my palm into hers, I squeeze once to help ground her. "No one is here, Cole. It's just us."

Her surprised look makes me smile. The immediate relief I see in the drop of her shoulders, however, tells me I have more work to do on this whole trust thing. I pull her to a stop right in front of the entrance to the bathhouse. Holding her left hand up, I twist her ring back around until the gem stone is facing up. "No more hiding this."

She hums in response, a flush crawling up her neck. In an incredibly impulsive—and not at all regretful—move, I lean down and lick the blushing skin from her throat to her ear.

"Benjamin!" She growls. "Did you just lick me?"

With no remorse whatsoever, I reply, "Yes, I did. Let's go."

Shouldering the door open, I pull Colette in behind me. We're greeted by a young woman at the front desk which immediately puts Cole on high alert. "I thought you said there wasn't anyone here." She narrows her eyes at me.

"Okay, so there are a few people here, but no other patrons. I rented the space out for the day."

"You… You rented the entire bathhouse out?"

Before I can answer, the receptionist—Marcy, according to her nametag—whispers in that way they do at spas, "Mr. and Mrs. Bardot, lovely to have you join us at Bay State Bathhouse today."

"Russell," Cole corrects, turning toward me. "If—and that's a *big* if, like the fate of the world depends on our reluctant nuptials kind of *if*—we get married, we're taking my last name."

"We can make up an entirely new last name if that's what you want, Red. Doesn't matter to me."

"Of course it doesn't," she mutters.

"Right," Marcy continues. "Changing rooms are just this way." She gestures to two doors that blend fairly seamlessly into the wood paneled wall at the back of the reception area. "You may undress to your comfort level. There are robes and slippers provided. Once you're done, you may exit from the only other door and make your way into the relaxation room."

Leaning toward Cole, I whisper, "My comfort level is completely naked, but if you need to wear your swimsuit that's an option." There's a challenge in my tone, and I can't wait to see if Cole rises to the bait.

Marcy raises her pointer finger in the air, stopping me before I can walk into the locker room. "Ah, I apologize, Mr. Bardot."

"Russell," I correct, winking at Cole who rewards me with an eye roll.

"Right," Marcy whispers, her smile strained. "Mr. Russell. Dress to your comfort level includes a swimsuit in the baths. Fully nude areas include the saunas and the gender specific locker rooms."

"I see, thank you for the clarification, Marcy. See you on the other side, Red," I call over my shoulder, disappearing into the changing room.

————

Cole makes me wait in the relaxation room, because of course she does. This woman does nothing but build my anticipation in any scenario we're involved in. I left my phone in the changing room, but the longer she takes, the more I'm worried that she broke into the men's changing room and stole the car keys, leaving me stranded at a bathhouse in the middle of Massachusetts.

I wouldn't put it past her.

The relaxation room is nice… It would be incredibly relaxing if I wasn't anxious about the fact that Cole still hasn't joined me. Tightening my robe around my waist, I sit down on one of the plush loungers before immediately popping back up when a door opens. It's just Marcy though, with a tray full of tea service.

"Mr. Russell," she whispers, adapting quickly to Cole's earlier correction. "Would you like a cup of tea?"

"Oh. I—Sure." I tap my fingers against my thigh as Marcy sets the tray down on a nearby table, flips one cup over, and starts pouring. "Did… Did Mrs. Russell—"

I'm saved from completely embarrassing myself when Cole finally enters from the door to her changing room.

My favorite long ponytail sits on the top of her head, red strands cascading over her robed shoulders. The fluffy white robe, with the Bay State Bathhouse logo embroidered onto the pocket, is snug around her waist. I can't tell if she has her bikini on underneath or if she's chosen to forgo any item of clothing so we can head straight to the sauna.

Honestly, either option has me already sporting a semi. Not something that will be easy to hide here in a minute.

"Mrs. Russell, welcome," Marcy mutters. "Would you also like some tea?"

"No, thank you, Marcy."

Marcy's thin-lipped smile tells me she disapproves of Cole's choice, but she doesn't say anything else as she hands me a cup of steaming tea and quietly slides out of the room.

Inching closer to Cole, I admire the freckles across the bridge of her nose. "She's a little creepy, no?"

The corner of Cole's mouth tips up. "Yeah, I'm a little worried we are involved in some sort of intricate murder plot."

"You watch too much *Dateline*."

Her shoulder lifts and falls as she says, "Probably. It's my hyperfixation."

"What makes you think we'll be murdered, though?"

Cole's eyes scan the serene room. "To clarify, I don't actually think we'll be murdered today. Marcy's just very good at her job and her job is to help us relax. But… if there was something nefarious going on, you would have about two minutes before your poisoned tea started making you feel extremely dizzy and then about thirty more seconds before you'd lose consciousness."

She looks at me pointedly as I take another sip of tea, biting back a smile.

"I want to be on your team when we play *Clue*."

"There are no teams in *Clue*. You figure the mystery out on your own."

"We could be on a team."

Cole's sigh is long-suffering. "I suppose you *could* play on a team. I, however, do not." She turns so suddenly, her ponytail would have smacked me in the face if I was just a little bit closer. Snuggling onto a lounger, she tucks her slippered feet underneath her and asks, "What now?"

"Now we relax. In the relaxation room."

Her pursed lips say *Duh!* but she doesn't move from her tightly coiled position. "Listen to the music, Colette." I set my teacup down before sitting on the end of her lounge chair. My first attempt to coax her legs out from under her is met with a light smack to my hands. "Let me help," I mutter, trying again. This time she allows me to tug her legs free. I place them in my lap, removing her slippers and smiling at the cherry-red polish she has on her toes.

"My favorite color," I remind her.

She tips her head back, and I watch as the column of her neck stretches with a gulp.

With a firm grip, I massage up and down her calves all the way to the arch of her foot. I know I have a hair fetish—well, only with her hair—but I might have a foot fetish too because her painted toenails are so damn *cute*.

We spend a few minutes that way—silent aside from the spa music as I help Cole unwind a bit. Her breathing evens out but her eyes are open, watching me, so I know she hasn't fallen asleep.

"Why are you doing this?" she suddenly asks.

"Massaging your feet? Because I could tell you needed some—"

"No, not this," she interrupts, gesturing down to where my hand is wrapped around her ankle. "I mean *this*." She moves her hand up to motion between the two of us and then circles it around the entire room.

"Mmm." I nod, resuming my ministrations. "I'm not sure you're ready to hear the answer to that question, Colette."

"'Mmm' indeed," she replies, her gaze assessing. "I think I'm ready for the baths now."

I slide her feet off my lap, turning to lean on the arms of the lounger, boxing her in. My nose dips slowly, waiting for her protests. When they never come, I slide my nose across her jawline, down her neck, back up until we are nose to nose. "Can I kiss you?"

Her hazel eyes flash up to mine, and what I see there is pure *want*. I know my expression matches hers, and when we kiss it's a tender strike of the match. Burning, but not quite igniting. Slow, gentle.

Then rougher, harder, more more *more*.
Finally, we explode.

Chapter Twenty-Six
ALWAYS ON YOUR KNEES FOR ME
Cole

GOOGLE SEARCH

Q Are there cameras inside of a bathhouse?

I don't think we've done this before. Kissing for kissing's sake. Because our lips fit. Like the pieces of the jigsaw puzzle that litter my coffee table.

And, God, it's satisfying. Finding that perfect fit. The perfect piece.

Wanting, needing, feeling like you should spend the rest of your life attached at the lips, exactly like this.

My hands weave into the hair at the base of Ben's neck. It's silky against my skin, and would it be weird to have shirts made out of his hair? Probably yes.

I think I'd want it anyway.

Ben's fist wraps around my ponytail, tilting my head so he has better access to my neck. I'm torn. I immediately want his lips back on mine, but why does this feel so damn good too?

They're sloppy and wet and loud, like he doesn't care who hears us.

We'll scandalize poor Marcy.

"We," Ben says with a kiss. "Should probably—" Kiss. "Go to the baths." Kiss.

The what? I can't focus past the suck of Ben's lips against my neck, feral, marking me.

"Colette." A firm hand comes to hold my hips down. I guess I was shamelessly grinding up into him. I'm not sorry for that. "You're going to make me…" His breathing is heavy as he yanks himself away from me.

My brain is moving too slow because by the time I try to pull him back to me, he's already across the room, back to me with both hands on top of his head. His "fuck" echoes around the room.

Standing, I walk around Ben's front, laughing at his scrunched up face.

"Not funny, Red." But his smile says otherwise.

I lace my hands with his, guiding them off the top of his head. One more kiss sounds like a good idea so I pop onto my tiptoes and press against him again. He winds our tangled arms behind my back, drawing me in.

The puzzle imagery comes to the forefront of my mind again. I don't know how I didn't see it before. A perfect fit.

I'm the one to pull away this time. "Baths," I remind him when his brow furrows in concern.

"Baths," he repeats, like it's a brand new word he's never heard before.

Stepping back, I let go of one of his hands but keep the other one hostage. We open the double doors that lead into the actual bathing part of the bathhouse and my jaw drops.

It. Is. Stunning.

The massive room is lined floor to ceiling with elegant green-grey tiles. There are skylight domes over about half of the baths around the room, casting magical rays of sunlight onto the small pools, making it look like the water is glittering. Six hot-tub-sized baths are dotted throughout the room, each wrapped in the same tile with a small set of stairs that leads to the bath itself. Little plaques with temperature information are fastened to the edge of each structure, but I don't need to read each of them to tell which ones are the hottest.

Large billowing steam twists and turns out of two near the center of the room. Obviously, I beeline straight to those.

"No sauna?" Ben pouts.

"What? No, I hate the sauna. This bath, however, is calling my name."

He looks like someone blew out the candles on his birthday cake before he was able to make a wish. "Why are you pouting Benjamin?"

"The sauna is the nude area."

In lieu of replying, I untie the belt at my waist that's holding my robe together. Slowly, the robe slides down my arms, revealing the fire-engine-red bikini that doesn't do much in the way of covering all of my important bits.

Ben quickly assumes his favorite position: on his knees for *me*.

"Colette," he groans, his lips skimming the waistband of my swimsuit. He bites at the fabric and tugs, letting it go with a resounding *snap* against my skin. His lips make their way to where my thigh meets my hip, planting more sloppy kisses against my inner thighs.

Tugging Ben's head back, I pivot around him and into the water before he realizes what just happened.

The water feels phenomenal, and I relish being wet in more ways than one. I've never had a partner that can pull this reaction out of my body the way Ben can.

It's terrifying.

I'm quickly becoming obsessed.

Ben gets his wits about him, finally disrobing to reveal—"You're naked!"

I cover my eyes, and Ben's responding laugh echoes around the room, surrounding me with his unfiltered joy. "You're observant," he volleys.

"Marcy said bathing suits in the baths!"

"Marcy is also being paid a pretty penny so that we have the ability to do whatever we want in this bathhouse."

"If we actually do get murdered they are going to find you fully nude. Do you really want an investigative team looking at your flaccid dick?"

He chuckles again, and I hear him wade into the water. Said dick—very much *not* flaccid at the moment—pokes me in the stomach as he sidles up next to me. His hands slide up my arms, peeling my hands away from my face. "It's nothing you haven't seen before, Red."

"Yes, but we are in public!" My reply is indignant.

Ben hums. "Not an exhibitionist then? The little show in the relaxation room tells me otherwise."

I bite my lip, looking up at him. "I don't mind a little exhibitionism." I shrug. "But there's no one else here! We can't even be discreet! Hide in the middle of a crowd—that sort of thing!"

"Fuck discreet," Ben replies. His dick seems to agree, insistent against me as he draws closer and closer. His eyes zero in on my neck and he grins, leaning in to bite the juncture between my neck and shoulder. "Don't be pissed," he starts, "but you may or may not have to cover this hickey for the next couple of days."

"Hickey?!" I shove Ben off of me, which he takes in stride, submerging himself fully in the bath. He resurfaces with a huge grin painted across his stupidly beautiful face. Water drips from his hair, and I can't even be mad at him when he shakes his head like a dog coming in from the rain. My hand finds the side of my neck, tracing the spot Ben left his mark on me. "I can't believe I'm going to have to cover a hickey in this heatwave, you asshole."

"Don't cover it." His long arms hook behind my legs, tugging me back toward him. "I like it almost as much as I like seeing you wear your ring," he tacks on, speaking to himself more than me.

"I have to cover it," I laugh, pushing back. "I'm starting classes soon. No one is going to take me seriously if I have a giant bite mark on my neck."

He doesn't answer me, instead swimming toward me with only his head and neck above the water. With my feet planted firmly on the steps, he's eye level with my navel. Which is exactly where he puts his chin once he's close enough. He kisses my stomach, asking, "What about here?"

"Hmm?"

He looks up at me through long lashes, drops of water snaking their way across his face, over his nose. He's unfairly pretty when he smiles, and I get the feeling that he knows exactly what he's doing to me. "Can I bite you here, Colette?"

"Oh."

Ben nips right next to my belly button, and goosebumps erupt across my flesh. "I think I'd like to mark you here and maybe..." He drags a finger lazily down the seam of my bikini, moving closer and closer to my inner thigh.

"How do you always end up on your knees for me, hmm?" I ask, increasingly distracted by where his hands are going.

"Very, very intentionally, Red."

"You can, by the way."

"Can what?"

"Mark me." That's all the permission he needs. His strong hands come around my waist, hauling me up to set me on the wide ledge of the bath. He shoves my legs open, sending me off balance before I can steady myself by grabbing onto the outer lip of the tub.

Ben's lips latch onto my inner thigh right at the juncture of my hip, and he *sucks*. Hard.

Immediately I'm met with images of him sucking on other things, and the heat pooling low in my belly is demanding to be released.

As if he can read my mind, his mouth closes over my clit and he sucks again. My head is spinning in the most delicious way, and I'm right back to wanting more, just like our earlier kiss.

Without removing my bathing suit bottoms—as if he's too lust crazed to create time for such a frivolous act—he hooks his finger in them, moving it to the side so he has full access to me. He returns to his task with gusto, and I appreciate his dedication to being perfect at everything he tries, I really do. It is absolutely working to my benefit at this moment as Ben's tongue swirls methodically. He teases my entrance with a finger as his other hand comes up to tweak my nipple.

That's all it takes. Somehow this man's tongue has become the key to my orgasmic bliss, and I don't know what I'm going to do without—

Holy shit. As the last waves of my orgasm are cresting, Ben returns to my navel, sucking a mark right next to it, too. Something about seeing how feral he is, in addition to the fact that two of his fingers have found that perfect spot inside me, has me falling quickly into a second orgasm.

My moans echo off the tile walls around us, and I'm praying to every god in the universe that this room is soundproof.

Ben kisses his way up my heaving torso, stopping to leave one more hickey on the underside of my breast—he's insatiable.

"I can't believe I just let you eat me out inside of a bathhouse." I cover my mouth as a bubble of laughter threatens to erupt.

Ben's answering grin is playful, puppy-like. "I can. We know a bath turns you on, Red. No one is surprised by this."

Fine, maybe he's right.

When Ben is dropping Ernest and me off at my apartment later that evening, I expect him to try to stay.

Instead, he gives me the most tender kiss on my forehead, draws a single line down my palm, and says, "One down, four to go."

Then he's gone.

And maybe I'm a little disappointed that he didn't stay.

Chapter Twenty-Seven

TWO ENGAGEMENTS AND A HICKEY

Ben

GOOGLE SEARCH

🔍 gifts for when you royally fuck up with your sort of fiancée   

Come to family dinner tonight.

RED

No.

Yes. I already told everyone you're coming.

RED

I told Thea I'd help her get the nursery ready.
Apparently she's surprising Jules.

Perfect, I'm helping too. I'll pick you up.

And family dinner is at Jules' house tonight.

See you soon *kissy face emoji*

In a surprise to absolutely no one, Jules and Thea are madly in love. I'm glad they figured that out before the baby came. I'm sure there will be enough to focus on once he makes his grand entrance.

Because we are all happy for the two lovebirds, Bardot family dinner is a particularly jovial affair.

I, too, would be thrilled if it weren't for the fact that my fiancée isn't wearing her ring and has a goddamn scarf around her neck to cover up the hickey I left there.

"Why do you look like someone peed in your Raisin Bran?" Bex, my younger sister, is not one to mince words.

"One, I don't eat Raisin Bran—"

"Yes you do," Gabe pipes up.

"And two," I continue, completely ignoring Gabe, "why are you even here?"

Bex and Anders' newest addition, Molly, is strapped to my sister in some confusing contraption that would take me an hour's worth of YouTube videos to figure out, and their older daughter, Elodie, is running around causing chaos, I'm sure.

"It's *family* dinner." She says the words slowly, enunciating each syllable before pointing between the two of us and then around at the rest of the room. "We, Benoit, are a family."

My sigh could probably move mountains. "I know that, Rebecca. But you, the giant redheaded man, and these cute little cherub babies live almost four hours away. So again, I will ask: Why are you even here?"

She shrugs and then walks away, still not answering my question.

"Something weird is going on," I murmur to Gabe.

"Agreed." Gabe eyes me. "You do look like someone peed in your Raisin Bran. Is it Cole? Is that why she's here?"

"She's here because she has an open invitation to join our family dinner any time she wants. And because she's friends with Thea."

"Is that all she is?" he asks, his tone knowing.

This is the hardest part about the arrangement between Cole and me. I would happily tell the world that she's mine—and I'm trying to do just that in any way she'll let me—but she's not ready. She's still wrapping her mind around us. And not *us* in the way she's always known, but the new *us* that could be if she wants it.

Before I can answer, I see Mom cornering Cole. I hand my drink to Gabe without looking at him so I can interfere before Elaine Bardot starts one of her famous lectures.

"Dear, take your scarf off! It's unseasonably warm. I can set it by the front door!" I know Mom is trying to help, but I would be able to see Cole's mortified expression from Mars.

"No, that's okay, Elaine! Thank you, though. I get very… cold… indoors." Cole's face is flushing even redder than normal, betraying her lie to anyone with functioning retinas.

Before I have a chance to jump in and save her—and honestly I'm not moving very fast because I *am* mad she's not wearing her ring—Thea pops out of nowhere. "Cole! Come to the bathroom with me." She rubs her belly obnoxiously as if to emphasize her next statement. "Pregnancy means I constantly have to pee! So sorry, Elaine. I'll bring her right back."

The two of them escape to the bathroom, so of course I follow. I'm not the only one, though. When I round the corner, I see Bex has ditched Molly and has her ear pressed to the bathroom door. She puts a single finger to her mouth and then slides it across her throat.

She'll kill me if I speak. Got it.

"When did you get so scary?" I mouth. But it's pointless because Bex has failed me by never learning how to read lips.

I lean my ear against the door, matching my mischievous little sister. Thea and Cole's words are garbled, but I can hear it clear as day when Thea asks, "What's wrong with you? Why are you being weird?"

"I'm not being weird," Cole replies, and I can practically see the way her arms cross under her perfect tits and her hip juts out to the side with those four words.

"Yes," Thea hisses, "you are! It is eighty degrees outside and you're wearing a scarf. We were rearranging the nursery earlier and I thought you were going to pass out."

"It's fashionable," Cole argues, and I have to bite my tongue to keep from laughing. Cole has worn the same uniform including some variation of sweaters and plaid skirts since high school. The last thing Colette Russell is worried about is what is currently considered fashionable.

I hear a gasp and a smacking noise. Bex raises her eyebrow at me as if to ask *Should we intervene?*

"Quit it!" Cole says at the same time Thea exclaims, "You're burning up!"

There seems to be a bit of a struggle between the women before everything gets quiet and Thea cries out, "Is that a hickey!"

It's not really a question, more like an observation because after one look there's no mistaking the mark on Cole's neck for anything other than what it is. Bex's eyes widen as she looks back and forth between me and the closed bathroom door.

"Who gave that to you?" Thea's tone is incredulous.

Cole answers but she's too quiet for me to hear, but Bex smooshes her face against the door even harder in the hopes of catching the name of the perpetrator.

Except I don't need to know who did it. I was there.

"Excuse me?" Thea's voice is shrill. "I thought you didn't like him! Y'all hate each other!"

Now that catches my attention. I lean in closer to hear how Cole is going to reply when Bex—*fucking Bex*—runs out of luck, knocking her elbow hard against the doorknob. The interior of the bathroom falls silent, and I haul ass out of there.

"Apologies ladies! Need to use the restroom when you're finished," I hear Bex telling whoever had the misfortune of opening the door. Unfortunately, her follow through isn't great because she follows Thea and Cole around the corner, earning confused looks from all three of us. "What?" Bex asks after catching the look on my face. "Oh! Bathroom, right..." And she turns on her heel and leaves.

Thea eyes the two of us, ultimately throwing her hands into the air. "I'm not getting involved in this! You two"—she points at Cole and me—"figure your shit out."

"Yes, ma'am." I salute to an answering eye roll from Cole. And then Thea leaves too, and I'm finally alone with Cole for the first time since we got here.

"Hey, Red," I murmur, taking a step toward her. "I noticed you didn't have your ring on. You had it on when I picked you up."

"Of course I don't have the ring on," she hisses. "I put it in my purse. We are with your entire family. You don't think one of them would have noticed? Your mom has already tried to get me out of this scarf fifteen times tonight."

With another step, I'm close enough to run my fingers down the curve of her neck, pushing the stupid scarf down to see what she's hiding. "You should take it off. Let them talk." I shrug.

Cole answers with a scoff. "I would threaten to turn your neck into one giant hickey but something tells me you'd get them permanently tattooed there."

"Damn straight I would. I already have a—"

"Dinner's ready!" Jules calls from the kitchen, and thank fuck because I was not ready to admit what I almost let slip. Something I've held close to my chest for so many years. I can—I should—wait a little while longer before I play all my cards.

Cole gives me a quizzical look, seeing too much, but I catch the moment she decides to drop it, heading for the cramped dining room instead of asking questions.

We all settle around Jules and Thea's dining table—the entire Bardot family, including Chloe and Hank. They've been a welcome addition to the Bardot chaos. Thea and Chloe especially were exactly what Jules needed—a family of his own to nurture and love. One thing that's always been different between me and my twin. Jules has always desired to be a dad, to have a family of his own.

I would be exceptionally happy with one singular person to call my own.

And she happens to be sitting right across the table from me.

Dinner is excellent, per usual, and conversation flows around the table. I watch Cole more than I probably should. She's beginning to relax around my family. I know she's slow to trust, slow to open up, and it does something inside my chest seeing how seamlessly she fits into my world.

"You're staring," Bex whispers in my ear. "Tell me what's going on."

"So," I say, expertly pivoting the conversation again. "Are you going to tell us why you're here?"

"For fuck's sake," Bex replies. "Oops, sorry." She looks at Chloe, who has already narrowed her eyes at Bex's language. "We are—"

Anders cuts in before Bex can continue. "We're moving back!" He's practically vibrating in his seat, biting back a smile. They've been in New York City for the last several years. I know it's been hard on them, but I also know Bex was more than willing to support Anders as he's been killing it on Broadway.

"Well, shit!" Gabe jumps up, matching Anders' excitement. "Hell yeah! I've missed having my best friend around." They pat each other's back in a huge bro-hug.

"And your sister," Bex adds. Gabe ignores her.

One look at Mom tells me she already knew Bex and Anders were moving back. She claps her hands together, exclaiming, "All my cabbages back together again!"

"Hawthorne wants me to come back as an artist in residence, and we knew we couldn't refuse an offer to come back to Sassafras," Anders explains.

"That's amazing. I'm happy for you both." And Jules does look happy. He's got his arm around the back of Thea's chair, stroking her shoulder in a way that sends a pang of longing through me. I look over at Cole, but she seems overwhelmed by everyone talking over each other and won't meet my eye.

"Thanks, JuJu," Bex replies. "Added bonus: the girls will get to grow up close to their new cousins."

The entire table looks between Chloe and Thea, the latter of whom looks like she might burst into tears at any moment. The Roses are good people, and I know they've had a rough go of things. I hope Cole can see how easily she would also be accepted into the Bardot family—is already accepted here.

"Do you already have a house?" Gabe asks, interrupting my thoughts.

Anders is the one who answers. "Not yet. This has been in the works for a bit, but I had to figure out some stuff with *Hercules*, to make sure they could replace me. It was time, we did the whole New York thing and we're ready to come home." He pauses to smile at his wife and their two girls. "We weren't sure if we were going to be able to make it work so we're staying at Elaine and Hugo's until we find a place."

"Hell yes," Gabe replies. "Sleepover at Mom and Dad's!"

Mom and Dad exchange an excited look. I think they would buy land and build a compound if we would sign off on that.

Before they can respond, Bex's phone starts ringing. "Oh! Luci is FaceTiming! I told her and Riz to call me so I could tell them the news."

All of our eyes swing to Gabe, and I guess I'm not the only one who knows about his history with Bex's best friend.

"I'll just..." Bex looks apologetic as she excuses herself to take the call.

The tension in the room can be cut with a knife, so of course I do something a little bit impulsive. That's my role in this family, isn't it?

"I also have an announcement." I push from the table, tapping my glass with my knife even though everyone is already staring at me.

Cole knows me a bit too well because she's the first to respond. "No. You don't."

I think her glare could castrate me and I'd enjoy every fucking second. And probably thank her for it afterwards.

"On the contrary, Colette," I grin. "I absolutely do."

This is a risk, but so is everything I've done with her. Looking at Jules and Thea, I know, *I know* how much Cole would fit in perfectly here all the time, not just at the occasional dinner. Fit into my life all the time. She just needs a little… push.

"As many of you know, Cole recently turned thirty," I continue. "A little over a month ago."

"We were supposed to celebrate! Cole! You've been avoiding me!" Thea smacks her hands on the table in mock-outrage, but Cole has yet to look away from me.

"Birthdays are stupid," Cole replies, answering Thea without looking toward her.

I hold back my laughter, knowing it won't help my cause, opting to tip my glass toward her instead. "Eloquent as always, my dear," I say to her, before turning to the table at large. "Colette and I are—"

Now Cole decides to respond. "No!" Her favorite word. She pushes back from the table, and it wouldn't surprise me if she decided to leap right over it.

She doesn't get a chance however because Bex bursts back into the room and exclaims, "Luci's engaged!"

Perfect. "So are we!" I add. Cole is fuming… and I'm turned on.

She has a death grip on her butter knife, and Jules, always the practical one, reaches over to dislodge it from her grip.

No one speaks. The only sound in answer to either of those proclamations is the scraping of Gabe's chair as he storms out.

"Probably should have done that differently." Bex winces. I'd have to agree with her but it's too late to turn back now.

Anders, who has been Gabe's best friend for over a decade,

gives a sympathetic look to his wife. "I've got it, Baby Bardot. He just needs a minute." And he follows Gabe out of the room.

Bex looks relieved for a moment before she registers what I said. "Wait, you two are also engaged?" She points between me and Cole, looking confused as hell.

"Yes!" I reply at the same time Cole says, "No."

Her eyes narrow at me. "Benjamin. I will *never* marry you."

I'm obviously fucked up because it sounds more like a challenge than a promise.

"That's not what you said last night, Red."

She's irate, and that's when it hits me, the weight of my miscalculation. Now it's her turn to shove back from the table, storming to the doorway. Once she's there she pauses, taking a deep breath before she turns back toward the room.

Her eyes find my Mom and Dad. "I apologize for my swift exit Mr. and Dr. Bardot. I'll call you tomorrow—" She turns to Thea to say this and then reluctantly faces me. "And fuck you."

Then she's gone.

I throw back the rest of the wine in my glass. With more confidence than I feel, I say, "I love when she's feisty," and then I follow her out.

Chapter Twenty-Eight
SICK IN THE HEAD
Cole

GOOGLE SEARCH

Q Help, I might be catching feelings.

I slam the door behind me as I leave Jules and Thea's house.

As anticipated, it's only a moment before I hear the door open and close again.

"Go back inside, Benjamin," I call over my shoulder. The last thing I want to do right now is talk to him. Not after he just embarrassed me in front of his entire fucking family. And his mom who is colleagues with all of the people who will determine my future success. I'm frantically searching for my car so I can escape this nightmare but I can't find it anywhere.

"Red, c'mon." His long legs carry him to me entirely too quickly. I couldn't escape even if I tried.

And I am trying. But this fucking scarf is making me so damn hot. I'm extremely overstimulated and I need to be home with Ernest, not here with the man who sends my nervous system into overdrive. *Where is my fucking car?!*

Ben catches ahold of my wrist, turning me back toward him. I wrench my arm free, yanking my scarf off as well. A crease forms between Ben's brows as he takes me in.

"You are sweating, Colette. Let me take you home."

"I can take myself home, thank you."

"I drove you here," he calmly replies, taking the stupid scarf out of my hands.

Right. That's why I can't find my car.

My entire body deflates. I'm hot and numb and I really do just want to go home.

"Fine. But I'm not talking about this right now."

"That's fair." Ben guides me by my elbow toward his car, opening the door and helping me in. I don't have the energy to bat him away. In fact, my traitorous body melts into his touch. Once he's buckled me in, like I'm a damn toddler, he brackets me in, leaning closer than strictly necessary. "I am sorry, for what it's worth. I had this wild thought, looking at how happy Jules and Thea are, hell even Bex and Anders who have been sickeningly in love for so damn long. And I want that with you. I wanted to..." He shrugs. "Rip the bandaid off? Maybe you'll never speak to me again after this, and that would—"

I kiss him.

Mainly because I need him to shut the fuck up. But also because he's—ugh, I don't want to admit this—not wrong. I am the kind of person who would need a bandaid ripped off or I'd keep things with Ben just as they are for the rest of eternity.

That's not what he wants, though. He's been more than upfront about that from the time he waltzed back into my life.

So I kiss him. It's slow, tender. Not quite an acquiescence but maybe something close. "Take me home, Benjamin."

"Yes, ma'am," he whispers.

When we get back to my apartment, the lights are perfectly dim. Ben ushers me to my couch, surrounding me with piles of blankets and pillows. He lets Ernest out and then walks over to the kitchen to make a cup of tea. "Music or TV?" he asks when he delivers the steaming mug to my little nest.

"TV, please."

Ernest jumps onto the couch with me when he's been let back in. I expect Ben to leave, but he surprises me by sitting on the ground in front of me, his focus on the new puzzle I laid out yesterday.

He doesn't say anything else, but he's here with me. And that's more than I could ever bring myself to ask of him. I snuggle in, getting comfortable. So much so, I drift off into one of the best naps of my life.

I wake up an undetermined amount of time later, confused about why I'm moving. I'm hot again, plastered against something… no, some*one*. Cracking an eye open, I see that I'm moving through my hallway toward the bedroom. Well, being carried through my hallway by Ben's strong, capable arms.

"Go back to sleep, Red," he whispers against my temple. When I ignore his instructions and look up at him, I see he's put on his reading glasses and his hair is more rumpled than usual.

"I like the glasses," I murmur sleepily. I feel his chest rumble in response.

"I think you made yourself sick, Colette."

I start to shake my head but fuck, that hurts. Maybe he's right. I scowl. He's been right too much lately, I need to figure out a way to remedy that.

"Head hurts. Pain meds in the bathroom cabinet." He nods, placing me delicately on my bed before fetching some medicine.

The bed dips as he sits next to me. I curl toward him, now fully aware that I'm very feverish. Cold then hot, head pounding. A general desire to keel over.

"Open up." Ben taps lightly under my chin. I push up to a seated position and take the proffered pills and glass of water. "All because you had to hide your hickey," he admonishes.

"That's not how sickness works."

My eyes are closed, but I can feel his shrug. "That's what I'm blaming this on. Next time, just wear the ring and show off the hickey."

"Aye-aye."

"Oh my God," he whispers. "Are you agreeing with me? You must be sicker than I thought you were."

"I am really fucking sick in the head, obviously. That's why I haven't kicked you out yet."

He hums, standing up. I miss his proximity instantly.

"Wait," I mutter.

His chuckle sounds distant. "I'm not leaving, Red. Be right back."

There's a distinct possibility that I drift off before he returns, but I'm awoken by a cool washcloth being placed across my forehead. It feels really, really nice. Both the washcloth and being taken care of.

He comes around to the other side of the bed, and I can hear him shucking clothes off before he slides under the covers next to me.

"You're staying?"

"Of course I'm staying, Colette."

He's quiet for a long time, rubbing reassuring circles on my back. It feels good... it feels right.

Right before I fall back into blissful oblivion, I hear his deep voice say, "I'm staying as long as you'll let me."

I might have been imagining it.

I'm probably imagining it.

My dreams are full of glasses and floppy hair and strong hands and tally mark tattoos.

———

The next morning, I wake up in a pool of sweat with an expanse of cold sheets next to me.

Disappointment crashes into me. I'll just shove that down to be dealt with... never.

Groaning, I sit up. My fever broke, but I still feel like shit. I could use some more pain meds for my head, and a bath sounds divine. My stomach, however, disagrees with that order of events, letting out an obnoxious growl. I'm dreading how long it's going to take me to get to the kitchen. If someone walked in right now and told me I was hit by a bus yesterday, I would believe them.

I'm about five seconds into my pep talk when my bedroom door slowly creaks open. A shaggy-haired, glasses-wearing, jawline-that-could-cut-glass man creeps into the room carrying a tray full of something. Ben is so focused on not dropping anything that he hasn't realized that I'm awake. He walks over to the dresser and carefully sets down what can only be described as a full feast of home remedies.

He turns toward me, practically jumping out of his skin when he sees that I'm awake. "Holy shit, Colette! You scared me!"

"I scared you… By sitting here in my bed…"

The corner of his mouth lifts, even as he continues to clutch his chest. "Glad to see you're feeling better."

I huff. "I wouldn't go that far." Craning my neck, I try to see what all he's brought in. "Is that for me?"

"No, it's for Ernest," he deadpans. "Of course it's for you. Sit back."

He places the tray in front of me, and maybe my physical state is affecting my emotional state, but I think those are tears pressing at the corners of my eyes. There's a bowl of chicken noodle soup that looks homemade, another cup of tea, an assortment of medications, a pedialyte popsicle, and plain crackers.

"You slept until midday. How are you actually feeling?" he asks, pushing my sweat-soaked hair off my brow.

"I look like shit, don't I?" I ask, instead of answering his question.

He grins down at me. "Yeah, you do. And somehow you

have the ability to make looking like shit also extremely hot. I shouldn't be surprised."

"Gross. You should leave me to wither away in peace."

"Not going to happen, Red. Eat. I'm going to clean up the kitchen and then we'll get you into the bath, okay?"

A completely unfair question because he knows that I can't say no to that. "Wait!" I call once he gets to the doorway. "Is this soup homemade?" I know for a fact that I did not have the appropriate ingredients for a full-ass chicken noodle soup.

He responds with a lopsided grin. "Eat up, Red."

I do, and of course it's delectable. I think one bowl of this soup could heal me from anything. Upon closer inspection, Ben used shredded chicken and a minimal amount of vegetables. The egg noodles are perfectly cooked, not long spaghetti noodles which I hate, and I think I might want to bathe in this broth.

Dammit.

When he comes back in, I've devoured the entire bowl, half of the crackers, and the popsicle, because logically I know that I need to hydrate. I feel like Oliver Twist when I offer my bowl up to him requesting more.

"Bath first, then you can have more soup."

"Bossy."

"You're welcome for taking care of your pathetic ass."

I raise my eyebrow at him. "I remember you quite liking my ass."

He groans, taking my shoulders to guide me into the bathroom. "No more ass talk. Only very innocent, very practical touching until you feel better. Got it, Red?"

"Yes, sir."

"Hmm... Yeah, I need you back to your dominant self."

That surprises a laugh out of me. "Don't like it when I let you take control?"

"Turns out I prefer a snarky, controlling woman who knows exactly what she wants." He bends down to adjust the taps on the bath. "I live to serve," he adds, smirking over his shoulder.

Once the water is warm, not as hot as I usually like it but Ben was insistent, he carefully strips off the sweat-soaked clothes I wore to bed and helps me into the tub. He lights my favorite candles and then instructs me to "Relax."

He comes back about fifteen minutes later with two towels folded in his arms. "Fresh out of the dryer, but if you aren't ready to get out yet, I can pop them back in."

I pull my legs in close to my chest and observe him. "Why are you doing this?"

Ben sets the towels on the counter and then has a seat on the edge of the tub. With a sigh, he says, "What are you really asking, Red?"

"I—" I'm not sure. "I'm still mad at you for that stunt you pulled yesterday."

"Obviously." He smirks.

"Has your family said anything about your... announcement?"

"My sister and Jules called me an idiot, and Mom is the one who sent over the recipe for the soup because she's so worried I fucked everything up with you."

"Hmm." I sink lower into the bath, unsure what to make of that.

Ben lets me think, gives me space to examine all of the thoughts running through my head. He's antsy though because a few minutes later he asks, "Did I?"

"Did you what?"

"Fuck everything up."

"What would you do if I said yes?" I look up at him, a lock of his chestnut hair falling across his forehead. He's so handsome, it makes every molecule in my body buzz.

He contemplates my question for a moment. Tentatively, he reaches out to trace my jawline, over my cheekbones, around the shell of my ear. His touch makes me feel... *precious*. Like I'm precious to him.

"If you said yes..." he starts. "If you decided that I had

fucked everything up, I would have to come to terms with going back to how it was before. I would respect your decision and loathe the fact that it would send me back to square one." He twists my ponytail around his fist, tilting my chin toward him. "I've been at square one with you before, Colette. I'm not itching to go back, but I will. I would do it all over again if I could earn even just one more minute in your presence. One more of your scathing glances."

His lips quirk. And damn, that answer was perfect.

I lay my forearms across the edge of the tub, resting my head on top and looking up at Ben. "No."

"No?" he questions.

"No, you didn't fuck everything up, Benoit."

"I… I'm glad, Colette." He smirks.

"Can I have some more soup now?"

"Yeah, sweetheart," he concedes. "You can have more soup now."

Chapter Twenty-Nine
HE'S IN LOVE WITH YOU
Cole

GOOGLE SEARCH

After a week of what turned out to be a nasty sinus infection, I'm finally starting to feel like a human again instead of a tin can in one of those large crusher machines. As satisfying as those videos are, I would like to never feel that way again.

Not only did I have an absolutely horrendous week, I also completely missed the entire first week of classes for the fall semester. Ben offered to go sit in all my classes and record the lectures, but I would rather have another full week of tin-can-crushing headaches than sending him into my classes like that. A full-body shiver runs through me just thinking about how I would explain that to my professors.

The fact that he offered, though…

And that damn soup. It was really good soup with the perfect kind of noodles.

It's been one date and I'm already entirely too close to just saying "Fuck it!" and accepting his proposal for real.

Which would be idiotic. Rash. Insane.

Right?

Right.

"Good morning, Ms. Russell. Glad to have you back this week," my forensic psychology professor, Dr. Daly, greets me.

"Thank you, please let me know the best way to make up what I missed last week."

He nods genially, but I get the sense that he's annoyed by my request. "I'll email over the slide deck, but I would suggest schmoozing one of your classmates into giving you a copy of their notes. Our first assignment is due on Friday, and the first of eight application-based assessments will be next week."

Lovely. Jumping right in, I see.

I've spent so much time with Ben lately that I didn't have the opportunity to comb through each syllabus or skim my textbooks before the semester started, like I usually do. With this grant on the line, I really need to get my shit together so I don't have to go back to working at the coffee shop.

"I will be sure to catch up immediately, Dr. Daly. Thank you for sending those slides over." I turn to face the classroom. It's a much smaller group of students now that we've split into our respective cohorts. In a shock to no one, I haven't spent much time making friends with my classmates, but right now I need someone's notes.

I decide on a beautiful Black woman with vibrant purple braids who I've definitely been in classes with before but I've never said a word to. For some reason, Ben's voice pops into my head with, *"You can do this, Red. You aren't as offputting as you think."* I can imagine the wink that would accompany this encouragement.

Walking over, I rehearse the introduction in my head. *Hi, I'm Colette. We've been in classes together before. Will you remind me of your name?*

Sliding into the seat next to her, I say, "Hi, Colette!"

Shit. Fuck. No.

"Sorry," I laugh and, thank God, she laughs with me. I think. "I mean, hi, I'm Colette. Or Cole. What's your name? I know we've been in class together so I apologize if we've met before."

I can feel the flush creeping up my neck which is one of the main reasons I avoid social interactions. My constantly color-changing skin is a neon sign above my head that says, SHE'S UNCOMFORTABLE!

"Hey, Cole, I'm Sahara." She laughs again. "And don't worry, I definitely did not remember your name either so thanks for introducing yourself. Those things are always awkward." She leans in conspiratorially. "Like, we're all supposed to just know each other? They don't do get-to-know-you games on the first day of grad school."

I get a vision of all of us standing in a circle, passing a ball around so I can hear Joe Schmo tell me his fun fact is that he went fly fishing in Alaska this summer. Gross.

"Thank God we don't have to do that. I think that would cause me to drop out of grad school completely."

"Hell, me too," Sahara adds, toothy grin on full display. "Well, to get it out of the way, my name is Sahara—you already knew that—I'm twenty-five from Pittsburgh. I did my undergrad at Penn State, and I'm a dog person. I think those are the highlights."

"Cole, thirty… from here, actually. I did my undergrad at Stanford and stayed out in California as an engineer for a few years before deciding to completely upend my life and start grad school. I'm also a dog person, you can come meet my rescue sometime."

"Oh my God, you have a dog?" Sahara squeals.

"Yes, his name is Ernest and he's only got three legs. He's the only man I like." Which used to be true but feels more and more like a lie. "I'll let you meet him, but can I ask a favor in return?"

"Anything. I need some puppy snuggles to lower my cortisol levels."

"Can I borrow your notes from last week? I was out sick and now I feel like I'll never be able to catch up."

"Easiest yes of my life." She grins. "So is Ernest the only man in your life? Or woman, or person."

The blush is back.

"Oh my God," Sahara continues. "He's not! Is it someone in our program?" She looks around the classroom as if she's trying to test her investigative skills.

"No! Stop looking! No, it's..." It's what? Dr. Daly starts projecting his slide deck, saving me from having to continue. "Complicated," I finish.

Sahara opens up her laptop, looking at me sideways. "Meeting Ernest, and a girls night. Those are my terms."

And that's how I end up making another friend.

———

Thea, Sahara, and I are in the middle of a rousing game of Yahtzee when the front door to my apartment opens.

"Red, why is your door unlocked? Anyone could walk in, it's dangerous! Don't they teach you that in—oh. Hi, ladies!"

Benoit Bardot is back to being the bane of my existence.

"Benjamin, what the fuck? Just because the door is unlocked doesn't mean you can just waltz in!"

"That's exactly what it means." He grins. He's got his glasses on and his hair is floppier than usual, which is doing funny things to the cadence of my breathing.

Massaging my temples, I eye Sahara and Thea, who of course became fast friends. Right now they are both looking ecstatic to see the very topic of conversation I've been avoiding all night.

Sahara stands up first, moving Ernest from his spot on her lap. "The famous Benjamin, so nice to meet you. Sahara." She points to herself. "I'm in class with Cole."

"Famous you say?" Ben asks, shaking Sahara's hand.

"Well, not as famous as I'd like you to be. Cole is keeping her lips sealed." She narrows her eyes at me playfully.

Ben *tsks* before bopping me on the nose, not at all bothered when I bat his hand away. "You know I like those lips nice and open."

"How you and Jules can be identical in looks and so incredibly different in personality is astonishing," Thea chuckles.

"I think Jules got all of the brain cells," I chime in, to an exaggerated frown from Ben.

"Wait." Sahara holds up her hands. "Explain this dynamic again? You"—she points at Thea—"are with his brother? Twin?"

"You know Dr. Bardot from the Marriage and Family Therapy department?" I ask.

Sahara tilts her head. "The sex therapy professor? Yeah."

I flourish my hands toward Ben. "This is one of her sons, Ben. He has a twin, Jules, who is the father of that fetus." Thea rubs her belly for emphasis.

"Shit, I see the resemblance now," Sahara says, nodding toward Ben. "What's it like growing up with a mom who is a sex therapist?"

"Enlightening," Ben deadpans.

"Dr. Bardot is much more interesting than Ben," I say. "We'll have to invite her next time. Benjamin"—I turn toward him—"thank you for coming, you can see yourself out."

Instead of listening, because he *never* listens, he pulls out a chair and sits down next to me.

"Nope, nope nope nope. We are having a girls' day and last I heard, you identified as a man."

"Have you confirmed?" Thea waggles her eyebrows suggestively.

"Thoroughly. In *all* aspects," Ben confirms with a wink.

"Out!" I cry.

"Fine, but I did come over for a reason. We are booked at a cabin in upstate New York for next weekend. I'll pick you up on

Friday after your classes." Ben blows me a kiss before finally exiting my apartment.

"That could have been a text," I mumble to the closed door. When I turn around, both Thea and Sahara's eyebrows are sky high.

"Complicated, huh?" Sahara laughs. "Doesn't seem complicated. Seems like you're dating Dr. Bardot's hot son."

"We aren't—" *dating*. But that's not true, is it?

"Aren't what, Cole?" Thea asks, her voice gentle.

Plopping down into my chair, I sigh so loudly Ernest wakes up from his nap.

"What was the whole engagement thing about?" Thea pushes. Meeting her eyes, I see why she's such a great mother. She's questioning but not in a judgemental way. Curious because she cares.

"Engagement thing?" Sahara pipes up, glancing down at my empty ring finger.

So, for the first time, I tell someone about the pact Ben and I made twelve years ago. The pact I thought Ben had forgotten about until about ten months ago. The pact that apparently he was dead serious about calling in.

Thea and Sahara gasp and swoon in all of the right places, it's freaky.

"So, he's in love with you," Sahara concludes.

"What?! No. No, I mean—"

Thea's laugh interrupts me. "Men don't just propose, Cole. He might not have admitted it to you yet, but obviously he's all in here."

I think back to all of our interactions over the past few months. He *is* all in. He's shown that time and time again—hell, he's said as much multiple times. But not like that. Right? He's not in love.

"I—" I have no idea what to say. That Ben box in my brain is so far past being destroyed. I'm currently trying to repackage it, but I'm not there yet. I feel like I'm still missing something, and I hate that feeling.

"I feel so in over my head here," I admit.

Thea's hand slides over mine. "Ditto." She smiles. "These Bardots are hard to resist, aren't they? Despite our best efforts."

"Are you going to the cabin with him?" Sahara asks.

Of course I am. The fact that it wasn't even a question in my mind should tell me something, but I'm still not ready to listen. I nod in answer to Sahara's question before groaning and banging my head lightly against the table in front of me.

"What's the holdup?" she continues. "Seems like a hot man with big dick energy wants to wife you up and take you on extravagant cabin dates. Are there any other Bardot brothers? I want one."

"There is another one, actually," Thea chimes in. "But it seems he's also hopelessly in love with a woman who is engaged to another man."

Sahara waves her hands in front of her face. "Sounds messy, no thanks."

"It's all fucking messy," I mutter from my face-down position.

Someone hums in acknowledgement.

"So…" Thea starts. "Can we see the ring?"

Chapter Thirty

IT'LL HAVE TEN BATHTUBS

Ben

GOOGLE SEARCH

Q houses for sale near Sassafras, Massachusetts   🎤

Band of (Bardot) Brothers

> Ok, I really need to lock things down this weekend

JULES

Lock what down?

> My relationship with Cole. What else would I be talking about?

BEX

Seeing as we all just learned about this relationship a few weeks ago, excuse us for being confused.

Bex changed the name of the conversation to Bex + Her Idiot Brothers*

GABE

That's not very nice, Bexy

BEX

If the shoe fits…

Can we get back to me please?? Cole and I are going to a cabin this weekend and I need to convince her to marry me

JULES

Do you know that you don't actually have to abide by a pact you made when you were 18?

Of course I do, no take backs.

GABE

Come in the living room and I'll teach you the move that's guaranteed to lock her down.

BEX

Fucking gross

I'm not sure I should be taking advice from you, Gabriel.

GABE

single tear emoji

JULES

Just be yourself, I thought Cole hated that version of you but apparently you did something right if she's agreed to go on an overnight trip with you.

Too true. I am amazing. Thank you for the advice, Julien.

BEX

eye-roll emoji

JULES

Anytime, brother.

You're late to work.

———

The next Friday, we arrive at the cabin just in time for dinner. Cole hops out of the car, stretching her arms above her head, her ring glinting in the light from the setting sun. It looks almost as good as her ass in those leggings.

I think I'm going to like Cabin-Cole.

Ernest jumps out of the back seat as soon as I open the door for him. He immediately starts sniffing everything within snouts reach, his tail wagging rapidly.

"He likes it here." Cole smiles, crouching down next to her dog. "Don't you, bubba? We need to get you out into nature more often, don't we?" she coos.

"I'll buy us a house with some land."

Cole looks up at me, incredulous. "I have no choice but to believe every asinine thing that comes out of your mouth, Benoit Bardot, so do not go home and buy an entire damn house because I said Ernest needs to get into nature more."

I shrug, eliciting a growl from Cole. "I need a house anyway. Don't want to live in Gabe's apartment forever. Real estate is a good investment."

She falls back onto her ass dramatically. "You aren't going to listen to me, are you?"

"Would you hate moving out of your apartment? Are you particularly attached to it?"

"I've worked really hard on decorating my apartment, thank you very much."

"That's not what I asked, Colette."

She huffs, standing to follow Ernest into the cabin. "It has to have a bathtub."

I wipe the smile off of my face. "It'll have ten bathtubs," I call after her.

She flips me off in response.

I chase after her like the fool that I am.

"This place is nice." Cole walks over to the back window that takes up the entire wall. The early October weather makes it the perfect time to be out here. The trees are painted in deep oranges, bright reds, and vivid yellows—with the sunlight it gives the illusion of the forest being on fire.

Cole's matching orange ponytail swishes as she looks over her shoulder at me. "Beautiful," I murmur, but I'm not looking at the foliage anymore.

"It really is." Her lips tip in the barest of smiles. "Thanks for bringing me out here. I should be studying," she adds. "I've only barely climbed out of the hole I dug myself by missing the first week."

"Your health is more important. And I made you flash cards based on the chapters in your textbook that you'd tabbed."

Her mouth drops open. "You... I can't... you are so confusing to me."

I walk toward her, my arms snaking around her waist from behind. She leans back against me, her entire body flush against mine. "What's confusing, Red?"

She sighs. "My entire life I've had to work really hard to figure people out. No one ever really says what they mean... with autism it almost feels like the general population is speaking in code, sometimes. So with you, I keep trying to apply the same code. But... you just say what you are thinking. No fucking around, no double meanings. It's refreshing honestly, but also confusing when I've been conditioned to interpret conversations with neurotypicals my entire life."

Kissing her temple, I whisper, "I will never purposely

confuse you. And you should always feel free to call me on it if I do."

She smiles up at me, twisting in my arms so we are facing toward each other. "Thank you. It means a lot that you would accommodate me."

Scoffing, I roll my eyes. "It is quite literally the least I could do—communicate clearly."

Cole shrugs. "I know it's not easy being—"

I cover her mouth with my hand because I don't want to hear that nonsense. "You, Colette Russell, are the easiest person in the world to be with. Don't let anyone tell you otherwise, got it?"

"Got it," she replies, voice muffled by my hand. She nips at it playfully before placing a kiss in the center of my palm. I move my hand so it's cupping her cheek instead, leaning down to take her lips with mine.

It surprises me, every time we kiss, just how perfect it feels. I hope it never stops surprising me.

I'm ready to pick Cole up and take her straight to the bedroom when her stomach lets out a loud growl. Her cheeks flush a pretty red color, so I kiss there too for good measure. "I'm going to start dinner. You study, yeah? Get a blanket and go sit on the back porch."

"Can I help with dinner?"

Shaking my head, I point authoritatively to the pair of rocking chairs on the other side of the windows. "Go," I repeat, giving Cole a quick smack to her ass.

She takes her backpack and a blanket from the couch, finally listening to my instructions. Ernest lopes after her, tail still wagging. I prepare the burgers and then join her on the porch, firing up the grill.

The fading sunlight makes Cole look like she's glowing, and I almost burn the burgers because I'm too busy staring at her. Half of her face is illuminated, her sprinkling of freckles in stark contrast to her pale complexion, even in the warm light. Her nose slopes to the cutest little point, and I want to run my finger up and down it. I'm sure she'd find that annoying, which would make her face scrunch up. Everything she does is adorable.

I'm so fucking gone.

She looks up at me then. "I can feel you staring, Benjamin."

"So what if I am?"

"It's distracting," she chides. "And you're supposed to be making dinner."

I flip a burger, showing off for her. "See? I can stare at you and make dinner. I'm multitalented."

Cole hums, her attention returning to her textbook. But I don't miss the way her full lips curve up.

"Just cheese?" I ask, ready for her attention to be back on me.

"Yes, please."

Ernest perks up from where he's laying across Cole's feet. His nose sniffs the air as he walks toward me, obviously searching for some dropped morsels.

"Don't feed him," Cole commands.

Ernest and I both whine in response.

"That's pretty rude of her," I whisper to Ernest.

"I can hear you," Colette responds.

She's still not looking at me when I ask, "He's not allergic to human food or anything, right?"

Shielding her eyes from the sun, she glares at me. "No, Benjamin. Ernest the dog, whose ancestors have survived for many centuries living off of what they could hunt and scavenge, is not allergic to people food."

"Just checking," I tease. And then I feed Ernest a few bites of hamburger.

"I see we're ignoring my requests today," Cole mumbles.

I laugh and add some cheese to our patties. "I'm not ignoring you, I'm just selective. And you aren't paying enough attention to me. I'm like Ernest here, I simply require your love and devotion. And some perfectly grilled burgers from time to time."

She slams her textbook closed. "You're the one who told me to study!"

"And you have studied!"

Cole looks at her pretend wristwatch. "For like twenty minutes!"

"Well, now it's time to eat. Burgers are done." Her head hits the back of the rocking chair, an exasperation only I can draw from her is evident in the dip of her eyebrow and quirk of her mouth. "Outside or inside?"

She stands, abandoning her textbook and wrapping the blanket around her shoulders. "Outside, you menace."

"Excellent choice." I pop open a diet cherry cola, placing it at her spot on the table.

We eat with the sounds of wind rustling the fallen leaves and the call of some unidentifiable bird as our background music. "I think there's water nearby," Cole comments. "Can you hear it?"

I sit in silence for a moment, and sure enough, I can hear the faint trickle of water. "Should we hike and try to find it tomorrow? Too bad it's not summer, we could have gone for a swim." I pump my eyebrows obnoxiously which receives a flick to my nose in return.

"I've been thinking," Cole says after another bite of her plain cheeseburger. "Do you really not want kids?"

"Woah, coming out with the big questions tonight, Red." I smirk.

She looks out to our temporary backyard. "You don't have to answer. I've just been curious."

"Oh my God, Colette Russell. Have you been thinking about a future with me?"

"No," she deadpans.

"You have!" I jump up, rounding the table so I can sit next to her instead of across from her. Taking her blanket, I wrap it around both of us so she's cuddled in close to me on the bench seating. She doesn't push me away so I test my luck even further by urging her onto my lap. With a huff, she acquiesces, straddling me and arranging the blanket so we are in our own little cocoon.

"You like me," I sing-song, kissing her so she doesn't have the opportunity to respond. "And no."

Cole pulls back, confused. "No?"

"No, I don't want kids. Hence the whole vasectomy thing," I joke.

She looks between both of my eyes in a way that tells me she's contemplating what to say next. "When did you decide to do that?"

"Uh..." I tilt my head side to side, deciding how truthful I want to be in my answer. "A few years ago."

There. A vague answer should be good enough.

"How many years ago, Ben?"

My mind flashes to the smile she gave me after I told her that I would do my best to communicate clearly with her. Such a simple fucking ask.

"I..." I clear my throat. "I read an opinion piece about three years ago now that finally convinced me to do it, though I'd been thinking about it for a while. The article made many thoughtful points about how men should have more involvement in the prevention of unwanted pregnancies and how there's a movement of couples who are choosing to be childfree. The author talked about how they came to that decision for themselves and it honestly was such a... relief. A relief to see that someone else felt the same way I did. I love kids, hell I am a kid, but I've never felt the desire to have my own."

Cole stares at me. For a really long time. Without saying a single word.

"Say something, Colette. Are you upset? I thought you didn't want—"

"How'd you come across that article?" she interrupts.

Fuck.

I look over her shoulder, scrunching up my face as I pretend to think about it. "A friend of mine posted it to their Instagram story, I think."

"Hmm." Her eyes are searching. She *knows*, but she doesn't

know how to ask. Finally she comes up with, "Does this friend have red hair and happen to be sitting in your lap right this very second?"

I nod.

"You got a vasectomy for me?" Her voice is quiet. Uncertain.

I nod again.

"What if you had met someone else?" she whispers. "What if you changed your mind? What if I had met someone else?"

She's shaking her head now, frantic and a bit panicked.

"Hey, hey. Shhh, it's okay." I run my hands up her back, over her shoulders until I'm cupping her neck. My thumbs firmly hold the side of her face, fingers pressing against the base of her skull. She's looking up, but I can see her eyes beginning to water. "Look at me, Cole."

After blinking a few times, she finally makes eye contact, a single tear tracing down her cheek. "Don't cry, Red. It's fine, really." I take a deep breath before admitting, "There was never anyone else. I wasn't going to change my mind. If you had met someone else I would want to know you were happy. If you were, I would regret walking away from you when we were eighteen for the rest of my life. But that would be my problem to deal with, okay?"

"I'm overwhelmed," she admits. "We hated each other. We—"

"I never hated you."

Cole lets out a sob at that, burying her face into my neck.

"Sweetheart, it's okay." I continue to rub soothing strokes up and down her back. "We're good, we're here. Yeah? It's okay."

She pushes back, tears streaming down her face. "I just need a minute," she says, and then she's gone, through the backdoor and into the cabin.

Before I can register what's happening, before I can pull her back onto my lap, she's simply gone.

Chapter Thirty-One

BE MY WEIGHTED BLANKET?

Ben

GOOGLE SEARCH

Q how do I stop myself from coming too early?? 🎤

I follow Cole into the house, wanting to respect her space but also wanting to make sure she knows I'm here if she needs me. I find her starfished on the king bed in the only bedroom in this cabin.

"There's only one bed," she mutters. Her eyes are closed, but she must sense me standing in the doorway.

"I figured we were past the point of sleeping in separate rooms, but I can take the couch if you need me to."

She shakes her head side to side. "Can I ask you something weird?"

"Nothing can top me admitting I got a vasectomy for someone I wasn't even speaking to at the time," I joke.

"True..." She gives me a soft smile, opening her eyes to find me. "Will you—it helps sometimes to have like a weighted blanket, but we don't have one of those here so can you..."

Cole gestures down toward her body in a limp way, as if it's taking a lot of effort just to raise her arm.

"You want me to be your weighted blanket, Colette?" She nods, so I crawl onto the bed, over the top of her, lowering myself slowly so she's getting some of my weight on her but not all of it.

I can feel Cole relax underneath me. "It's stupid."

"What is?" I ask.

"The fact that I need this. I get annoyed sometimes that my body seems unable to cooperate."

"It's not stupid. I'll be your weighted blanket anytime, *mon chou*."

Her hands wrap around my waist, tugging me down further. "No idea what that means but I've heard your mom say it before so I'm assuming you're being nice. You need to stop being nice to me."

Turning my head, I plant a firm kiss on her cheek. "No."

"Is there more?" she whispers after a moment.

She doesn't elaborate but I know what she means. Are there more things I haven't told her? More things I'm hiding? "Yes."

"Will you tell me?"

"Not yet, but I will. I promise."

Her sigh is deep. "I don't like that. I don't like feeling like I'm missing something."

"I know you don't. Can you let me give you information in doses, please?"

She doesn't agree so I release my elbows and let my entire weight fall on her.

"Benoit!" She squirms. "You're—*crushing*—me!"

"Oops, sorry about that!" I'm not sorry. I roll off of her so we're laying side by side. We both stare up at the ceiling, quiet as she processes.

After a moment, she props herself up on her elbow, turning to face me. I look up at her beautiful face, trying to decipher the look she's giving me.

Leaning close, she runs her nose across my jawline. Once she reaches my ear, she whispers, "I'm going to fuck you now."

"Yes, please," I beg.

Cole climbs on top of me, straddling my hips. She grinds down slowly, finding me hard already. That perfect brow arches. "Eager, are we?"

"Always, Red. Always."

She falls forward, kissing up my neck and across my face. When she sits back up, she pulls me with her, removing my shirt before lightly shoving me back down. "Your abs are stupid."

"So stupid," I repeat. "I'll start skipping core day."

"If you do that, I will contemplate murder."

"Doubling core days, got it," I mumble, distracted now as Cole also strips off her own shirt. She's got some sort of sports-bra situation going on and her tits look too restricted. "Take this off," I say, sliding my finger under the bottom band.

Cole smirks, pulling it off and sending her ponytail swishing behind her. "Your body is anything but stupid, don't change it," I tell her.

"It will probably change as I get older," she replies, factual as ever.

"And it will still be perfect." I cup both of her breasts in my hands, rolling her nipples between my thumb and forefinger. She moans, tossing her head back and arching into me. My dick is straining against my jeans, but she seems to enjoy the friction through her thin leggings. "Can I taste you?"

Dazedly she nods, shuffling her knees toward my face. She realizes around the same time that I do that she's still wearing pants. Hopping off the bed, she strips the rest of her clothes off until she's standing there looking like a goddess. My eyes jump back and forth between her bouncing tits and swaying hips, frantic to drink the entire picture in.

She climbs back on top of me, stopping when I take her nipple into my mouth. She grasps my chin and holds me to her, taking exactly what she wants from me. "Good boy," she whispers before maneuvering so her knees are on either side of my face.

"Sit," I command. "Please," I add when I hear her scoff.

"I love when you beg, Benoit." She lowers herself partially down, waiting.

"Fuck," I mutter. "Please, Colette, I want to taste you. Please sit on my face." I turn my head and nip at her inner thigh.

Finally she drops her full weight onto me, and I fucking devour her perfect cunt. She cants her hips in time with my tongue, chasing the orgasm already. Cole tastes like honey and sunshine and *mine*.

I grip one of her thighs so hard she might have finger-shaped bruises tomorrow. I groan, lightening my grip, but she moves her hand over the top of mine and squeezes, urging me to stay firm. My other hand moves to her ass, gently teasing her rim.

"Fuck," she whimpers, griding down harder. I might suffocate in her pussy, but what a way to go.

She's so close, I can feel her thighs tightening around me. I push slightly harder against where my finger is playing with her ass, and she explodes. Her legs clamp around my face, and I suck hard on her clit as she convulses above me, crying out my name.

My mind is rotating through, *Fuck she's so good* and *God, Benoit do* not *come*.

Cole slowly comes down, collapsing onto the bed next to me, a thin layer of sweat coating her body. I kiss and lick my way to her mouth, planting a peck there. She forces my mouth open with her tongue, tasting herself on me. "Thoughts on meeting me out in the hot tub?"

She nods, clearly still lust addled. Unwillingly, I peel myself off of her, shedding my clothes on the bedroom floor too. When I look at Cole, her bottom lip is trapped between her teeth and her eyes are trained on my hard length.

"If we move to the hot tub, do I get that?" She nods toward my dick.

"Haven't you figured it out yet? You get whatever you want, Red."

The hot tub was already warming up, but I turn on the jets before scrambling in because its fucking freezing when you're buckass naked. Cole saunters out a minute later with the entire duvet cover wrapped around her. She drops it right inside the door and then beelines to the hot tub stairs.

"Oh my God, this feels amazing," she says, sinking into the water across from me.

I reach my arms out, unable to touch her where she's sitting. "Come here," I request, giving her grabby hands because I'm a desperate motherfucker.

She gives me a wicked grin before turning her body out toward the forest, leaning over the edge of the hot tub so her ass is in the air toward me.

"Red," I warn. "Put that ass down or I'll have to do something with it."

Cole looks over her shoulder feigning innocence. "What will you do with it, Benjamin?"

Moving through the water, I open my mouth and take a big bite out of her right cheek before going back to where I was sitting. Cole's pout is so adorable I'm tempted to do it again on the other side.

"Is that not what you wanted, Colette? You have to use your words, sweetheart."

"I want you to fuck me, Benoit." She's so confident in her body, in her sexuality.

"Where?" I ask.

She laughs, turning to fully face me. She looks down hungrily at my cock, then slowly traces the tally mark tattoo on my hip. "We can do that too, but your ass is going inside to get the lube."

"Cunt it is," I reply. "But we're circling back to the other option this weekend."

Cole grins, returning to her previous position—ready and waiting.

I stand, teasing her slit with my tip. The cold air on the top half of my body juxtaposes with the heat bubbling below me, creating an elevated sensation as I push into Cole. She moans, arching back into me, pushing herself onto me.

Kissing up and down her spine, I whisper praise to her. "You're so fucking tight, so perfect, so good for me. Mine, mine, mine."

When I'm in to the hilt, I can't help but set a punishing pace. I want to make both of us come. I want Cole pliant in my hands. She takes all of me beautifully. Of course she's a vision of creamy skin against the now dark forest around us. I wrap my fist around her ponytail, using it as an anchor as I thrust again and again into her heat.

"Ben, fuck, that feels so good," she moans, and I can see her fingers turning white as she grips the edge of the hot tub. "Yes, yes. I'm going to come."

I can feel it, feel her tightening around me. She reaches down to touch herself, and I fall apart. My thrusts become ragged as she closes like a Vise-Grip around me, cresting into her second orgasm. It's euphoric, being with her like this.

We both catch our breath with a laugh. Cole mutters one last *fuck* before pulling herself out of the hot tub and waddling penguin-like back into the house.

"You've never been hotter, Red!" I call through the closed glass door, laughing as she flips me off and then sticks her tongue out at me before closing the bathroom door.

Later that night when we've returned the duvet to the bedroom and snuggled tightly underneath, Cole turns in my arms to face me in the pitch black of night. "Thank you," she whispers.

"For what?" I ask, curious as to how she'll answer.

"For never asking me to be anything other than exactly who I am."

"I like who you are," I reply. I more than like who she is.

"I know you do."

A few minutes later, her breathing evens out and I quietly voice the thing I've been scared to say for twelve years.

"I love who you are."

Chapter Thirty-Two

YOU LOVE IT WHEN I'M MEAN
Cole

GOOGLE SEARCH

Q Best ways to explore primal play.

"This hiking trail feels very murdery."

Keith Morrison's voice echoes through my head. *She lit up every room she walked into!*

I always felt like that had to be a lie—there's no way everyone who had an episode of *Dateline* lit up the rooms they walked into. What does that even look like anyway? They smiled at strangers? That seems to be what got them into the whole murder mess in the first place.

Ben's boisterous laugh draws my eyes to him. I made him walk in front of me, mainly because I like watching his firm ass in the short hiking shorts. He's paired the shorts—which I feel like could be at least two inches shorter—with a Hawthorne hoodie and hiking boots. We left Ernest back at the cabin because I wasn't sure if he'd be able to handle the hike. Ben is taking lots of pictures to "show him later," he said before giving Ernest extra belly scratches.

"Don't you think if I was going to murder you, I would have done it last night? Why wait until today?"

"Hmm… maybe you enjoy the thrill of the chase," I suggest.

He turns around, quirking his dark eyebrow at me. "Kinky."

"Whatever, I was always faster than you anyway. I could definitely outrun you if my life depended on it."

Ben stops dead in his tracks, but I'm so focused on not tripping over a tree root that I charge right into him. When he turns around, his slight elevation on the trail makes him tower over me more than usual. "Want to test this theory?" He smirks.

There must be something seriously wrong with me based on the excited swoop that flies through my stomach. Ben sees it on my face because he leans down to whisper in my ear, "You have until the count of five. Run."

He doesn't have to tell me twice. With a squeal, I take off, following the trail we were taking. Ben's voice grows farther away as he slowly counts to five, adding a *Mississippi* between each number. "Ready or not, here I come!" he yells, spurring me to run faster than I have in a long time.

But Ben apparently spends a lot more time on the treadmill than I do nowadays because it's not long before I hear his heavy footsteps catching up to me. Hoping he's not able to see me yet, I dart off the path in hopes of a place to hide.

A tree wide enough to cover me is only about ten feet away, and I try to quietly tiptoe behind it without crunching too many leaves. My heart is pounding and my breathing is heavy, but I can hear Ben pass my hiding spot before slowing down once he realizes I'm not in front of him anymore.

"Very clever, Red," he calls out. "You've got to be around here somewhere."

I chance a peek around the tree and see his back toward me, searching the opposite side of the trail. Looking around, I contemplate whether or not I should move to a different tree. When I look back toward Ben, he's gone.

My brow furrows as I lean further around the tree, straining to listen for his distant footfalls to no avail. "What the fuck," I mutter before deciding to change locations. Maybe if I get a bit closer to the trail, I'll be able to hear him. Quietly, I tiptoe back toward the path, cringing when a twig snaps beneath my boot. I make it back to the main opening, but there's still no sign of Ben. My mind is spiraling with worst case scenarios when a strong set of arms suddenly grabs me around the waist, twirling me not once, but twice.

"Got ya," says Ben's smug voice in my ear. I can barely hear him over my own scream. His hand comes over my mouth to muffle my startled screech. "Jesus, Red. You're going to make people think an actual murder is occuring."

"Youscaredtheshitoutofme," I mumble into Ben's palm.

"Yes, I caught you," he teases, dropping me back to the ground and crowding me up against the nearest tree. He leans in close, lips grazing mine. "What's my prize?"

"My undying devotion," I joke, taking his lips with mine.

"Deal. Sealing it with a kiss." And he does. A tender, affectionate kiss that communicates so many things that I'm not ready to hear. I think he knows this though, because he laces his hand through mine and wordlessly starts us back on the hiking trail.

A short while later we arrive at our destination. The waterfall we must have been hearing last night at dinner. It falls straight into a swimming hole that would be perfect for the summertime. Ben opens his backpack and lays out a blanket for us to sit on.

"This place is really nice." Though we can't swim, the fall colors are stunning and definitely make the hike up here worth it.

"We should come back in the summer." Ben says it so casually. As if it's just normal that we would be making plans together for almost a year from now.

I hum in response, joining him on the blanket.

"Does it freak you out when I make plans like that?"

Of course he caught on to that. "It makes me a little anxious," I admit.

He pats his lap indicating that he wants me to lie down. My head willingly meets his bare thigh—thank you short shorts—and he tugs at my hair tie. "Can I take this out?"

I do it for him, and he begins to play with my long locks. He braids and unbraids my hair several times before saying, "I don't want to make you anxious. I can come on… *very* strong. I know that. But I want to find a way to make you feel secure."

"It can take me longer to process things. It's not necessarily that I don't like the thought of coming back here with you next summer… oftentimes it just takes my brain a minute to wrap around new or surprising ideas."

He nods, which I can feel more than I can see. "So, give you processing time. Don't try to interpret your silence."

"That would be really helpful." My heart picks up speed again, this time from an emotional intensity rather than a physical one.

"Can I ask a hard question?"

"That seems more than fair, after last night." I laugh but Ben, for once, stays serious.

"You told me about your friendship with Maya and how things ended there. I noticed you don't really talk to your parents either—was it something similar?" he asks.

Surprisingly, this topic isn't too difficult to talk about, though I can see how Ben would assume so with the relationship he has with his parents.

"Well, you know that I moved to Sassafras when my parents divorced in middle school. After that I was pretty much estranged from my mother. I don't think she ever really wanted to be a mom, but I was the bandaid on a marriage that was in the middle of brain surgery. Surprise, surprise, a child does not make marriage easier. Especially not a child with undiagnosed autism."

We're both quiet for a bit. I listen to the falling water as Ben continues to play with my hair. "My dad," I finally continue, "he is a pretty conservative guy. He retired to Florida a few years ago, and I haven't talked to him much since. Just the occasional obligatory check-in. I think he realized both the autism and the queerness weren't a phase." I shrug. "Maybe I would miss him more if he had ever tried to form a real relationship with me, but he didn't. And that's sort of the parent's job, isn't it? He didn't get the perfect child so he stopped putting in the effort."

"How the fuck could anyone think you aren't perfect?" Ben seethes.

"I'm not," I laugh. "Not in his eyes, at least."

"You were the goddamn valedictorian, Colette. Didn't you get a full ride to Stanford? What else did he want?"

"Your guess is as good as mine. It caught me by surprise at first. He hid a lot of his preferences away from me. I really had no idea he felt the way he felt, probably because I'm not good at interpreting nonverbal communication. It's why I struggle with feeling like I'm missing something in other social relationships I've formed. Between that and my fallout with Maya, you know?

"I'm thinking when I came home and told him I had a girlfriend instead of some macho jock that wanted to wife me up and put two point five babies in me, he finally realized I wasn't going to follow the path he had laid out for my life." I sigh. "The irony of all of this is that he would have loved you. Floppy hair and athletic, put together, a real guy's guy."

Ben scrunches his nose and I laugh. "Gross, please never call me a 'guy's guy' again."

"Fine, you goof." I spin in his lap and look up into his disgusted face. "If it makes you feel any better, now that I know you I can wholeheartedly say you're a girl's guy."

His hand comes over his heart. "Thank you."

"What about you?" I ask. "Tell me more about your relationship with your parents. They seem great."

He nods in confirmation. "They are great. With both of them, what you see is what you get. They are loving, down to earth, overly affectionate and way too involved in their children's lives. But we all agree how lucky we are to have them as parents. Both Mom and Dad just want us to be happy. They love big family dinners that seem to grow each Sunday. The more the merrier has always been their motto."

"I was so envious of your dynamic in high school," I confess. "The Bardots were everything my family wasn't. I felt like the only thing I had was school… achievements. I think I hated you because you threatened the one thing I felt like I had any control over."

"That makes a lot of sense, Cole." He pushes my hair away from my face, twisting a piece slowly around his finger. "I never hated you."

I scoff. "Fuck off, yes you did."

He grins, shaking his head. "No, I didn't. I wouldn't have tried half as hard in school if it wasn't for the opportunity to spend more time with you. I admired your work ethic—still do. And yeah, I enjoy friendly competition." His hair flops onto his forehead when he looks down at me. "But really I was just trying to get your attention. Albeit, I would go about it entirely differently now."

"No you wouldn't," I tease. "You got off on me being mean to you."

He groans, tipping his head back so his Adam's apple is on full display. "Fuck, I really did. Well… do," he corrects.

Then both of us are laughing. Full belly laughs, something only Ben is able to pull from me. He falls back until he's lying flat, stomach moving up and down in silent laughter. Catching my breath, I crawl on top of him to give him a proper kiss. Ben makes me excited to touch, to laugh, to play. There's freedom in that, something I could easily get used to.

He takes my left hand, kissing the ring there before he maneuvers me off of himself and pushes to standing. "Let's get back to Ernest. I want to show him the pictures I took for him," he says, completely deadass serious about showing my dog his photographs.

"Okay, Benoit." I hop up to join him, and we work together to fold the blanket. "Should I stop calling you Benjamin?"

"Hell no." His reply is instant. "You're the only one who is allowed to call me the wrong name. I love it. Love your sass."

I blush and he clocks it, tracing where my skin is turning red. "Love this too."

"That makes one of us." I roll my eyes. "C'mon. I'm hungry and I have some more studying to do. But maybe tonight we can get back in the hot tub?"

"And do some butt stuff?" Ben suggests.

"Oh my God." I shove him as we start back down the trail.

"What? Never hurts to ask." He smirks, pinching my ass in emphasis.

"Maybe I want to do butt stuff to you," I tease.

"Colette." He sighs. "We've been over this a million times. My answer to you is always yes."

Damn, tonight is going to be fun.

"Race you down the trail? Last one to the bottom gets to be the bottom," Ben winks before taking off.

Spoiler: we take turns being the bottom.

Chapter Thirty-Three
THE LOUDEST ANIMAL ON EARTH
Ben

GOOGLE SEARCH

Q what's the size of a blue whale tongue?

"I think this counts as dates two and three—we were gone an entire weekend together!"

"Absolutely not," I argue. "It counts as one date and I get three more."

"Three?! I don't have time for three more dates, Benjamin." Cole is currently in her bra and underwear, sitting on top of the bathroom counter and painting her toenails while I take a bath. She's absolutely right about how relaxing they are.

"I'm in no rush, Colette," I drawl, leaning my head against the rim of the tub. When she doesn't respond, I crack one eye open to see her narrowed eyes glaring at me. "Let me?" I ask, nodding toward the red polish in her hands.

She scoots over on the counter letting her feet rest on the edge of the tub. "Have you ever painted nails before?" she asks, amused smirk on her lips.

"Never. How hard can it be?"

Really hard, it turns out. "Why are your toenails so fucking tiny?"

"You're using too much polish," she replies. "It looks like you yanked all of my toenails out and now they're dripping bright red blood."

"That is a visual I could've gone my entire life without having. Did you bring any of the remover?"

"No," she laughs. "I wasn't expecting to have to remove a bloodbath from my feet."

I stop what I'm doing to admire the way she giggles. It's so rare with Cole, this lighthearted side of her, and I've seen so much of it this weekend. It only makes me crave more, just like anything new I learn about her.

"What are you looking at?" she asks after I've stared at her a beat too long.

I shake my head. "Nothing… just you seem happy. Lighter somehow."

She purses her lips together. "Have you heard of masking?" she asks. "The conscious, or sometimes subconscious, decision to suppress any of my neurodivergent 'quirks.'"

It's like a lightbulb goes off in my head because of course that's what's going on. "Yeah, actually. I was reading about it the other day. Do you think you've been unmasking more around me?"

"Maybe. Probably," she admits. "Does… does it bother you?"

"What? No, absolutely not." I give her a cheeky grin. "I fucking love that I get a side to you that no one else does. I like that you're comfortable around me."

"I am. Don't fuck it up," she deadpans.

I hold three fingers in the air. "Scout's honor."

"You are no Boy Scout, Benoit Bardot," she teases. "I'm going to the porch to put my feet in the sun in hopes that the entire bottle of nail polish you used on my toes dries eventually, and then we need to pack up. C'mon, Ernest."

The dog follows her obediently out of the bathroom, and I don't think I've ever related to a dog more. I would also follow Colette anywhere she told me to go.

Sighing, I sink further into the hot water. It's been a perfect weekend and I don't want to leave. I want to stay holed up here with her and Ernest forever.

Unfortunately, reality is calling and we have to answer.

———

I've been doing the weekly story time at the Sassafras Public Library ever since this past spring when Ethel volun-told me. There was a week I couldn't make it and I recruited Gabe to take my place, so now he and Jules join me every so often.

When Chloe started Kindergarten last month, I begged to swap to the afternoon slot so we could still hang out. I'm pretty sure Ethel pulled a few strings in the way only she is able to do, but I'm not going to question her tactics.

I'm setting up the puppet theater when Jules and Chloe bust into the room. Well, Chloe busts… Jules scrambles in behind her looking a little dazed. He really got thrown into the whole dad thing—baptism by fire and all that.

"Benjamin!" Chloe calls, adopting the nickname from Cole.

She drops her backpack unceremoniously on the ground next to me. She has one pigtail that's hanging by a thread and the other one has fallen out completely. Her shirt is only half tucked in, and there's an unidentified brown smear near the collar.

"Hey, Princess Chloe! How was school today? Did you have some chocolate in your lunch?" I raise my eyebrows questioningly at Jules.

"It was SO good! I love school. Did you know that blue whales have tongues that weigh as much as an elephant and their heart is the size of a car? They are also the loudest animal on Earth." She lets out a loud cross between a moan and a screech. "And yes, JuJu put M&M's in my lunch today. How'd you know?"

I clutch my chest after Chloe finishes her diatribe, exhausted just from listening.

"Yes," Jules answers my unasked question. "This is what it's like every day after school."

"It's a good thing you are an excellent listener," I joke before turning my attention back to Chloe. Now that I know it's chocolate on her shirt, I pick her up and twirl her around. "I had no idea about blue whales. That's so cool, Chlo. We should find more books about whales while we are here."

She perks up. "That is a great idea!"

"How's Thea?" I ask Jules. He immediately takes his man bun out and reties it, his nervous tic.

"She's good. Ready to have the baby. Only a few more weeks." He shoves his hands into his pockets, rocking back and forth.

"How about you, bud? How are you feeling?"

He nods a few times before answering honestly, like I knew he would. "Absolutely terrified."

I clap my twin on his shoulder. "It's going to be great. I'm excited to be an uncle again!"

"We're uncles again?" Gabe asks, hustling into the story room with Anders and his daughters right behind him.

"Not yet," Jules answers. "Soon."

Gabe looks back and forth between Jules and I. "We already knew that, didn't we? That Thea was due soon? This isn't, like, new information."

"No, Gabriel. We were just discussing it before you got here. Now, both of you grab a puppet and look over your lines before the rest of the kids get here."

"I want lines next time," Anders whines. "I'm kind of an expert at this sort of thing."

"Sure, Anders. You're welcome to join anytime," I acquiesce. "But right now, it's showtime—go sit down and enjoy."

Puppet story time is a huge hit, obviously. Gabe only misses one of his cues, but the kids all thought it was hilarious when he broke character. After we're done, we head over to Louie's for an early dinner, meeting Bex and Thea there.

"So, I heard good things about you and Cole's little cabin getaway," Thea tells me between bites of pickle.

"I want to know!" Bex chimes in. "Tell me about it!"

This bit of information from Thea is surprising considering Cole's desire to keep everything so close to her chest. "Did you?" I ask, ignoring my sister. I'm trying to stay nonchalant and failing pretty hard.

I told Gabe, Jules, and Bex about my pact with Cole after announcing our engagement at family dinner. Gabe obviously already knew about the feelings and Jules did not seem surprised at all. Bex, per usual, became feral, wanting to know anything and everything about Cole.

"I remember her from high school, obviously. She's always been gorgeous and it's hard to miss that hair. But I want to know"—she had slammed her hands down on the table—*"everything!"*

Thea interrupts that memory with a shrug. "I mean, it's Cole. I didn't get a ton of information out of her but she did mention that you made *very* good use of the hot tub."

Jules puts his arm around Thea, pulling her in close to him. "I did not need to know that, Rosie girl."

She groans in response. "I miss being able to get in a hot tub. Take a scalding hot bubble bath. I need this baby out of me!"

"Oof, I feel that," Bex says, sending a comforting smile Thea's way.

Chloe pushes her stomach out and rubs it obnoxiously, mimicking her mom. "Get this baby out of me!" she mocks, to peels of laughter from Elodie, Bex and Anders' two-year-old.

"Okay, you." Thea laughs, poking her daughter's stomach. "Let's go get some ice cream at the shop next door and leave these boys to chat, yeah?"

"But I like chatting," Chloe whines.

"You also like ice cream," Thea reminds her.

"Fine." She hops out of her seat, sliding her hand into Thea's as they head toward the exit.

"I'll go with you." Bex stands, baby Molly strapped to her chest and Elodie by her side, following closely behind Thea and Chloe.

"So," Gabe starts as soon as they're out of earshot. "Thea heard good things about you and Cole's trip to the cabin." He bounces his eyebrows up and down a few times. "Do you think she's any closer to accepting your proposal? For real this time?"

I cross my arms over my chest, leaning back against the booth. "We made a lot of progress at the cabin, but I don't quite think she's one hundred percent in yet."

"What do you think she needs?" Jules asks.

"Time." I shrug. "She's asked for time to continue to process all of these major changes happening in her life right now. The absolute least I can do is respect that desire." Jules gives me a nod of approval.

"When's the next date?" Anders asks.

"I'm not sure yet. But I think I have an idea of what I want to do. Do you think you all would be able to help me?"

"As long as Thea stays pregnant, I'm happy to help," Jules says.

"You know I love this kind of shit," Gabe chimes in, rubbing his hands together. "Let's fucking go!"

"I'm in, obviously. I've missed Bardot shenanigans," Anders adds.

Gabe places his hand in the middle of the table, me, Anders, and Jules piling our hands on top like we are back in little league baseball.

"Team Bardot on three," Gabe says. "One, two, three."

I grin at my brothers, Anders included, excitement filling my stomach as our plan begins to come together.

Chapter Thirty-Four
THIS IS A 1950'S MAFIA DEN...
Cole

GOOGLE SEARCH

"Why am I wearing this?" I look down at my black silk dress that reaches all the way down to the ground, hugging every curve along the way. My hair is down in loose waves and a pearl necklace—that better not be real—is lying just above my collar bone. My lips are painted a deep red, of course.

I look at Ben who is wearing a tux… almost. He neglected to put on a jacket and his bowtie is hanging loose, displaying the top buttons of his shirt that he didn't bother to do.

We look hot—*I have eyes!*—but I'm incredibly confused about where the hell we could be going. Especially when he turns onto his parents' street. We park outside Mr. and Dr. Bardot's house, and I'm surprised to see several other cars already parked out front.

"Benjamin, what is happening?" I ask, hoping to get at least some information out of this man.

"Patience, Colette. You'll find out momentarily."

I sigh. "You know how much I love surprises."

"I know, I know. This is a really good one, though. And if you absolutely hate it we can leave, no questions asked." He looks at me with those stupid puppy-dog eyes, and he seems genuinely excited about whatever we're about to walk into.

"Fine," I agree. "But if I hate it, we are leaving. And it will still count as date three."

"Deal. Let's go." He hops out of the car and then rounds the hood to my side, helping me out of my seat.

When we get to the front door, Anders answers. He is also dressed up, in a deep emerald suit with a black shirt and tie underneath. I spot a name tag stuck to his lapel that says "Vincent Castellano."

"Welcome"—he checks his notes—"Mr. and Mrs. Luciano. Here are your name tags, please step over here to have your photo taken."

"Anders, what the fu—"

"Ah, ah! It's Vincent, but you can call me Vinny. Thank you for joining our dinner party this evening." He smirks, ushering us into the house.

His wife is right inside with a polaroid camera, ready to take our picture in front of a beaded backdrop. She leans in conspiratorially, and I catch the name "Curly" on her tag. "Isn't this so fun?" she whispers. "We thought a mob boss theme would really—"

"Baby Bardot! Stay in character!" Anders scolds.

She rolls her eyes and then motions for me to step in front of the backdrop. I stand there, still confused as hell, but give her a soft smile anyway.

"Gorgeous! Your turn, Mr. Luciano," Bex says.

Ben steps up, pulling his suspenders away from his chest, giving the camera a wink.

Next, we move into the living room, which has been transformed into a 1950's style club... if you squint your eyes and tilt your head. The furniture is grouped in little vignettes and the lights are turned down low. It's really adorable actually. Jules, Thea, Gabe, and the two heads of the Bardot household are mingling about, dressed up just as much as we are with champagne glasses in their hands.

They each introduce themselves—well, their made up names for the evening—and then Dr. Bardot offers to pour me a drink.

She fills about half a glass before setting the bottle and glass down gently on the counter. With an extravagant flourish, she clutches her chest with one hand and covers her forehead with the other. "I—" She coughs dramatically. "I think I've been poisoned!" Then she sinks to the floor.

Staring at her for a moment, I look around unsure of what to do next. Thea slides up next to me, her large stomach looks about ready to pop. "It's a murder mystery party!" She smiles. "Isn't that the cutest thing?"

Gabe, realizing it's his part, rushes over to "check" his mom's pulse. He stands and places both hands on his hips. "There's been a murder! Everyone gets three clues throughout the night to solve the case. You will have until thirty minutes after the last clue has been given to submit your guess. Good luck and trust no one…"

I turn to laugh with Thea about Gabe's commitment to the bit, but she's now eyeing me warily and slowly backing away.

Ben takes her place, his arm winding around my waist. "Benjamin, this is unhinged. Is your mom just going to lay there all night?"

"Dead people can't move, Colette." He narrows his eyes in concern. "Are they teaching you nothing in your program?"

"Yeah, I've learned that if there's a murder, you shouldn't mill about the room trying to solve it on your own," I fire back.

"Well, this is a 1950's mafia den soooo…" He drags out the last word as if it should be completely obvious what the second half of his sentence will be.

"So what?"

He huffs. "So pretend like we're solving a murder. Let's go, Red. We have to get our first clue from Bex—I mean, Curly."

———

"It was Curly, in the powder room, with a poisoned bottle of perfume!" Hugo, Ben's dad, calls an hour later after presenting all of his evidence.

"How the fuck did he figure that out?" I mutter to Ben.

"I think we might have skipped a step..." Ben replies, flipping through the clue cards in his hands.

Elaine pops up off the ground, scaring the shit out of me—I had almost forgotten she was there. "Great job, *mon chou*! You did it! Now let's eat! I'm starving."

"Are you okay to stay for dinner?" Ben asks, tugging me close.

I look around the room, nervous energy buzzing through me at his very public display of affection. He loosens his grip and I instantly miss his firm touch. I lean into him, moving his arms back into place as I say, "Yeah, I'd love to. That was really fun, but maybe we should buy a kit next time instead of letting Anders and Gabe come up with the clues. I'm ninety-nine percent sure it was not actually Curly who did it."

He kisses the tip of my nose. "Next time?" He grins and I shove him off me.

"Wait!" Bex runs over. "Get back together, let me take another picture."

Ben puts his face right next to mine with a huge grin, and I flick off the camera. Once it's developed, Ben looks down at it like it's the most precious treasure he's ever come across. "It's perfect," he says, showing me.

I realize immediately that the star of the show is the giant engagement ring on my finger. It's front and center, a beam of light making it sparkle even in the poor quality polaroid. Honestly, I've been wearing it so often I forgot it was there, but this is the first time I'm seeing it on my hand through someone else's eyes.

"Can I keep it?" Ben asks, snapping me out of my thoughts.

I nod and he tucks it into his pocket.

We sit down at the dining table with the rest of the Bardot family. In keeping with the theme, tonight's dinner is a variety of Italian dishes. I actively avoid the spaghetti and meatballs—I really hate long noodles—loading my plate with lasagna instead. I'm content to observe as the chaos of Bardot family dinner unfolds around me.

Everyone jokes, tells stories, asks thoughtful questions. They care about each other's lives with no judgement. No expectations except that you show up.

I'm overwhelmed, so I'm quiet, but I reassure Ben that I do want to stay. I enjoy being around his family, and a sudden pang hits me when I think about what it would mean to say no to Ben and this stupid pact. It would mean not only losing out on him, but also on a family that I could one day, hopefully, call my own.

This is so much more than just Ben and me. So much more…

"I need some air," I whisper to Ben, urging him to stay seated when he gets up to join me.

I'm standing on the Bardot's front porch, freezing my ass off and wishing I was a smoker, when the door creaks open. "I told you not to follow me," I say, without even turning around.

"Apologies," comes a much older voice. Deep in the same way Ben's is, but… different. "I can go back inside if you'd like."

I whirl around, instantly embarrassed. "Mr. Bardot, no it's fine. Please stay out here, I can go in!"

He grins, looking so much like his sons in this moment. "I was hoping to talk to you, actually. Want to sit?" He gestures toward the porch swing, and that's when I see a heavy coat draped across his arm.

"Only if that's for me." I nod toward the jacket, and he holds it up for me to slide my arms into.

We sit on the porch swing, rocking quietly for several

minutes. It seems that Hugo Bardot doesn't mind the silence, either. I inhale, looking up at the starry sky, debating whether or not I should be the one to start the conversation.

"We can be a lot," Hugo says, right before I was about to excuse myself back inside.

"Hmm?"

"The Bardots. It can be a lot to try to… acclimate."

"Oh, no. It's fine, really." I say it more as a comfort to him than anything else.

Hugo chuckles, obviously picking up on my discomfort. "It's okay," he says. "I am also an only child. All four of them came out so rambunctious. Well, not Jules. He's always been stoic, an old man from birth. But the rest of them—absolutely nuts. It was a lot for me to get used to. Still is, sometimes," he admits.

"How'd you handle it when the noise became too much?" I ask, curious about how the quieter Bardots fare amidst the chaos.

"Exactly like this," he states, his arms spread wide to indicate the porch swing and the stars above us. "I've spent a lot of time in this exact spot. You can still hear their chatter inside but it's not quite so jarring. It helps me feel connected while still taking a little time for myself."

"I hope you don't mind me joining you," I reply.

He smiles warmly. "Of course not. Jules, and even Bex, will join me out here on occasion."

We fall back into comfortable silence, the back and forth motion of the swing soothing my nerves. A few minutes later, Hugo speaks again. "This might sound odd, but I remember the day you moved to town."

"That does sound odd," I joke. "Seeing as it was, what? Almost eighteen years ago."

He hums. "Something like that. Sassafras is a small town, as you know. We don't get a lot of newcomers. I met your father first, actually. Elaine heard someone was moving in a few streets over and that he had a daughter that was the twins' age. She volunteered me to go greet you both that day. Do you remember?"

I shake my head.

"No, I suppose you wouldn't. There was a lot going on and I only stayed briefly because Ben and Jules came zooming by on their bicycles and Ben lost control, ramming into a tree maybe three or four houses down from you."

Now *that* I remember.

"Ah, I see the spark of recognition."

I huff a laugh. "Yeah, a lanky pre-teen boy with blood running down his face definitely leaves an impression."

"I'm surprised he walked away with the gash on his head but nothing else. He could have easily broken his nose or his arm." Hugo tuts. "He was quite distracted by a beautiful young lady that day."

My scoff is automatic. "No, we didn't even talk that day. I don't think he noticed me."

"Mmm. Maybe… but I do distinctly remember him asking what your name was while we were in the ER waiting room. You're right, though. He probably didn't notice you." Hugo winks, belying his sarcasm.

We go back to swinging silently as I process what he's saying.

"It's a strange feeling," I sigh.

"What's that?"

"Rewriting my memories. Well, not rewriting necessarily but looking at them from a different perspective, which has always been hard for me." Hugo, like his son, senses that I have more to say and gives me space to process. "Ben does this a lot—it shouldn't surprise me anymore. I'll tell him a memory the way I remember it and he'll let me know how he was actually feeling at the time…"

"It's a lot to take in," Hugo concludes.

"Yeah…" I fiddle with the ring on my finger. "Ben knows that it has been a struggle for me. He's working on being more straightforward and communicative. I know it's a lot to ask—"

"It's not," he cuts in. "That's part of being in a partnership."

Just then, the man in question pops his head out of the front door. "Red, do you need—oh! Hey, Dad. I was wondering where you wandered off to. I'll let you both…"

Hugo stands, patting me a few times on the shoulder as he does. "No, I was about to head back inside. Come sit with Colette."

He squeezes his son's arm on his way inside, and Ben does indeed take his spot. His arm casually drapes around me, tugging me in tight. "Hey, Red," he whispers, planting a kiss on my temple. "Did you have fun tonight?"

"I'm pissed we didn't solve the mystery," I tease—kind of. "But I did have a great time. I can't believe your family threw all of this together just because."

"Not 'just because,' Cole," he says. "It's never 'just because' with you."

I smile to myself, snuggling deeper into the sweet, surprising man next to me. We rock back and forth for so long, I almost nod off. Until I hear a yell coming from inside the house.

"What the fuck?" Ben asks, standing up to rush inside.

Before we can make it there, Jules and Thea come bursting through the front door.

Thea looks calm, serene even as she looks at me and says, "So sorry to leave early! My water just broke."

Chapter Thirty-Five
I WANT TO KEEP YOU
Cole

GOOGLE SEARCH

Q What does it mean when someone calls you mon chou?

Thea's water breaking was not how I envisioned ending the evening. Things are never boring with the Bardot family, that is for damn sure. Jules and Thea rushed to the hospital and the rest of the party dispersed pretty quickly after that.

Ben drives me home, letting himself into my apartment without even asking if he's allowed to stay.

He is, of course. But I do marvel at how the fuck this happened. How he wiggled himself so thoroughly into my life, so perfectly under my skin.

"Diet cherry cola?" Ben asks, opening up my fridge like he owns the place. Technically, he did stock the fridge and the pantry for me last week. So I guess he does kind of own that part of the place.

"Sure, I'm just going to change clothes." I start to walk toward my bedroom when his heavy footfalls sound behind me.

"Wait, wait, wait!" His hand slides across the silk of my dress. "Don't change yet..." He holds my hips, angling me away so he can eye my body up and down.

"Really?" My eyebrow quirks. "Someone's water breaks in the middle of a dinner party and you're still turned on?"

He bites his lower lip. "I'm always turned on by you, Red. There could be a zombie apocalypse happening outside and I'd still want you."

"Okay, that's kind of hot actually. Do you think next time you can arrange a zombie apocalypse party?"

"I'll hire a party planner," he jokes, nipping at my exposed neck, kissing across the pearl necklace. "We can have a party once a month—once a week, if you want."

I scowl. "That sounds horrible. I don't want to see people that often."

His chuckle rumbles up my neck. "I think we should take the ties back out tonight," he mutters, continuing his perusal of my body.

My mind flashes back to the first time we had sex. I was so worried that as soon as Ben found out I wanted to tie him up, he was going to run as far and as fast as he could. That was the beginning of his surprises. He didn't run at all—he embraced the sexier, more erotic version of me, even when that was all I was willing to offer.

"You're thinking very loud," he teases.

I shake the intrusive thoughts out of my head. "You want to be tied up, Benoit? I'll tie you up. How about a blindfold? A gag? You do tend to run that mouth more than you're supposed to."

Ben pulls back to look at me, panting, a lock of his hair falling across his forehead. "I'm at your mercy, Colette."

Placing my finger under his chin, I tilt his head up. "Good boy. Now, strip."

He steps back from me, removing his suspenders and pulling off his already loosened bowtie. I take it from him, knowing it will come in handy in a few minutes. Slowly, he begins to unbutton his shirt, revealing abs that I would love to lick. He's got one of those stupidly seductive man V's that points straight down to his long cock, straining against his zipper.

Heat settles in my stomach—lower—as he shucks off his pants and boxers, leaving him completely bare for me.

It feels more even this way… he's completely naked physically, and I feel emotionally stripped down, too.

My entire chest seizes when I meet Ben's eyes and see—no, there's no way.

"Turn around," I rasp. Using the abandoned bowtie, I tie a secure knot around his wrists. "Remind me what our safe word is?"

"Foudroyant." He rolls the syllables around his mouth, tasting each and every one.

"Right," I gulp. "On your knees."

Without hesitation, he faces back toward me and drops to his knees in the middle of the hallway. It's not easy with his hands tied behind his back, and I definitely think he'll have bruises tomorrow, but he doesn't seem to care.

I run my own hands down my dress, loving the soft texture of the silk. Down over my hips, across my stomach, up toward my breasts. Ben watches with rapt attention, hanging on every small movement I make. I hike the long dress up, revealing the strappy stilettos Ben chose before the party. They have a leather bow that ties about halfway up my calf—they're probably the sexiest pair of shoes I own.

Delicately, I place my—now neatly painted—red toes onto the center of his chest. He moans, leaning down to kiss wherever he can easily access.

"Uh uh," I tsk, pushing him away with my foot. "Did I say you could touch?"

Ben shakes his head, lust so palpable he might boil over at any moment. I look down and see a bead of precum dripping from his dick. It makes me feel powerful, beautiful—he makes me feel those things.

"What do you want, Benoit? Maybe if you're good, I'll give it to you."

"To marry you," he replies, instantly. His eyes drop to my ring finger before bouncing back up to my shocked expression.

Recovering quickly, I roll my eyes. "Tonight, Benjamin. What do you want tonight?"

He grins cheekily. "I want that tonight. But I also want to taste you, fuck you, spend the night with you."

"Fine, untie my shoe." Ben looks down meaningfully at his restrained arms. "With your mouth," I clarify. "Put it to good use."

His teeth catch the leather string and he tugs, loosening the entire shoe until I'm able to kick it off. He moves to the other foot, licking where the strap criss-crosses up my leg before he unties the second bow. I throw my calf over his shoulder and lean back against the wall. My dress is fitted but I still manage to work it up high enough that Ben can duck his head underneath.

I can't see his face, can only feel as he licks a slow line down my center, over my underwear. He uses his teeth again to pull them down so he has full access to me. I move my leg off his shoulder, adjusting so the underwear tangles around my standing leg. Ben maneuvers back under my skirt and my head falls back as he nips and teases my clit, working until he can pull an orgasm from me. I buck my hips against his face and he groans in pleasure.

"Love—" His voice is muffled, currently being suffocated by my cunt. "Love tasting"—*lick*—"you."

Fuck. I've never been with a partner who has been this enthusiastic about eating me out, and I can't say I'm mad about it. It's a delicious burn as the stubble on Ben's chin rubs against my thigh. He sucks hard and I'm immediately tossed over the edge, gripping Ben's shoulders to stay upright. If his knees aren't bruised tomorrow, the claw marks I'm leaving on his shoulders definitely will be.

When Ben pulls away, coming back out from underneath my

dress, there's a vulgar sheen of *me* across the bottom half of his face. The asshole licks his lips, attempting to suck down every last taste.

"You're disgusting," I pant, not really meaning it.

"And you, *mon chou*." He pauses for another pass of his tongue. "Are mouthwatering."

"What does it mean?" He knows what I'm asking.

"Literally, it translates to my cabbage." He shrugs, leaning in toward my thighs. "But when I'm talking to you… it means sweetheart"—*kiss*—"honey"—*kiss*—"love." He pulls back and meets my eyes. "It means I want to keep you."

Instead of responding, I bend down to help him off of his knees, turning his body so it's the one up against the wall now.

"Stay here," I whisper before hurrying to my bathroom so I can reapply my lipstick. I decide to go ahead and bring the whole tube with me, tucking it into the top of my dress. When I walk back into the hallway, Ben is exactly where I left him. I take a moment to admire the strong line of his body. His thick thighs and hard cock. He rolls his head toward me and smirks, knowing exactly what he's doing.

"Your turn," I whisper.

Chapter Thirty-Six

INAPPROPRIATE USE OF LIPSTICK

Ben

GOOGLE SEARCH

Q can you get lipstick stains out of clothes? 🎤

"Your turn," she whispers, dark red lips parting into the sexiest smile I've ever seen. She saunters toward me, her eyes drinking me in.

Do I flex a little to show off? Absolutely. She bites her lower lip, and I can't help but imagine her biting into my lips instead. Her hands find my pecs as she comes to stand in front of me. My arms are still secured behind my back, but I'm so desperate to touch her.

She smirks, tweaking my nipples, causing my hips to buck. Precum drips from my tip, dropping down onto my thigh.

"Hmm…" She hums, watching eagerly. I'm desperate as Cole leans in, planting kisses across my collar bone and down my abs. I want all of the red marks she's leaving permanently tattooed on me. An even better reminder of her than the one I currently have.

When she gets down to my hips, she kisses right over the tally marks there. It's incredibly erotic, and Cole doesn't really even understand why.

She dips lower, licking up where I've dripped onto my leg and then pulls a tube of lipstick from her cleavage, causing images to pop into my head of other things between her perfect tits.

One swipe, and another, of my favorite color painted across my favorite mouth. Then, her perfect pout is wrapped around the tip of my cock, and I swear this is what heaven feels like. The wet heat of her mouth paired with the red lip marks she leaves behind, I am incredibly glad I whacked off earlier today to prevent me from coming the instant Cole touched me.

"Colette," I warn as she sucks me all the way to the back of her throat. I strain against the bowtie that's holding my hands behind my back, itching to plunge my hands into her gorgeous hair.

"Colette," I plead when she does it again. "Please, I want to fuck you," I beg.

I swear I see her eyes crinkle at the corners, a tear escaping down her right cheek. She pops off to say, "Don't come," before sliding me right back into her mouth.

"Fucking hell, you're making that extremely difficult." My head tilts back and my eyes squeeze shut, hoping that if I can't see her it will slow the heat that's building in the base of my spine.

If her mouth wasn't wrapped around my dick, I think she would laugh. Take pleasure in the pain she's causing me. Fuck she's so hot and I—*no!* I yank my hips back, trying to get as far out of her mouth as possible. Which is not very far seeing as I'm up against the wall.

She shuffles forward, continuing to suck and lick and tease.

"Please," I whine. "I'm going to—don't make me—"

Cole pulls off a second before I'm about to explode, stopping all sensation completely.

"Fuck!" I roar, doubling over, trying to suck down any air left in the room.

Colette looks like the cat that ate the mother fucking canary, red lipstick smeared outside of her lips. "Dammit, Colette," I pant. "I've never been edged so hard in my life."

She laughs—laughs!—carefully untying my hands. Once I have them free, I spin her around, undoing the zipper on her dress one tooth at a time. I need to even the playing field, so once she's completely naked, I pick her up and move her until she's resting against the opposite wall with her legs wrapped around my waist.

Adjusting myself, I thrust into her in one punishing movement. She gasps and then moans, letting me fill her completely. I fuck her hard and fast, the frames on the wall bouncing haphazardly around us.

My thumb comes between us to circle her clit while my mouth covers her nipple. I bite and tug, sending Cole over the edge.

As soon as her pussy clenches around me, I can't hold on anymore. My thrusts become erratic as I push and push and push into her, wringing out my orgasm. The primal side of me wants her to leak for *days*.

"Fuck I'm going to be sore tomorrow," she rasps, struggling to breathe.

"And the next day," I reply, licking a bead of sweat off of her neck.

"Menace." She smirks. I let her slide down the front of my body as she gets her feet back under her. Taking her mouth in mine, I kiss her thoroughly, not wanting to break away from her.

We rinse off together in the shower and a pang of sadness hits me square in the chest when the last of Cole's lipstick washes off.

"I want another tattoo," I tell her later, once I've settled onto my side of the bed. She looks up from the doorway, scowling at

Ernest who is curled up next to me. I think I'm his new favorite after I took pictures for him on our hike.

Her eyes flick to my face. "Where'd you get those?"

I touch the reading glasses I put on after we got out of the shower. "I left a pair here for when I spend the night. Obviously," I tease.

Cole sighs before joining me in bed. "You can't just start leaving all of your things here."

"You're right." I pick up the romance book that I definitely left here, pretending to read. "We should go look at houses soon. Then all of our things can be in one place."

She tilts her head, trying to get a good look at the cover of my book. "That book isn't mine either," she grumbles.

"I know." I wink. "I left it here."

"Oh my God, you're insufferable."

"Thank you."

"And we can't go look at houses. I can barely afford school and this apartment."

My brow furrows. "You shouldn't be paying for school. And I have enough saved for a house."

Her head tilts side to side. "I'm not technically paying for school with that new grant, but after my scholarship suddenly went away last semester, I'm not taking any chances. Any extra money I have is staying in my bank account in case of emergency."

"There won't be an emergency."

"You don't know that." She meets my eyes, tucking the quilt around her before scratching the top of Ernest's head.

"Yes, I do."

"What if something happened to Ernest? What if I needed a medical procedure done? What if the apartment springs a leak and I lose all of my furniture?"

"If there's an emergency," I correct, "you won't need to dip into your savings. I'll take care of it. I'll take care of you."

"How do you have all of this money anyway? Am I allowed to ask that?"

"You, Red, are allowed to ask anything you want."

Cole gives me a *go on* gesture.

"As you know—and so affectionately refer to me—I was a dreaded Finance Bro after college. I didn't have anything else to focus on except for my job so I rose pretty quickly through the ranks. In fact, I'm pretty positive they were about to put me on the partner track when I left." I look down at Cole, my brain flying through the many different ways my life could look different right now.

"Anyway, I lived in a tiny apartment that was haphazardly furnished with hand-me-down furniture. My only travel was coming back here to Sassafras to see my family. Most of what I made, I saved or invested. A few of my investments continue to do really, really well. I think I just got lucky, honestly."

"If I know you, you worked your ass off to get where you are." Cole eyes me. "And probably also got lucky," she adds, grinning.

"It's enough to live comfortably for a while. I can pretty much live off of what I make from Bardot Brothers Coffee Co. and use my savings for bigger purchases. Different kinds of investments." I take Cole's hand in mine, examining the ring I put there.

"You're nuts, do you know that?"

I kiss her knuckle, right under the dark gemstone. "Thank you, *mon chou*."

She's silent for a moment, frowning down at where our hands are clasped. "I don't ever want to be indebted to you."

"That makes perfect sense."

"It does?" she asks, surprise in her tone.

"Of course. You are fiercely independent, Colette. You've lived so much of your life on your own terms, and I don't ever want you to change that part of you." I twirl a piece of her hair before tucking it behind her ear. "I'm not trying to take it away from you, either. You can do all of this yourself—absolutely you can. But… I can also help, if you want. Or buy a house"—I shrug noncomittally—"and move all of your things into it."

"If I want?"

"Ehh… I will probably do that regardless," I joke.

She smacks my hand away and then falls back on her pillow. "Just give me time," she whispers.

"I've got nothing but time, Cole."

A forever that I'm ready to spend with you.

Chapter Thirty-Seven
HE LOOKS LIKE A NAKED MOLE RAT
Cole

GOOGLE SEARCH

Q Are newborn babies supposed to be that wrinkly? 🎤

The next several weeks are a whirlwind. Emmett Henry Rose-Bardot—a damn mouthful of a name—was born after fourteen hours of labor. The entire Rose-Bardot family is happy and healthy, obsessed with their pink and wrinkly newborn.

I swear something evolutionary skipped me because he looks a bit like a naked mole rat. And, yep, still no maternal desires surfacing. Squinting at the picture Thea sent me, I decide the best way forward is lying.

THEA

Look at how cute he is!

It's a picture of Emmett curled up on Thea's chest. He's a bit splotchy and very bald.

So cute!!!

THEA

Too enthusiastic, Cole. We have to work on your lying skills.

Shit, sorry. I just don't understand how we're supposed to think he's cute right now. Maybe in a few months?

THEA

skull emoji

He's just so little and squishy!

Hmm...

THEA

Come on, you have the world's ugliest dog. You have to think this baby is cute!

Yes, world's ugliest dog. I do not think Ernest is cute but I still love him.

THEA

I'll take it!

Another text comes across the top of my screen.

BEN

Did you also get an ugly photo of Emmett?? I mean, I'm his uncle, obviously I'm obsessed with the kid but when they are so fresh it's just…

Creepy.

BEN

Exactly! I knew you'd get it!

Do you want me to add you to the family group chat? We're all talking about it!

Dear god, please don't.

I hate group chats. They are so stressful.

BEN

LOL you are so cute Red

I'll just recap the messages before bed every night

I think that's worse than just being in the group

BEN

Noted

A few minutes later, a new notification pops up.

Benjamin added you to Cabbages

THEA

Oh my god, yay! Cole is here!

Fuck. No! I don't want to be in this group chat. I move back to my texts with Ben.

What the fuck

BEN

You said this would be better than me recapping the messages!

I didn't mean for you to add me!

Cabbages

BEX

Yay! More women!

GABE

Welcome, Cole!

Colette left the group

There. For some reason being added to the family group chat feels like more of a commitment than moving in with Ben. It's not something that can be done this casually!

BEN

Gabe thinks you left the group because of him

I left the group because of you, Benjamin!

BEN

That's not what Gabe thinks

> Then tell him it's because of you! I didn't want
> to be in the group!

BEN

Poor Gabe. He's going through a rough time
right now, too.

Goodbye Benjamin.

I toss the phone onto the other side of the couch and go back to studying. This semester has been difficult but invigorating at the same time. I love that we are finally diving into criminal psycho analysis and applying our learning to real world case studies.

This is exactly what I've been itching to do for as long as I can remember. Following this career path feels more *right* than engineering ever did. Honestly, it feels like so many things are lining up exactly the way they are supposed to.

So much so, I might even let Ben add me back into the family group chat. After I process what that would look like and maybe have Ben do the recapping thing for a few weeks…

Baby steps.

————

Since missing the first week of classes, I still feel like I'm playing catch up so I decide to pop into Dr. Daly's office hours the next Monday morning. His office is cozy, with a large wooden desk and two leather chairs across from where he sits. Mismatched textbooks line the shelves behind his desk and a photo of him, another older man, and a dog sits framed among the various knick-knacks scattered around him. Unlike Dr. Winthrop's office, Dr. Daly's feels lived in—welcoming.

He greets me with a smile and we have a rousing conversation about Eysenck's theory of criminal personality.

"Don't you think Eysenck completely overlooks the whole nurture part of nature versus nurture? I mean, he's scientifically accurate when it comes to some of the biology of criminals if we were to look across a wide pool of subjects, but what about their background? Previous trauma? Education? We can't overlook those things when thinking about actual humans and not just case studies."

Dr. Daly beams at me across his desk. "Excellent point, Ms. Russell. I wholeheartedly agree with you. Indeed, Eysenck had some good points and many researchers used his work as a jumping-off point, but there is a gaping hole, in my opinion. We don't have all of the pieces to the puzzle if we don't take external factors into account."

"Precisely!" I agree, closing my laptop. "Thank you, this was really helpful."

"Anytime, Ms. Russell. I appreciate you stopping by. This is one of the main reasons I went into academia—getting a chance to converse with brilliant minds." He chuckles jovially, pushing to stand.

"Well, I will definitely be back then. I'm a verbal processor so talking through the reading a bit helps create a deeper understanding," I say as I stand as well.

He crosses his arms behind his back, leading me to the doorway. "Excellent. Looking forward to seeing you in class soon."

I thank him again before exiting his office, deciding to take the stairs down instead of the thousand-year-old elevator. Bonus points because I'll have to pass by Dr. Bardot—I mean, Elaine's office on the way out, and I've been rehearsing a conversation in my head with her for the past week.

Dr. Bardot, thank you again for having me over to your home. The murder mystery party was great. Yes, sorry, I promise I'll start calling you Elaine. Congratulations on your newest grandchild, he's very cute!

The last part is a lie, hopefully she won't see through it.

When I get close to her office, I realize it's a different familiar voice that's drifting into the hallway. A voice that whispers the dirtiest words to me followed by nonsensical French endearments. A voice that sounds distressed.

Several thoughts run through my head at once. I should just keep walking but I want to say hello, and it's Ben, so why am I nervous? Maybe I should hang out in the hallway and wait until he leaves, act surprised to see him coming out of his mom's office. I should, I should, I should…

What I definitely shouldn't do is plaster myself to the wall and lean as close as I can to the open door without announcing myself. I definitely should *not* do that.

However, that is exactly what I decide to do.

"Ben, you need to tell her." Dr. Bardot's voice is calm, drifting through the open doorway. It's the complete antithesis of how my body reacts to the phrase she just uttered.

I can picture Ben running his hands through his hair, picture as it flops back against his forehead while he lets out a sigh.

"I know," he agrees. "I know that. Every time I've tried, I imagine the worst possible reaction and I freeze. She's asked me to go slow and I've gone anything but. I don't want to push her away now when she's doing so well."

Doing so well?

They're talking about me, they have to be.

"How many days was it?"

"Four thousand four hundred. I stopped counting when I proposed," he replies.

"You stopped counting?" There's a note of surprise in Dr. Bardot's voice. "Do you still keep your journals?"

"Do I still have them? Yes. Do I still use them? No."

"You're that certain?" she asks.

There's a long pause and I know I should leave. The appropriate thing to do would be to walk away and bring this up to Ben later. What I really want to do is walk away and shove this entire day way down deep into the recesses of my memories and never think about it again.

"I need to tell her," he finally says, a non-answer to his mom's question.

A chair screeches across the floor which is enough to spook me out of listening to any further conversation.

So I run. Backpack and all, I sprint across campus through the neighboring streets until I'm back at my apartment. If people stare, I don't notice. I'm so locked in, so focused on getting anywhere but the psychology building, a full production of *Spamalot* could have been happening in the quad and I wouldn't have noticed.

Once I let myself into the apartment, I drop my things and slide down the door until my ass hits the ground. I sit there, panting in a terrible attempt to catch my breath.

Only, I might be having a panic attack because I still can't breathe. I rip my sweatshirt over my head and press my back against the door. My hands find the cool laminate below me and I squeeze my eyes shut, focusing on the sensations around me. Ernest trots over, nudging me with his nose. I can tell he's distressed so I scratch behind his ears, tugging him into my lap.

It takes a few minutes but I start to calm down, right as a knock sounds on the door behind me.

My traitorous heart immediately assumes it's Ben, though there's no way he'd be able to make it all the way here unless he also sprinted like a lunatic across town.

My adrenaline is crashing and I feel numb all over. I debate not answering the door but whoever it is knocks again. Slowly, I drag myself to standing, not even bothering to look through the peep hole before I answer.

Swinging the door open, I see the last person I ever expected to find on my doorstep.

"Dad?"

Chapter Thirty-Eight
SURPRISE VISITORS
Ben

GOOGLE SEARCH

how to support your partner if their estranged father randomly shows up

My mom's advice is ringing in my ears as I leave her office. "Be honest with her, my cabbage."

Be honest.

I am honest with Cole. Mostly.

I answer every question she asks. It's the age-old conundrum: Is it a lie if it's by omission?

Really it's my attempt to protect her, to take things slow... ish.

Feeling antsy, I check my watch. She should be in classes the rest of the day but maybe I can let myself into her apartment, hang out there for a while, and have dinner ready for her when she gets home.

With a quick change in direction, I head toward Cole's apartment. I've never thought twice about letting myself into her apartment but, in light of the conversation with Mom, my stomach flip-flops when I reach for the spare key I had made. Only, her door is already unlocked.

My brow furrows as I push the door open. "Colette?"

She steps around the corner, a look of shock on her face. "Cole, what's wrong?"

There's a flash of... is that frustration in her eyes? She looks as if she's about to run into my arms but something stops her. I'm not sure if it's my anxiety or the fact that she's home when she's meant to be in class, but it feels like the few feet between us is rapidly widening into a full on chasm.

"Cole?" I question for the third time.

She opens her mouth to answer me when another voice cuts in. "Colette, who is here?"

Cole winces as a man joins her in the entryway. It takes me a moment to place him because I haven't seen his face since high school, but the faded auburn hair and sprinkle of freckles across his wrinkled face gives him away.

"Mr. Russell," I say, extending my hand. "It's... uh, it's good to see you?" It comes out as more of a question than a statement, and one glance at Cole doesn't give me an answer.

She's put her mask back on, that's apparent. She looks like she did when we ran into each other last Christmas—hard, cold, indifferent. Not a trace of the warmth I've drawn out of her in the last few months.

"Ben Bardot," booms Mr. Russell. "It's good to see you too." He claps a hand on my back, patting twice before he lets go. "What are you doing here?"

"Funny," I mutter. "I was about to ask you the same thing."

Cole's eyes widen and her head shakes imperceptibly.

"Well, a father has every right to visit his daughter, does he not?" There's an edge to his voice that wasn't there initially. He doesn't like his motives being questioned, and it's obvious he feels some sort of entitlement to Cole's time and energy. To Cole, period.

"When that visit is agreed upon by both parties, he absolutely does," I reply. "Cole, was this agreed upon?"

"I—"

"Excuse me, but what gives you the right to walk in here and monitor visits between me and Colette?"

This statement finally jump-starts Cole. Except, instead of going after her dad like I thought she would, she comes after *me*.

"Don't answer that." She points at me, hiding her hand when I notice there's no ring on her finger. "You need to leave, Ben."

"Me?" I ask, honestly shocked that I'm the one being asked to leave this unhappy little reunion. "What about him?"

"Young man, this is uncalled for," Mr. Russell says. I make eye contact with him over the top of Cole's head. It's clear he is fucking clueless, which just confuses me even more.

A small hand comes to the center of my chest, urging me backwards. "Please, Ben."

It makes me physically ill to leave her with a man who has caused her so much heartache. But one of the things I love about Cole is that she can hold her own, always has. "You'll call me if you need me?"

"Probably not." She shrugs.

"Dammit, Colette. Tell me you'll call me if you need me or I swear to God I will sit outside your door and eavesdrop on the entire conversation."

For a moment Cole looks guilty and then she nods, acquiescing. "I'll call you if I need you," she says through gritted teeth. "Now, go."

I back up, hands in the air in surrender. Without another word, I turn and leave Cole with a sinking feeling that everything is about to change.

———

From the moment I was born, Jules has been the one person on this planet who knew me better than I knew myself. The one person that I knew wouldn't feed me bullshit when I needed advice. The one person I could sit in comfortable silence with for an entire day if we wanted to.

Until Cole, my brain adds unhelpfully.

He doesn't look surprised to find me when he opens the door to his house. He does, however, look exhausted.

"Shit," I mumble. "Should I go? Were you taking a nap? Is Emmett taking a nap?"

He huffs a laugh. "What is sleep?" Jules waves me in, shuffling to the kitchen. "I was about to make another coffee. Want one?"

"Sure, thank you." I take a seat at their kitchen table.

Jules works quietly. He's never felt the need to fill the space with chatter. With him, I don't either. He places a double espresso in front of me and I raise my eyebrows. "This feels excessive."

He glares at me. "Does it, Benoit? How long did you sleep last night?"

"Fair, I'll shut up now." That lasts for about thirty seconds before I ask, "How is my nephew?"

"I will be happy to answer that question as soon as you tell me why you're here." He takes a slow sip of his own coffee, content to wait as I decide what to say.

"Just… feeling a lot of feelings."

"Helpful," Jules deadpans. "Care to expand on that?"

Thea walks in then, a squishy Emmett in her arms, hair piled high on top of her head. She looks like she got about as much sleep as Jules but at the same time she looks more content than I've ever seen her.

"Hey, Ben, I didn't know you were coming over."

"He didn't tell us," Jules answers. "Coffee on the counter for you," he tells Thea, a warm smile aimed her way.

She gives Jules a kiss on his cheek before handing him their son. "Can I sit with y'all or is this secret twin time?"

"Have a seat!" I say, eager to continue avoiding why I came here.

"If she sits, you still have to talk," Jules says, seeing right through me.

I sigh. "Fine, it would probably be helpful to have a woman's point of view anyway."

"I'm glad to be the only woman in the vicinity." She smiles. "Should we ask if Bex wants to come over too?"

"God, I think she'd pass out if we did that," I joke.

Thea starts texting before I have the opportunity to stop her. Jules' hand comes over the top of Thea's. "We aren't waiting for anyone else. Spit it out, Benoit."

"Full-naming me, are we, Julien?"

He doesn't respond, just waits.

"I'm not even sure why I came over here," I admit. "I went to Cole's and her dad was there and she asked me to leave and I didn't want to go to my apartment so now I'm here."

"Cole's dad?" Thea asks. "The one who lives in Florida?"

I nod. "I don't get it. He's barely been in her life for years at this point. I don't really understand how he knew where she lived or if she's communicated with him recently. I was fully expecting to… I don't know, defend her honor? And she asked *me* to leave."

"Does Cole's honor need defending?" Jules asks.

"No." I scrub my hand down my face. "She can fight her own battles. I guess I was hoping she'd want me to help." My head hits the table in defeat. "I want her to want me to help," I whisper.

Thea rubs my back in an extremely maternal gesture. "I'd wager that she wouldn't mind the help but doesn't know how to ask for it. The sudden appearance of her father had to be jarring."

"I know you're right." Emmett lets out a little cry in agreement and then snuggles right back into Jules' chest. "I also need to talk to her about something important, and I'm a little bit pissed that he's blocking me from doing that."

"Maybe it's not the right time," Thea suggests. But I hear the implied *Don't overwhelm her, you idiot!*

"Fuck. I know… It's important, though," I repeat.

"We don't doubt that it's important," Jules cuts in. "But you can't argue that maybe it's not the right time to talk to her about whatever it is."

I look out their kitchen window, fiddling with the coffee cup in front of me. "I'm worried. About her. About us."

"Hang out here for a bit," Thea says around a yawn. "Then you can call her to check in. But give her space right now—it's what she asked for."

"It's what she's always asking for," I mutter.

"I don't think she always means it though, when she asks for space," Thea says. "I think she doesn't know any other way. And it's your job to continue showing up for her, to continue showing her what it's like to have a true partner by her side."

"Holy shit your kids are lucky." I smile at Thea and Jules in turn. "You sure you don't mind if I hang out here for a while?"

"Absolutely not," Jules says. "You take the baby, we're going to lay down."

My gaze swings over to Thea who simply shrugs. "Advice tax."

"I don't know what to do with a baby—"

Bex chooses that moment to bust into the kitchen. "Sorry, let myself in." There are no boundaries in this family. "What did I miss?"

Chapter Thirty-Nine
OUTSIDE OBSERVER
Cole

GOOGLE SEARCH

"Why did that young man burst into your apartment like he owns the place?" my dad asks.

He's always been like this. On the surface he's polite, unassuming. A man who got dealt a bad hand the second the divorce papers were signed and he had sole custody of a pre-teen daughter.

But, in what I assume was an effort for him to control what felt out of control, his word was law. The result was me learning that if I stayed out of the way, if I stayed quiet and compliant, he generally left me alone. I was an easy kid for all intents and purposes.

That's probably part of the reason he was so surprised when I started pushing back. Accepted my diagnosis, accepted my sexuality, accepted *myself*.

He didn't like that.

It was out of his control.

"Colette, answer me." His tone turns harsh.

"He has a key," I reply. "He's allowed to be here."

"Is that so?" He raises a single eyebrow at me, and I know it's a look I've given Ben hundreds of times. Damn him for ruining it.

My sigh is long-suffering. I don't know why Dad is here. I don't really give a fuck, if I'm being honest. The conversation between Ben and his mom is still running through my head. I would rather be getting answers to that than figuring out how and why my dad is at my apartment right now.

"Yes, it is so," I reply. "And he wasn't wrong to question why you were here."

"I'm your father," he quickly replies.

"In name only," I fire back. "And that was your choice."

He gives me a frustrated look. "That's not fair, Colette. I raised you. You owe me the decency of spending time with me when I come all the way here."

"I made sure I wouldn't ever owe you anything again after I left for college. I owe you nothing," I reply. "When was the last time we spoke to each other?"

He's sitting across the dining table from me, rubbing his hands down his thighs. He doesn't know the answer to my question but he'll never admit it.

"You didn't even bother to call me on my birthday," I continue. "I said all I needed to say to you the last time we talked. Wasn't that before you moved? So unless you have something revelatory to tell me, you can leave."

He thinks for a moment but doesn't show any indication that he's going to comply with my request. "I was right about it being a phase, wasn't I?" he finally asks.

"I'm not following."

Dad waves his hand in front of his face. "You know. The dating girls thing. What did you call it? Not gay but something else."

"You have got to be kidding me." I rub my temples, already sick of his bullshit.

"What?" He feigns innocence. "Ben seems very comfortable around you, and I know for sure he is a man. I remember watching him at your track meets on occasion—great athlete. Does he still run?"

"For fuck's sake. I need you to leave."

His face hardens. "Don't speak to me like that, Colette."

My hands slam down on the table, shocking the both of us. "No, you don't speak to me like that. You haven't changed at all. You're still questioning my sexuality—queer is the word you were looking for, by the way, and no, it was not a phase. I still very much like men and women and non-binary people, but I do not owe you or anyone else an explanation for that."

"But Ben is—"

"A man, yes! But I didn't have a choice with him. He is... actually, I'm not talking about this with you!" I shake my head. "Is that why you are here? Just to have the same argument we have every time we see each other?"

He holds up his hands in surrender. "No, I was actually nearby and I thought I'd drop by."

"I'm afraid to ask, but why were you nearby?"

"I was in Boston," he continues. "Visiting your mom."

My nails scrape across my scalp, digging in until it's almost painful. "Why?" I grit out.

"We've been talking, you know."

"I don't."

He looks at his hands. "Right, well. We started talking again a while back."

"As soon as I wasn't in the way, you mean? I was always the problem in your marriage, wasn't I?" My anger is reaching a boiling point, and it's like watching a trainwreck—I couldn't stop it if I tried.

"That's an exaggeration, Colette. You always overreact." He

gives me a one-two punch with two of my favorite triggering phrases.

"Amazing," I reply, sarcasm dripping off each syllable. "So happy that you and Mom are back together. Fuck, that's what every divorced kid dreams of, isn't it? You two can go ride off into the sunset. Please don't invite me to the wedding."

"So dramatic," he sighs. And I see Ben's favorite color—red.

"Get out."

He continues to stay seated.

"Get out, Dad. I'm so fucking for real, I will call the police."

I can tell he doesn't think I'm serious because he moves at a glacial pace as he pushes back from the table and rises to his full height. It takes everything in me not to scream at him again, but I can see he's resigned himself to leaving, he's just going to test every shred of patience I have in the meantime.

When he finally gets to the door, he turns to me. Stupidly, I have the smallest shred of hope that he'll apologize for all of the damage he's caused. Instead, he says, "Call me when you come to your senses."

The door shuts, and I beeline straight to the couch where I snatch a pillow and finally let out the scream I've been holding in.

———

BEN

Red, are you ok?

I would really like for you to answer so I stop worrying.

I don't want to intrude again but I will if you don't start answering my calls.

I'm trying to respect your wishes but I'm losing my mind over here.

On my way over.

I wake up to the sound of my apartment door opening. I can't remember if I locked it after Dad left, and it would really suck if someone was coming to murder me right now. Snuggling under my blanket, I listen to see if I recognize the sound of the intruder's footfalls as they walk further into the space.

The fact that Ernest doesn't bark should be my first indication, but it's not until I hear a familiar, "Red?" that I realize I'm not about to be brutally murdered in my apartment.

"Over here," I call, poking my head out from under the blanket.

He throws his jacket over the back of the chaise and hurries around to where I'm lying on the couch. "Red, what the fuck? I've been trying to check on you for over an hour!"

I scrub the sleep out of my eyes. "Sorry, I must have passed out after my dad left. I was so drained after our conversation..." I look down and realize I didn't even get my shoes off before I fell asleep. "What time is it?"

"Close to five," he replies. "Here, let me help you."

He starts to untie my Doc Marten's when I have the sudden realization that I'm mad at him, too. "Wait!" I say, sitting up so I can face him. I've got to rip the bandaid off before I lose steam.

Ben looks at me with a bemused expression. "Wait to take your shoes off?" he asks, a furrow in his brow.

"No, I don't care about the shoes. I—" *Shit.* "What do you need to tell me?"

This apparently doesn't clear things up for him. "What do I—?"

"I heard you," I interrupt. "Talking to your mom this morning. In her office."

A look of genuine surprises crosses his face. "You did? How much did you hear?"

"Enough to know that you have something to tell me and your mom thinks you need to go ahead and do it. So, come on. What is it? You've just been fucking with me this entire time? It's all a big joke to you? Is that it?"

Ben's expression turns stern. "Absolutely not. I would never be that cruel."

"Wouldn't you?" I ask. "Aren't you the one who tricked me into this whole pact situation to begin with?"

"Twelve years ago? Okay so high-school me was a bit immature, big surprise there." He scoffs. "But now? You know better than that now." His voice is imploring. He wants me to agree with him but I can't, not until I know what he's hiding from me.

"What is it then? You know honesty and transparency is all I've asked of you. Just tell me."

We're both standing now, facing each other. I'm just waiting for the other shoe to drop.

"I have been honest with you," he replies.

"But?" I prompt. He hesitates, fighting a battle that I'm not privy to. And I'm so fucking tired of living on the outside of my own damn life. "Just fucking tell me!"

"I funded your grant."

"You…" I take a step back, a step away from him, but the lace on my shoe that Ben untied trips me, and I'm falling. Ben tries to catch me but he's not fast enough. I land hard on the edge of the coffee table, flipping it sideways so the puzzle on top goes flying, scattering pieces all over my living room.

You know when something is so surprising, even if it's not the worst thing to happen to you that day, it sends you over the edge? The last puzzle piece falls into my lap and it's like a rock hitting a window.

I shatter.

The first tear falls before I even realize what's happening. It slides off the edge of my nose, dropping soundlessly.

"Cole, talk to me." Ben is kneeling in front of me now, his mouth tight.

I shake my head, covering my mouth before an embarrassing sound comes out. It's not even necessarily his revelation, though I'm not thrilled about it, but the fact that he kept it from me. That

I didn't have a choice in the matter. In something that affects *my* life.

Again, I have the feeling of being an observer of someone who looks like me and acts like me but isn't allowed to make her own decisions.

"You had no right," I say, pitifully splayed out on the floor like a toddler.

"I only wanted to help," he pleads.

But I'm manic now. "I don't need your help! I don't need anyone's help! People do nice things and then they… they hold it over your head as if you owe them."

"That's not what's happening, Cole."

"Then why? Why do that? Why not ask if I wanted help?"

Ben's face waivers between anger and frustration. "Because I love you, Colette!" he yells. "Because I love you and I'd do whatever it takes to make you happy!"

He pushes his hair off his forehead only for it to flop back down.

"I've told you," I whisper. "What would make me happy is you communicating with me. Asking me for permission before you make life-changing decisions on my behalf."

"You needed a push," he says, and I think he's trying to convince himself more than me.

"I needed a partner," I correct.

He looks back and forth between my eyes, searching. "I can be that for you," he finally says.

"Yeah?" I ask. "What else are you hiding from me?"

His wince is microscopic, but I catch it anyway.

"For fuck's sake," I cry. "I need you to leave."

I'm having déjà vu after having to repeat that same phrase over and over again today.

Ben stands and I follow, kicking my shoes off so they don't trip me again.

"At least let me help clean up," he says, looking down at the mess.

"No," I reply, pointing toward the door.

He's resigned when he says, "I'll check on you tomorrow."

"For once in your life, listen to me. I. Need. Space. Please respect that."

Ben, the man that is perpetually happy, doesn't have a smile line in sight. His hand brushes against mine and my palm aches. When we reach the door, Ben's eyes are red rimmed. "I wasn't trying to hurt you."

"I know. But you did." His pinky loops into mine and he raises my hand, planting a quick kiss on my empty ring finger. "Shit. I should—let me go get your ring."

I pull my hand away from his but he only grasps me tighter. "No," he replies, a command and a plea. "No, if you—" His voice cracks and my last thread of control snaps.

"Okay, I won't. I'll keep it," I quickly reassure.

He clears his throat. "I'll give you space. But please don't forget about me."

"Impossible."

His smile is devastation incarnate. He wraps his free hand around my head, pulling me in to plant a kiss on my forehead.

"Goodbye, Ben."

"See you soon, Red," he replies.

And it sounds a whole lot like a promise.

Chapter Forty

MISSING PIECES
Cole

GOOGLE SEARCH

"Thanks for stopping by. I could really use a completely objective third party."

Sahara has her feet curled under her as she works on the jigsaw puzzle that I finally picked up off the rug earlier today.

It's been a week since my father lost his mind and tried to… I don't know? Form a relationship with me? And since I found out about Ben… Time and distance really are a helpful tool. But as I've continued to parse through my feelings when it comes to him, I end up just as mixed up as I was when he left my apartment with the promise to see me again soon.

I will hand it to him though. He listened to my desire for space. Ben hasn't stopped by, he hasn't texted, he hasn't presented any more over-the-top jewels to me. I really hope he hasn't bought a house. But I wouldn't know even if he did, because he's respected me. Respected my space.

I hate it.

Sahara finishes placing the edge pieces, giving me a nod. "Of course. Let me just clarify what's going on really quick. You and Ben are kind of engaged—we went over that last time, though it's still confusing as hell—and now you just found out that he is funding your entire tuition. And you are upset because he hid that from you. Is that the jist?"

"Yeah." I sigh, flopping back onto my couch.

"Alright," she continues. "As the completely objective third party, it was pretty shitty of him to hide that from you. But also, like, extremely romantic? Not the hiding part. But the sexy billionaire that falls in love and wants to take care of his partner part? Sounds like a rom-com movie I would totally watch."

"Ben's not a billionaire. I think."

She waves me off. "Whatever, you get the picture. I know I only met him briefly, and believe me, I'm not one to defend a man, but he seemed like a good one."

"I think he's hiding other things from me too," I admit.

Sahara hums, starting to group the puzzle pieces by color now. "It seems like it's hard for you to trust anyone, period. And with your dad showing up unexpectedly? That's a one-two punch. So it makes complete sense you would have trouble trusting Ben after this." She pauses, stopping to look me in the eye. "It really is up to you on whether you'd like to let him earn that trust back or if you'd feel more comfortable walking away."

"The question of the hour, isn't it?" My smile is wry and my heart is heavy. "I miss him."

"He's important to you."

A traitorous tear trickles down my cheek. "Yeah," I whisper. "He is."

Sahara pats my leg before refocusing on the puzzle. "There's your answer then."

She stays for dinner and we chat about our love of true crime and our hope to one day do something meaningful in the world with our degrees. We finish the puzzle only to realize there's one missing piece. After searching the entire rug, under the couch, upturning the cushions, we never find it. Long after she leaves, I sit there staring at the beautiful mountain scene with one small piece missing right at the peak.

It drives me crazy.

When I fall asleep later that night, I dream of hiking up that same mountain, only to fall into oblivion as soon as I reach the top.

———

It takes another three days for me to work up the courage—or maybe it's to rage against how respectful Ben is being—to track Ben down for a conversation.

Starting at the coffee shop, I walk by the front windows several times to see if I can spot him working behind the counter. On my third pass, Thea comes out with her little-old-man baby strapped to her chest to shoo me away.

"He's not here, stop being weird!"

"I fear I'll never be able to stop being weird," I reply. "Do you know where he is?"

She shrugs. "He's off today, I'm pretty sure. He's been particularly mopey this past week and a half. Are you about to put him out of his misery?" She waggles her eyebrows.

"Don't do that"—I wave toward said eyebrows—"again. It's very creepy."

Thea's shoulders hunch. "I'm sleep deprived. Be proud that I'm not having this conversation in a baby voice."

"I am very grateful for that..." I clap my hands together. "Okay, I'm going to try his apartment next."

"Good luck." She smiles her warm, maternal smile as she lets herself back into the coffee shop. I watch as Jules rounds the counter, pulling a chair out for Thea and Emmett. He gives both of them a kiss before returning to work.

I want that.

Well, minus the baby. But stick Ernest in his place and, yeah. I want that.

Ben lives just down the street, so I leave my car at the coffee shop and walk over to his apartment. I knock and Gabe opens the door to greet me.

"Oh, hey, Cole!" He leans casually against the door, a smirk on his lips.

"Will you stop fucking doing that?" Ben calls from the couch, not even looking over his shoulder. "It's fucking mean to keep getting my hopes up."

Gabe gives a look that says, *Ball is in your court.*

"*Tsk, tsk,* Benjamin. It's not nice to talk to your brother that way," I tease.

Ben's head immediately whips toward me and he's up and over the back of the couch in seconds, shoving his brother out of the way. He's got his glasses on and his hair looks like he hasn't brushed it in several days. He's so achingly handsome, it hurts.

"Sorry, sorry." He's breathless. "He's done that five different times this week and it's always one of our siblings or a very confused delivery driver."

I stick my hands out in what I know are really lame jazz hands. "Surprise." When he doesn't move, I ask, "Can I come in?"

"God, of course. Sorry." Ben pushes the door open, guiding me past the living room and into his bedroom. "Can we talk in here? Is that okay?"

"Yeah, this is fine."

"Can I get you a diet cherry cola? Some chicken noodle soup?"

My eyebrow quirks. "You have chicken noodle soup? With the egg noodles?"

"No, but I can make some. I'll make some for you," he rushes out, standing with nervous energy dripping out of every pore.

I huff a laugh. "No, don't go make me soup."

"I would," he whispers. "I would do whatever you want."

"I know." And I do.

"Listen, I'm so sorry about hiding my involvement in the grant," he starts. "It was wrong to keep that from you, no matter how good my intentions were."

I nod, biting my lip. He takes a seat on his bed and I sit across from him, swinging side to side in his desk chair so I have something to do. I have to sit on my hands so I don't reach for him—something that was unfathomable a year ago and has now become second nature.

"There's no way for me to trust that something like this won't happen again," I start.

Ben slides off his bed and onto his knees before me. "I will tell you everything from now on, I promise. I'll—"

"Wait." I hold up my hand to stop him. "Let me finish."

He nods, sitting back on his heels with a furrow between his brow.

"Like I was saying, there's no way for me to trust you other than allowing you the time to rebuild that trust. Allowing *us* the time to continue to build the relationship we've started. I want to do that, you are worth doing that with."

There's a look of relief that flashes across Ben's face that quickly turns to panic when I say, "But I need you to explain the tattoo." I have a weird feeling that his tattoo is meaningful in some way, and I think it's the other thing he's been hiding, but I can't be sure.

He gulps, running a hand through his hair and breaking eye contact with me for the first time tonight.

"What are you afraid of?" I ask, quietly.

"That I'm going to scare you off," he confesses, his tone just as gentle as mine.

"Ben, you proposed to me when we weren't even dating. I think if I was going to be scared off, you would have done it by now." The corner of my mouth lifts. A peace offering. An encouragement.

After a moment, Ben begins. "To explain properly, we need to go all the way back to that party after graduation. Even further back, if I'm being honest."

"Okay…" That's a long-ass time ago.

"You know how we always hated each other in high school? But how I actually didn't hate you."

"We've talked about it, yes," I confirm.

"And when we made that pact, I had already been in love with you for quite some time." He says it so matter-of-factly, like it was something as easy as breathing for him. "I knew you and knew that you wouldn't be able to turn down a challenge. I also was fairly confident that you had never played a game of beer pong in your life."

On that, he's not wrong. "I didn't exactly have time to learn," I reply in mock defense.

"Fair." He smirks and my heart skips a beat. Looking at him feels like when I drink cola too quickly—fizzy and effervescent, but it burns a little bit too.

He's quiet for a long time. It's unusual for this man who always knows what to say. I get the sense he's gone somewhere uncomfortable in his mind, somewhere difficult to relive. He takes off his glasses, pinching the bridge of his nose before he continues.

"It didn't start right away. After the party, I mean. I had to go back and add some of the ones I missed." I'm not following, but I hold space for him to parse through his thoughts. "College was hard. I was still here but you were gone. It felt like high school but wrong somehow. Broken. I didn't have a name for it at the time, but I fell into a depression. I spent a lot of time alone, numb, feeling like I was aimless or purposeless.

"Jules and my parents jumped in pretty quickly, and I was able to start therapy with the campus health center. One day my therapist asked if I could think of something I was looking forward to." He rubs his jaw, the light stubble there. "Do you know what instantly came to mind?"

My breath hitches because I think I do.

"You," he says, answering his own question. "You and our pact and, I know it sounds insane, foolish even, but the thought of you at thirty, standing in a white dress, ready to marry me. I was really, *really* looking forward to that."

I'm crying now. I was hopeful all of my tears had dried up, but I was wrong because big ugly teardrops are falling, and I couldn't stop them if I tried.

Ben's laugh is derisive as he continues. "My therapist asked if there was anything in the more immediate future so I made some shit up, but when I went home that night, I started my journals. I had to count backwards to figure out how many marks I needed and then calculate twelve years into the future to see what number I was working toward."

He stands, walking toward his bookshelf and pulling one of the moleskins down. He flips open to a page and then hands the journal to me. At the top there's a month and a year and at the bottom two numbers written out, labeled "days passed" and "days remaining." But what catches my attention are the rows and rows of tally marks.

"There were four thousand four hundred days between the night we made that pact and the day you turned thirty," he explains. His voice lowers as he reaches out to brush a tear off of my cheek. "Every single one of those days has been documented in a journal. I've been foolishly yours for as long as I can remember, Colette."

"Why?" I ask, my breath unsteady. "Why did you wait?"

We could have had so much more time together.

His smile is sad. "Do you really think you would have welcomed me with open arms if I had tried to pursue you before now?" He doesn't give me time to answer before he says, "Five tally marks because I wanted a reminder of you and getting over four thousand seemed a bit excessive. But now it's five tally marks for five dates with you. Five dates to try to convince you to be mine." He pauses, taking a deep inhale. "That was my last secret. The last piece of me that I was hiding from you. Now you have all of me, for as long as you want me."

I don't know what to say, don't know how to express what Ben means to me. He knows that, of course he does. He kisses my forehead and it's tender, full of so much care.

"I want you to go home and think about everything I've shared with you. Think about how you want to respond—if you want to respond. And let me know when you're ready. When you're sure." He gives me the smallest tilt of his mouth, a gift. "I've waited over a decade for you, I can wait a few more days."

I nod, mostly because I'm paralyzed with overwhelm, not because I want to leave his side. But I need to collect myself, make sure I can give this man everything he's so willing to give me.

Ben walks me to his apartment door, our hands threaded together. Everywhere we're touching feels like it's on fire, like my body is trying to fuse itself to him. He opens the door and then spots something on the entryway table.

"Oh, I almost forgot," he mutters. "I found this attached to my shoelace when I left your apartment the other day."

He places something delicately in my open palm.

My missing puzzle piece.

Chapter Forty-One

A GOAT FOR ERNEST

Ben

GOOGLE SEARCH

Q appointments for a courthouse wedding 🎤

RED

Meet me here at 3pm?

Red dropped a pin

Are you going to murder me?

RED

Undecided.

When I turn down the street toward the location Cole shared with me, it does feel slightly murdery. We're just outside of town where homes sit on a few acres of land instead of right on top of each other like the neighborhoods closer to campus.

My GPS chimes with a helpful "You've arrived at your destination!"

My destination appears to be an unlocked and open gate with a long driveway that leads to the quaintest looking home I've ever seen. The most surprising thing I see: a For Sale sign staked up by the main road.

Maneuvering my car down the driveway, I realize Cole's car is also here along with a vehicle I don't recognize. As soon as I get out of my car, Cole steps out onto the wraparound porch with a white woman that could be my mother's age. Her brow is furrowed and her arms are crossed under her chest as she nods along to whatever the woman is saying.

The car door slams shut, drawing both of their eyes to me.

Cole lifts her hand in a tentative wave, the gemstone in her ring twinkling in the afternoon sunlight.

I shove my hands in my pockets so I don't do something absolutely ridiculous, like suck her ring finger into my mouth, and I walk up to meet them on the porch. The older woman holds her hand out in greeting. "Hi, I'm Barbara! It's nice to finally meet you."

Looking toward Cole, I mouth, *"Finally?"*

Barbara continues, not picking up on my confusion. "I just showed your fiancée the house, so I'll let you two wander around for a bit."

"Fiancée?" I mouth again, and Cole gives me a playful eyeroll.

"As a heads up, it needs a bit of work, but Colette didn't seem to think that would be a problem. It's four bedrooms, three bathrooms, and sits on just under two acres of land." Barbara smiles warmly. "Let me know if you have any questions!"

"Thanks, Barbara," Cole replies, opening the front door for me.

Barbara wasn't lying, the home needs some work. We walk into a large entryway with peeling floral wallpaper. A dining room is to our left and a hallway is to the right.

"That leads to the primary," Cole explains, gesturing to the hallway but walking toward the dining room. "I don't know how you feel about a house that needs work or even being this far out of town, but it's got this amazing solarium off the kitchen and I think I would like a goat. For the yard. And Ernest."

She hurries ahead of me pointing out different things she loves or parts she would change. "And it's a great price because it's been on the market for a while, and I guess no one wants to put in the work but look! The details? You can't find these things in a new build."

Cole rushes into a round room that is fully windows with a view of almost the entire property. Windows and beams meet in a point right in the center of the room. Currently a dated light fixture hangs down but I can already see the vision as Cole holds her arms out, turning around the room.

"We could change the light but I love the stained glass details and I think it would be a perfect plant room but I'd need you to be in charge of the plants because I cannot keep them alive and oh my God, I just realized you aren't saying anything…" She looks worried as she faces back toward me, her arms falling at her side. "Do you hate it?"

Instead of answering, I prowl toward her, a man on a mission. My arm wraps around her waist, tugging her body flush with mine. She falls into me, soft and compliant. Something about it releases the pent up nerves I've been holding on to for the last few weeks. Like I'm taking my very first breath after surfacing from below the water.

Life giving.

Refreshing.

Overwhelming.

All of the things Cole does to me… for me.

My finger comes under her chin, tilting it up toward me. "Colette Russell. Do you want to buy a house with me?"

She nods, her eyes imploring as she tells me, "I want to do everything with you."

Our kiss is slow, gentle, familiar.

It makes me realize that even if this isn't the house we end up in, my home will always be with her.

Cole pulls away first, biting back her smile. "I can't remember the last time I told anyone this, but I love you, Benoit Bardot. I love how steady you are. I love the stupid way your hair flops onto your forehead. I love how you push me out of my comfort zone, push me to be the best version of myself. I love the slutty little glasses you wear. I love that you've loved me in all the quiet *and* loud ways over most of my life, without me even realizing it. I love you and I don't need to go on any more dates to figure that out. I don't want to give you this ring back. I want to keep it on my finger and I want you to have one too. I want to do all of the things in the complete wrong order with you for the rest of my life."

She finishes and her breathing is heavy. Her chest rises and falls, meeting mine with every breath.

"Is it my turn now?" I tease, eliciting a pretty red blush. "It's no secret now that I've been in love with you for as long as I can remember. What has surprised me, however, is how much joy I take in learning the best ways to love *you*, specifically. When I was young it was love, yes, but more of an infatuation. A desire to learn everything I could about you and to push your buttons just so I could have a moment of your attention. Now, I'm learning how to love the woman you've become. Strong, confident, kinky." I wink. "You're brilliant and I'm perfectly content to be in your orbit. I'm the moon and you're my sun— my light comes from you, Colette. I know you think you are difficult or cold or closed off, but for me? Loving you is the easiest thing I've ever done. I want my two more dates plus a million more. I want it all."

"Fuck, you're good at that." Her laugh is gurgled as tears fill her eyes, and I kiss her cheeks where the tears fall.

"So," I start, tilting her head back so it's angled toward me. "Do you forgive me for hiding things from you?"

She smirks up at me, wiping away any remaining tears. "Would I be here if I didn't?"

"No, Red. You would not."

Cole laces her fingers through mine, squeezing once. "Come on, Benjamin. Let's go look at the rest of the house."

I follow her lead, just like I always have.

Just like I always will.

ALL I NEED IS YOU
Cole

GOOGLE SEARCH

🔍 bathroom renovation inspiration 🎤

Four Months Later

"Benjamin! Are you home? Can you help me?"

We finally closed on our house a few weeks ago, and I've been slowly moving things from my apartment whenever I go into town. Thankfully, the inspection showed that most of the work that needed to be done was cosmetic, so Ben and I decided to go ahead and move in and work on a little bit at a time in order to make it the perfect home for us.

The front door opens and Ernest hops down the steps to meet me. Obsessed is an understatement when it comes to how he feels about his new yard. With three legs, he's never been very fast, but he spends most afternoons running circles around the land. Right now, he gallops right up to me, Ben not far behind.

He gives me a kiss and then rounds the car to pop the trunk. It's full of pillows and framed art because I didn't feel like hauling the boxes of books on my own. "I thought you were meeting Bex, Thea, and Sahara for coffee? I would have come to help if I had known you were grabbing a load from the apartment," Ben scolds.

"I just picked up a few of the lighter things," I reply. "It felt like a waste of a trip if I didn't at least get *something*."

"Well you go inside. I have a hot bath ready for you and I'll unload the rest of this."

"Were you tracking my location again?"

"Obviously." He levels me with a look. "Sue me for missing my fiancée when she's gone!"

I pat his cheek affectionately. "You're insane."

"You love it," he counters.

I hum before walking toward the house, stripping my clothes as I go. A definite perk of living somewhere a little more secluded.

Ben wolf whistles, and I may or may not shake my ass a little as I let myself in. The primary bathroom is dated but already has an amazing clawfoot tub that we are absolutely keeping. My favorite candles are lit on the counter, and when I dip my toe in the water, it's practically boiling. My favorite temperature.

I've only been soaking for a few minutes when Ben walks in, also completely naked, and squeezes into the tub with me. "Scoot up, Red. Let your hair down."

His voice is a mix of pleading and expectant. This is his favorite ritual. He brushes my hair over my shoulder, kissing down my spine before he massages shampoo into the long waves. It is divine and I take a deep breath, savoring the feel of his strong hands digging into my scalp.

"Mmm," I moan. "I think we should do it tonight."

Ben freezes.

"Tonight?" he repeats. "Are you sure?"

I nod, smiling even though he can't see my face from his spot behind me. "After family dinner, I think."

Everyone is coming over for the first Bardot family Sunday dinner at our new house. Ben has been fussing all weekend, making sure he has all of the ingredients for grilled kebabs and arranging our mismatched furniture so we can seat everyone.

"Tonight, then." I can hear the joy in his voice. Turning to face him, I see that he's biting his lower lip, a huge grin threatening to overtake both of us. "You have everything you need?"

"All I need is you."

He kisses me thoroughly, and yeah, I'm sure I want to do it tonight.

———

Family dinner goes off without a hitch. I think Ben's great mood rubs off on everyone in the room. Something that used to annoy me—that unending charm and charisma—has quickly become one of my favorite things in the world because I've learned he's so damn genuine. Every big feeling he feels is so real. Almost tangible.

I can't wait to—

"Attention everyone," Ben announces, standing from the table and clinking his knife against his wine glass. He looks absurdly handsome in navy pants and a striped button-down. It goes perfectly with the white sundress I slipped on earlier. Wary eyes all turn toward him as he says, "As you all know, Colette and I got engaged last summer."

"That's not quite how I remember it," Thea pipes up, taking a slow sip of her drink.

Ben ignores her. "And we've been debating the best time to finally tie the knot. As it turns out, the best time is tonight."

Bex gasps, dropping her fork as she covers her mouth in surprise.

Jules looks between me and his twin before asking, "Does Cole know about it this time?"

"Yes, Jules." I smirk. "It was my idea."

"Gabe, you're ordained after doing Bex and Anders' wedding—care to do the honors?" Ben clasps his eldest brother on the shoulder, giving him a wide grin.

"Is this even legal?" Anders questions.

"Absolutely not," I reply with a shrug. "But we'll go jump through all of the legal hoops this week. We've never done anything the 'right' way, and I don't think either one of us wants to wait to make it official. All of our favorite people are here tonight, so why not?"

"We really wanted tonight to be about the two of us..." Ben lifts his glass, gesturing to each and every person around the table. "And all of the people that mean the most to us."

Hugo stands up to congratulate us. Ben's normally quiet father looks thrilled to be welcoming another member into the family. "Men, let's go set up the back yard. Everyone grab a chair."

Thea and Bex take the kids to pick some of the early spring blooms from our haphazard garden—there aren't many yet, but it will do. Which leaves me with Elaine.

"How are you feeling?" she whispers, her smile warm and her tone conspiratorial.

I play with the engagement ring that Ben gave to me all those months ago. "Ready," I sigh. "He's a great man. He loves me so well, even when I don't feel like I deserve it. And he comes with all of you." I wave my hand to indicate the rest of the Bardot family, smiling and laughing with one another. Excited for and supportive of us no matter what. It's so unique. Catching lightning in a bottle is what joining this family feels like.

"We are the lucky ones, Cole," Elaine replies.

"God, please don't make me cry!" I fan my face, feeling the tears well up.

I do end up crying, however, when Hugo walks me down the

aisle. Chloe and Elodie throw their flowers as they walk right before us. Gabe and Jules stand next to their brother with Thea—cradling a much cuter Emmett now that he's grown out of his newborn stage—standing on my side.

Ben looks at me, his gaze filled with awe, and it hits me all over again. More than twelve years of love and devotion and *patience.* He did it all for me.

And I can't fucking wait to marry him.

ACKNOWLEDGMENTS

I wrote another book?! I think I can officially call this a *thing* now—it wasn't a fluke! Thank you all for picking up another Bardot sibling book! Or if it's your first time in Sassafras, I hope you enjoyed the trip and will take some time to go back and read books 1, 1.5, and 2. This world would not exist without readers so first I was to acknowledge YOU!

To Bryan, my forever book boyfriend: I came to you with a crazy idea and you didn't bat an eye. Life together is the most exciting adventure. Thank you for being the only man I like!

To my girls: It will forever be my honor to be your mom. I hope that you both continue to chase your dreams and that I can continue to set an example of what that looks like. Every time you write your own story and make an "About the Author" page, my heart bursts a little bit more! I'm so proud of both of you. You are my favorite Lainey and my favorite Emmy!

To my family: None of you are reading this but I'm going to thank you anyway! Every time I write a toxic family member, I think about how lucky I am to have grown up with y'all. Thank you for always supporting my dreams!

To my friends: Erin and Lindsay, this book wouldn't exist without Lindsay telling me I couldn't do it and Erin telling me that I absolutely could. Love you both! To Kelsey, thank you for always being my HBIC. You make everything more fun and I'm so grateful for you! To my book club, I am so sorry I never read the books. Thank you for not kicking me out and for supporting my writing with unwavering enthusiasm!

To everyone who made this book possible: Thank you to Amber, my PA, who keeps my life together for me and creates all of the beautiful content you see on social media! Thank you to my alpha readers who have been with me since book one: Jess, Wren, and Kalie—y'all are the real MVPs. To my beta and sensitivity readers: Chelsea, Morgan, Jenny, Bekah, Kelli, Vic, Ashlyne, Ange, Amilia, Rachel, and Kei—thank you for helping me treat these characters with love and care! To my wonderful Sadie: You are the editor of my dreams! Thank you for continually championing my work! To my cover artists: Isabelle who does the paperback illustrations and David who does the special edition illustrations. Thank you for always creating absolutely stunning covers! To everyone who helped market this book: Jess (Truly Yours Marketing), Rae and House of Hearts Lit, Samantha and The Smuthood, my fellow authors who shared about release (the girl's girls!!), and all of the bookstagram/booktok creators who helped promote! Thank you for loving Ben and Cole! I love you all!

ABOUT THE AUTHOR

Rachel Lewis is a fresh voice in contemporary romance following the release of her debut novel "Yours, Unexpectedly." With charmingly flawed characters and laugh-out-loud dialogue, Lewis' writing effortlessly blends witty banter, delightfully indulgent spice, and heartwarming found families that readers will want to call their own.

Beyond her own writing, Rachel champions the book community through Get Lit: Grown-Up Book Fair.

Rachel is a mother of two crazy girls, wife of a crazy husband, and crazy for some 90's country hits. She is a nostalgic TV watcher, lover of fan-fic, and is always willing to try a new color in her hair.

You can find her most frequently on Instagram: @rachel_mlewis.